SHADOWS OF LOVE
AMERICAN GAY FICTION

SHADOWS OF LOVE
AMERICAN GAY FICTION

edited by Charles Jurrist

Boston • Alyson Publications, Inc.

"Feedbag Blues" first appeared in the *Seattle Gay News*,
volume 12, no. 20 (May 17, 1985)

"Sea Gift" first appeared in *Out* magazine, Pittsburgh,
issue no. 125 (August 1987)

"A Faustian Bargain" first appeared in *The James White Review*,
volume 3, no. 2 (Winter 1986)

"Immortally Yours" first appeared in *The James White Review*,
volume 4, no. 3 (Spring 1987)

"Survival" first appeared in *The James White Review*,
volume 3, no. 1 (Fall 1985); and thereafter in *Stallion*,
volume 5, no. 5 (September 1986)

Published as a trade paperback original by
Alyson Publications
40 Plympton Street
Boston, Massachusetts 02118

Distributed in the U.K. by GMP Publishers,
PO Box 247, London, N15 6RW, England.

First U.S. edition: December, 1988

ISBN 1-55583-136-2

Shadows of Love
editor: Sasha Alyson
production and design: Wayne Curtis
proofreading: Tina Portillo
printing: George Banta Company

For Michael Whitney
*who was a star
and still shines*

Contents

Introduction

Over the decades since Stonewall, gay fiction (and particularly anthologies of short fiction) has tended to follow certain well-worn paths. Much of the published work has come from New York and San Francisco and, more often than not, out of self-conscious literary circles in those two cities. Particular subjects have also predominated: coming out, life in the urban fast lane, and, in recent years, AIDS. The voices of racial and ethnic minorities within the community have rarely been heard.

The present collection of fiction resulted from a desire to discover what else was "out there." It was our aim to assemble a group of stories that, while not surrendering any ground in terms of quality, would more accurately represent the geographic and ethnic diversity of gay America and the multifariousness of its inhabitants. We hoped, also, to offer new writers the opportunity to publish for the first time.

Alyson Publications sent press releases to every gay newspaper in the country, inviting submissions to this anthology. The response was enormous: one hundred ten writers from twenty-eight states and three Canadian provinces submitted some three hundred fifty stories. The sixteen stories that appear here represent the best of these.

This method of assembling the book — selecting the best out of hundreds of random submissions — meant that I could not shape the final result. For example, there are two wonderfully comic stories here, *A View of the Freeway* by William Reyes and Scott Peterson's *Feedbag Blues*. Yet they were among the very last pieces I received and, until they appeared, it looked as if there would be no humorous works in the collection.

In the end, however, that very diversity Sasha Alyson and I had hoped for when we began was achieved. The contributors to this volume live in small towns such as Ferndale, Washington and Toms River, New Jersey, and in cities as farflung as Toronto, Seattle, San Diego, Houston, and Atlanta. Regional voices are heard in stories like Bart Washington's haunting *Accountability,* and ethnic voices are here, too. In *Immortally Yours,* Guy-Mark Foster gives us a black man's takeoff on our mating rituals. Tomás Vallejos, a Mexican-American who grew up in Colorado, writes of the land and the people of his childhood in *Piñons.* Chilean-born William Reyes has a unique viewpoint from which to choreograph the comic dance of the four characters in *A View of the Freeway*: a second-generation Mexican-American, two recent (and illegal) Mexican immigrants, and a Japanese-American Ganymede who has refined upward mobility into a science.

The themes of these sixteen stories are, I am pleased to say, as various as their origins. While I am tempted to describe all of them, a few examples must suffice. Patrick Franklin has provided a delicious ghost story, *Sea Gift,* that is set in the time of the Great Depression. Richard Hall, a distinguished crafter of short fiction, explores the choices made by a married man when his life reaches a crossroads. And Alan Neff, in his first published story, chronicles the burgeoning of a romance between two mental patients.

Five of the writers in *Shadows of Love* are publishing fiction for the first time. Finding and presenting their stories has been by far the most satisfying part of my work on this project. For there are some astonishing debuts here. William Mann's *Cords of Love* displays his control of a style that is whipcord-lean and utterly assured. Lee Kincaid presents his tale, *Coloring Inside the Lines,* from within the consciousness of a little boy — a child of no more than four or five years old. I cannot imagine better writing or a more subtle imagination. Working with writers such as these has been both a pleasure and a privilege.

Coloring Inside the Lines is also of interest as illustrating one of the principal issues I grappled with in making my selections. This book is subtitled "American Gay Fiction"; and I am aware that there might be those who would assert that Mr. Kincaid's is not a "gay" story. It contains, after all, no sex, no gay relationship, no clearly gay character. True, there are suggestions in the piece that the uncle is gay; and the little boy's sensitivity to the smell of his uncle's t-shirt and the feeling of big masculine arms encircling him will recall for many of us the first stirrings of our own attraction to men. But *Coloring* is in this book primarily because it is a superlative work by a gay artist. It is our own loss (and really to our peril) if we fail to recognize and celebrate such works, for we then narrow our artists' options and force them to make invidious choices between art and community.

Overt sexuality was another thorny issue in the selection process. Our initial guidelines ruled out "stroke fiction" — the sort of stories printed by the slick magazines in between photo spreads of the lusciously endowed. But even those stories that endeavored to place sexuality in a larger literary context most often suffered from a distorted focus: introducing an important character in a paragraph, letting a couple of days pass in half a page, and then describing a thirty-minute sexual encounter at such length and in so much detail as to dwarf the surrounding material. Try as they might, the authors of these stories could not conceal the fact that the real goal of their writing was to get to the sex.

The two exceptions in all the hundreds of submissions were William Mann's *Cords of Love* and T.R. Witomski's *Within You/Without You,* stories in which sex, brilliantly employed, is part of their essential fiber. Witomski's eloquent howl of pain also speaks to one of the central concerns of men who now have to face AIDS as a fact of life. His narrator is one of those who practice safe sex but do not embrace it, regarding it as a pale substitute for pleasures that are now too dangerous. Possibly this is not the most enviable state of mind, but we cannot doubt that it is a very real one.

There is only one story here, Scott Humphries' *Tinky,* that is actually *about* AIDS. This, too, is by happenstance rather than design, and represents the most surprising result of our free-form selection process. When the call for submissions first went out, I fully expected to receive many such stories, possibly as many as a quarter of the total. But it didn't work out that way. There were days when the mail would bring ten or twelve submissions, stories about every conceivable subject — except AIDS. In quite a few pieces, of course, the disease *was* part of the characters' consciousness: they felt the need to be careful about meeting people, to take precautions during sex. In the end, however, fewer than a dozen of the three hundred fifty pieces I read had AIDS as their main subject matter.

The AIDS stories came almost exclusively from San Francisco and New York. The fact that writers elsewhere aren't yet working with this subject is not surprising; nor, on reflection, disturbing. As a group, our literary artists — fiction writers, playwrights and journalists — are certainly not avoiding their responsibility to deal with the issues raised by the epidemic. And those who write about other things are performing an equally important task: transmitting to that lucky generation who will come of age after a cure has been found the humor, the sensuality, the tireless imagination that are as much a part of their heritage as our present anguish.

Finally, I would like to acknowledge the help of a number of people who recommended potential contributors or otherwise aided in compiling *Shadows of Love*. My thanks to John Coriolan, Jerry Douglas, Freeman Gunter, Ed Iwanicki, John Preston, Sam Staggs, and Bob Summer.

SHADOWS OF LOVE
AMERICAN GAY FICTION

OTHER PLACES

Accountability

The Old Wake Woman stopped him in the middle of the road, looked him straight in the eye, and said, "Ye ain't got long, have ye?"

Birk thought she meant until he crossed the misty foam. (Born with a caul, she could sniff out death.) But he asked, in a voice still changing, "Long for what?"

"Till ye reach accountability," she said. "Ain't ye almost thirteen?"

He nodded that he was — just under a week until he turned, and none too soon. She shook her head and suctioned her tongue, the way she had when she laid out his daddy. He waited, frozen in the road, for more; but she walked on by, her black dress almost sweeping the dust.

At Nat's Store and Post Office, he hid his polio leg behind the bread rack and listened to the men, full of cars risking death around Sickle Curve. To the women, full of chow-chow they were canning up for winter. He didn't dare ask what accountability was. As a boy, he had picked up a hog nut from the road and, thinking it was a baby animal, had spread it for the traders at the Store. He got five years of knee slaps and giggles for that.

He was tempted to waste a dime on ice cream, but he fisted his money and looked ahead to Saturday, when he'd have more than enough for Haysi and the movies, sixteen long miles away. He left for the pool at Sand Rock to wait for his buddy Roy, who usually came, just before dusk, to rinse off the day's sweat and dirt. But Roy's stepdaddy, Emmit Lowe, was still cursing the mule in the tobacco field. Roy would have to work into dark. There would be no lying on the big rock by the river. No listening to talk of Roy's Saturday coming up — the Carnival in Haysi — or of when his real daddy, on furlough, had oranges in every pocket.

At the mouth of his own holler, Birk sat behind a clump of sassafras where he always hid his cane. He waited for Furley Cook to come home from the mines and the beer joints. On this night, Furley was just drunk enough to be company.

"What's accountability?" Birk asked him, as soon as his half-swivel matched Furley's steps.

Furley kept walking until they cleared a curve. Then he stopped to unbutton his britches. He aimed his eyes straight up while his fingers pulled out his pecker, which he kept covered in a condom to impress the mining crew. Birk turned his head.

"Boy, 'at beer goes right through a man," Furley said, the rubber rolled off and the urine gushing. Birk spat into a patch of ragweed.

"What's 'at now?" Furley asked, his head turned to rake Birk's face.

Birk said again.

"Easy," Furley said. "When ye can shoot jazz. Knock women up."

For a year, Birk had made full love to knotholes in trees, to moss banks. And he knew of others who could prove thirteen late.

"Ye gone thank ye tail's blowed off." Furley housed his pecker and pulled, from a back pocket, a half-pint of moonshine he kept for when the seam got tough. "Take ye a little sip," he offered.

Birk knew to refuse was to bring on a lifetime of mistrust. He took the bottle and lifted it. Fire scattered down his throat.

Back in walk, Furley named women Birk might try to use his power against, when it came. After every curve, Furley swigged at the bottle.

At the fork of their paths, Birk thanked him and hurried on to bring in wood and water, while his granny grumbled from her bed. He didn't ask her about accountability, for she rarely talked sense to any but those who had crossed over to the other side.

With his feathertick to hug on, he threw his dreams onto a screen — Dayton, Ohio. Roy and him fastening doors onto Frigidaires. Convertibles to wave from. Six or seven movie houses in a row. Beer joints for Roy, who could pass for eighteen.

Gasps from his granny broke the film. Her heart was reminding her she hadn't taken her medicine, and Birk had to get up to find it.

"Did ye see Gervais?" she asked.

Gervais Deel had been dead since Birk was a child, but he said, "Hoein' in his corn," to help her chase a memory into sleep. He could see double when he had to — yesterdays for her, tomorrows for himself.

The next two days he was hired out to Preacher Ezra Hess. Though he usually feared God's people, Ezra was an exception. He laughed at God as just another wayfarer. Some said he even took a drink of liquor at the Hardshell Associations. And he didn't ride up and down the road screaming brimstone from a truck.

Ezra and the mule Grunt were already plowing the balks of the tobacco rows that Birk — and later Ezra — were to hoe. Birk could not have made himself heard above the "verilies" and "thous" Ezra aimed at Grunt, the only mule who knew scripture. Birk forgot the Old Wake Woman . . . Turned the tobacco rows into paths of tumbleweed, way out West.

Dinner, at 11:30 A.M., was no time to ask. Ezra's wife Rithie, hurrying around the table to serve a multitude of two, named every pain that had stitched her last night and that morning. "Can't understand it," she said, and smacked her lips on air. "Why th' Lord doubles up on me."

"He don't give us more'n we can take," Ezra said.

"Kraut?" Rithie asked Birk, who nodded. He was wondering about Elden Howard, who blew his brains out after fire took his house and family. Of Harkis Colley, eaten by a cane-mill.

They got a thirty-minute rest on the front porch. "Let th' food settle," Ezra said, and tried to find justification in his limber Bible.

"My eyes," he said when he failed.

Rithie talked to and about the five kinds of dallies that bordered her yard.

Birk watched the regulars going to Nat's on the ribbon of road, far in the valley. He guessed what each expected the U.S. to bring them.

Grunt did not have to go back to work, the field now plowed. He stuck his head over the fence. His nose came perilously close to the dallies.

For the afternoon, Ezra took the first row since he was faster, especially at the beginning when the sun had not slowed him. A few feet back, Birk warmed up for his question by asking where the next Association would be. Ezra hoed, yards between them. Birk remembered the trick others had played — to get him to talk about Moses. He'd slow, and work would be easy all day long.

They were too far apart for talk. Ezra sang about those gone on or about children on the verge: a little girl eagles pecked the eyes from, and a boy who dreamt that his daddy would die in the mines, and twenty men did. The saddest in sound was "Loneson Valley":

You gotta walk 'at loneson valley.
You gotta walk it by yourself.
They ain't no one's gone walk it for you.
You gotta walk it for yourself.

Near the end of eight hours, Ezra lost some of his vigor, though he helped Birk hoe his row out every time. They were only about six feet apart when Birk asked him. Ezra leaned on his hoe. He cupped his ear, the way all Hardshell preachers did, to pick up what God was sending out. "What say?" he asked.

"Accountability."

Ezra shook his head side to side. Birk stared him head on, to show he could take it. Ezra motioned him to their resting place — an apple tree that a rockpile had saved from the axe. Birk started to sit but when Ezra continued to lean on his hoe, he followed suit.

"Most important day of yore life," Ezra said. He removed his hat. Swiped sweat from his forehead. Ran a finger around the sweatband inside the hat. "Day ye give up th' playpretties of 'is world," he said.

Birk's bird egg collection had already gone to Trellis Tiller, who slept on it and crushed every last one. His gravel flipper to Early Deel.

"Ye don't play leap-frog no more," Ezra said, his ear recupped. He let out a little giggle, like granny's when she stepped on a puppy's tail. "They lord God no. Ye don't roll a wheel on a wire, round an' round in a circle. No, honey." (As a cripple, Birk had never developed the habits.)

"Ye don't hunker an' shoot some marble from a ring. Good gracious no!" (Birk had 363 see-through marbles and eleven steelies, though he rarely played, and then with just himself.)

"Ever thought an' ever deed from 'at day on is recorded up yonder." Preacher Hess pointed to the one little cloud in the sky. "Hit don't matter, honey, if ye don't do th' deed. Just have one jumpin' around in ye head, an' angels up in 'at City Four-Square gone take it down." (Birk's granny had said that every hair on his head was numbered.)

"Ever thang up to thirteenth's just a play-party," Ezra said. His grin was like granny's when she petted a hanging coat for a ghost.

Birk's big foot covered the little one. "Ye go to heaven, in automatic?" he asked.

"Ontil thirteen," Ezra said.

His last teacher, a Free-Will, had ruled dead babies in hell. ("Lest ye be born again," she preached.)

"Atter'n 'at birthday, ain't no joy without knowledge." Ezra paused, to listen. "Ain't no knowledge without pain."

"Well, I thank ye," was all Birk could say.

"When is it, boy?"

"Sunday," Birk said.

"Well, ye'd better walk 'at straight an' narrer path atter midnight Saturday." The old man looked at his pocket watch and said, "Let's us take off a little early, till tomar morn." He counted out two dollar bills that smelled of hoarded sweat. Then he reached into his right overall pocket and pulled out an extra quarter, new as dawn.

"Buy ye somethin' pretty," he said and winked against the sun.

Birk saw ahead to half a ticket for Saturday's double feature.

With time on his hands, he waded the shallow ponds up the river, toward Sand Rock. He liked to feel the minnows play with the foot that had shriveled.

A large pond spread his mind out to sea — where Roy and he were in the Coast Guard. The seams of their white clothes whispered from starch. But what Ezra had said drowned out shore leave. Birk wondered aloud to jar-flies and snake-doctors why mamas and daddies didn't hold their children's heads under water, on the night of their twelfth full year. If Roy was talky, he'd ask him about heaven without teens, without growns. (Such questions they used to settle on Sundays, before Emmit took them for fencing.)

Birdsong pushed out eternity. Cardinals, thrushes, catbirds, and crows. He could copy some. Roy could fool them all, even bring them close to his hand.

On the bank of Sand Rock, he curled up in his nest molded from buckwheat and timothy. Hidden by willows, he could eavesdrop on the voices of traders walking home on the highway above. He knew their approach, for the birds lost their song. Old Square Dick stopped every few feet. (His cane, Birk knew, would be pointed at trees to blame them, as Democrats, for the mess in Washington.) Rubygay Rose threatened a switch on all her babies but the one she carried. They slapped at each other to get away.

"Tan yore hide," Rubygay yelled.

From their twine in the willows, Birk broke vines from wild grapes. (Roy and he smoked them, dried, for Luckies in the winter.) He now squeezed the juice over the mustache of his pecker, to help the fuzz along.

He closed his eyes tight to imagine Rubygay naked. He became Roy in the tumble. Then he let love rest to watch evening climb. Though accountability waited just around the calendar, he slept to the small breezes the willows caught.

Awakened by Roy's fighting the water, he shied out of his nest and into the open. He hunkered on the large rock that had been for divers till Emmit claimed it for his cows. (Roy told Birk to trespass, come hell or high water.) Though he couldn't swim — had never pulled his clothes off to try — Birk guarded for Roy.

"Goddamn sonofabitch," Roy said to the sloshes around him.

Birk kept his mouth shut. An angry Roy had called him a shit-ass once, just for nodding hey. He got the towel (a pair of ragged pants) from its hiding place under brush and handed it to Roy when he stepped naked from the water. Before Emmit left three scars on its back, it was the only body Birk had seen without blemish.

Roy lay on his belly and talked into the cave his arm made with his head. "Hope t'hell his back breaks off." Some said Emmit's bent back made him work Roy double. But he did let Roy drive calves to market in the pickup.

"Went back on his word," Roy said. "No truck for th' Carnival."

Birk counted the seeds of ragweed he shredded between his fingers. "Reckon could ye thumb?" he risked. He caught himself from saying "like me." (Roy enjoyed their times in the woods, from birch bark in the spring to possum grapes in the fall, but the four years between them stretched far on a Saturday night.)

Roy turned. Lay on his back. His front had not a scar. "Sumbitch said hoe th' crop an' I can go." From last year's Carnival, he remembered a man part wolf that ate up chickens raw. "Woman with a chin beard four feet long."

Birk was thinking of Rex Allen and Jimmy Wakely. So he could tell the nightbirds what the cowboys sang.

Roy said, "We could have yore pictures by day. Carnival in th' dark. An' beers before an' atter."

Birk's hand unbuttoned the bib of his work overalls. It trembled when he lit Roy's Lucky Strike. His own. He cleared his voice against crack and asked, "What time would we leave?"

"Ain't no use t' thank about it," Roy said. The white skin of chest and belly made little stitches as he blew smoke rings toward heaven.

A whippoorwill practiced for its shift. Katydids scratched. A bullfrog cleared its throat.

"Bet two could hoe it out," Birk volunteered.

"Might could," Roy said and scratched the cave below his ribs.

"Could start at daylight," Birk offered.

Roy eased a hip onto rock to face him. "Work into night," he whispered, as if they were going to break into Nat's Store again. He closed his eyes and guessed the number of rows they'd have to hoe each day, through Friday. Birk did not say he was promised tomorrow.

"'At big wheel," Roy said. And in a voice husky with sharing he told of men who ate fire and steel, a woman that slept on nails. Five beer joints — one for every twelve miners. To make sure they weren't playing, Birk asked the time on Saturday.

"Pick ye up at 11:00 sharp," Roy said, his voice still low. "Picture house opens at 12:00."

11:30 on a Saturday, but Birk didn't say.

Roy gave hours till the cafs closed at midnight. He shivered head to toe and rushed into the work clothes that would make him dirty again. "Daylight," he said, and disappeared into tall grass.

* * *

His eyes lowered, Birk knocked on Ezra's door to say, "Somethin's come up." Ezra asked about Granny and Bossy the cow. Birk shook his head. He held the quarter out, but the old man seemed not to see it.

Birk hurried back down into the valley. He was waiting in Emmit Lowe's tobacco before Roy arrived, wiping sleep from his face and coughing out night.

"This ain't buyin' th' baby no shoes," Birk said.

Without a smile, Roy started.

Birk followed.

Emmit, still plowing balks, didn't know till 12:30 — their dinnertime — that Birk was helping. He grunted that there'd be no pay.

"Helpin' me," Roy dared. "For th' Carnival."

Emmit spat as if he'd just sucked snake-bite. He walked on before them to the house.

Birk had never eaten at Roy's. For their Sundays, he whistled from the woods and Roy met him around the hillside. Roy's mama didn't even know who he was. If Emmit and Roy raised their heads, it was to look mean at each other. The mama ran around the table to cap Emmit's biscuits with sorghum.

Emmit allowed no rest time on the porch, to tell of olden times or what the future stacked up to be. But as they passed the cowshed, now a garage, Birk petted the fox tails fastened to a dead aerial.

Back in the field, there was no talk, no song to make work easy. At Birk's mention of the Carnival, Roy grunted — like the end of a pushup.

The plowing finished, Emmit took the third row. Though Birk couldn't keep up with Roy, a demon with his stepdaddy in the line, he did stay ahead of Emmit Lowe.

Furley had told Birk that the Carnival was going strong. A merry-go-round. A set of swings. Roy didn't even grunt to the information. He pushed hard to stay ahead of Emmit. Birk, in the middle, almost gave up the ghost. They had no time for Sand Rock. At dusk, Roy rushed to feed the stock. Birk staggered home to his chores and a bed that held no dreams.

Friday, Roy and Birk hoed into the night, with the moon to light them. Peckerwood boys passed on the road above and pointed to what they thought was Emmit Lowe. "Ole tightwad," they yelled down. "Ole wither-bone." They threw rocks into the swimming hole and ran away giggling.

"I'll be out of th' holler in plenty of time," Birk whispered at the end of the last row.

Roy nodded into moonlight.

* * *

Birk was hunkering in the sassafras by 9:00 A.M., every spot that covered him new and shiny, except for his socks and underwear which nobody could see anyhow. The right toe and heel of his new wing tips held corn silks and heart leaves, to take up the slack. His see-through nylon shirt sported an unopened pack of Luckies and a pocket comb. His cowboy belt twinkled every hue of the rainbow and then some. His billfold bulged on four greenbacks and a rubber rolled up into a golden coin. If cars and trucks had seen him, they might have thought "funeral" and stopped, but at 10:00 he eased out to the roadside to make sure Roy would not pass him by.

Two trucks honked their horns. The Wampler sisters threw up

their hands from the back of their daddy's pickup. A stray dog stopped on the curve and sniffed. At the first flick of Birk's wrist, for hello, it yapped and ran over the hill.

Birk felt the muscles of his arms for a week's hard growth. Soreness rested around the bone. He tried not to follow the path of the sun, but near noon his jaw slackened. A pain — a pinpoint — began in his belly. His throat tightened. He lit his first Lucky. Furley came out of the holler to find chewing plugs for his parents, liquor for himself. He gave Birk the exact time: 1:17.

Birk walked as fast as a bad leg and unbroken shoes would allow him, up the road to Emmit Lowe's and an empty cowshed. He yelled down to Roy's mama shelling beans on the porch.

"Emmit's fencin'," she said.

"Roy," he called.

She looked to both sides of her and, without answering, hurried inside with her lap of sheelies. He waited for words of another beating, of Roy's running off to sign up for Fort Jackson, but none came.

Birk thought he was going to be sick. Around the first curve, he sat in the ditch and breathed hard through his mouth. He wouldn't even let the pain bring snot. Then he jerked his back from hump and threw out his thumb at a load of miners, but they whizzed on by.

The wing tips soon brought blisters to both feet. He pulled them off and hid them in a drainpipe. Then he took another mile.

He rested under an oak. A thrush cried, "Pip-pip-pip."

"What-cheer-cheer-cheer," answered a cardinal.

The sun told after quitting time when he got his first ride — Vernon Deel, headed for Nervie's Place. "Ever little bit helps," Birk said. Vernon, dry, was not talky. Birk leaned his head out of the window. The fast air fanned his face.

Roy's truck had not smashed into Sickle Curve. It was not parked at Harricane Hole, where a line of baptizers waded into their watery grave.

The graveled yard of Nervie's Place was crowded with four vehicles, but not Roy's. Birk, inside before Vernon, hobbled up to a woman old but for jet hair. "See Roy?" he asked her and two miners at the bar. The drunkest of the men pulled his right eye out and dropped it into a glass of beer. "See this?" he said. "Gimme quarter I'll drank it."

Birk stepped back. "Roy," he said. "'Bout six foot. . ." The beer and the big marble disappeared in three swallows.

"Pickup with red fox tails," Birk said to Nervie.

"Lordy, dat boy honked me out first thang this mornin'," she said. "Left high's a kite at noon."

The miner laid the eye, an egg, through gums and lips made redder by the black around them. He put it backwards into its blue pucker.

"Any of youens goin' to Haysi?" Birk asked in a child's quaver he thought he had lost. Nobody answered. The miner removed his eye again and dropped it into his glass. "See this?" he was saying when Birk left.

The Long Mile, just below Nervie's, was supposed to be haunted but Birk paid it no mind. A truckload of Christians, wet from baptizing, stopped. He pulled himself up into the truck bed and sat beside a hollow-eyed woman clutching a boy about his age.

"You saved, mister?" the woman asked, in a voice too deep for her flesh.

"Ain't got a cigarette on ye, have ye, mister?" the boy said through circles of rot for teeth. The pack of Luckies held only four when it circled back.

"Ain't got a slab of gum on ye, have ye?" the boy said. Birk did not offer the unopened pack of Juicy Fruit in his pocket.

The truck stopped twice so that singers in the back could match harmony for the driver's lead of "Are You Ready?":

> Aaaarre you readyyyy?
> Aaaarre you readyyyy?
> Are you ready for th' Judgment Day?

Birk had to bang on the cab, else they'd have taken him onto a strange dirt road.

He stayed in one spot until a truck stopped — a farmer whose baby tried to hide behind his shoulders. All the farmer said was "Gyp-joint" for the Carnival, Birk's spoken destination.

At the sign that read "Haysi 1 Mile," Birk ran his comb

through his hair and shook both legs from the needles they had caught in rest. Two curves further, bright rings decorated the sky. Wheels grated and music cranked from boxes. Traffic was so slow that Birk got out before the farmer came to a stop. Straight ahead, a thousand lights drew the moths and mosquitoes of summer.

Roy had not told him there would be a fare, and a full one, for the ticket man would not take his word for twelve.

He stepped over wires and cables to the merry-go-round. The eyes of its riders were rounded but their lips curved down, as if they had guessed the breeze would go. Birk swiveled right, past booths of rifles and darts, wagons for hot dogs and cotton candy. "See Roy?" he asked. The few who noticed him seemed to think he was telling them to see more.

The ticket man at The Tent of Mystery said Roy was just inside. "Not too tall? Not too short?" he said. "Handsome?" Birk broke a dollar bill to find him. Inside, the tent was bare but for a woman and her youngens and, in the center, a jar that contained a dead two-headed baby. A sign underneath said it was a mystery. The man would not give him back his money.

In front of the largest tent, a hawker told of a man who could digest motorcycles, a woman with the hide of an elephant. Birk waited, but no one came out who resembled Roy. At the far end, where Roy had said the wheel would be, children stood in line for swings that twirled around and upward. Beyond the circle's turn, the hootchie-kootchie tent was coming down. Men were rolling it up.

One tent was still crowded — a ring of men throwing dimes into orange bowls, the prizes; or, if the winners preferred something living, one of the baby ducks huddled around a light bulb. Some had stretched out in death and the others gaped, for scratch or water.

The entrance was now an exit, for the ticket seller was taking down the Carnival's sign. He headed back up the road, though his mind argued with his legs that the Movie House might have gotten a late start — that the machine might have broken, the Carnival draining all its juice. He didn't lift a thumb for the trucks that filed by him, thick at first, the thinning to none far into night.

On a curve beyond Nervie's, he recognized Roy's pickup when it passed . . . and for a second Roy, alone, seemed to recognize Birk in the ditch, for the brake light flickered, the truck slowed. But just long enough for the foot to gather force for the gas.

Some time past the shift for night birds, he risked death to crawl into a big garden that faced the road. With his shirt for a sack, he picked tomatoes. Pulled a cabbage head. He waded the river to Harricane Hole where he sat on a log to feast. The cabbage had slugs, but the tomatoes held their own. He rubbed their acid into the salt from his sweat and tears. He stifled sobs with the goodness. Laughed into seeds.

"Teakettle, teakettle, teakettle," called an early wren.

He lowered his feet into the water, to soak them from sharp to slow burn, into a gentle numbness.

"Sweet-sweet-sweet-sweet," gave a sparrow.

Just as the three-noted robin helped with the dawn, he stripped his clothes off and scooted in deep enough to sit with all but his head covered. His arms, tired paddles though they were, swirled the water to fool other muscles and bones into thinking they didn't have eight long miles to go.

First Blood

By late spring the college was green again, though winter seemed to last forever each year I was there. In the 1960s, Williams had prestige, mountains, and no girls. It still has mountains and prestige. I chose it because I felt that if I joined an exuberant group of healthy peers, I could make up for not having had a real father. I would have friends I loved — loved appropriately, if slightly physically, with wrestling, laughter, pretzels, and beer. Then I could "graduate" to loving a real live girl.

Later. The girl would come later.

That was the plan. I would not be queer, no. I would pass through that. My plan virtually required an all-male school, though. No Swarthmore, no Berkeley would do. I wasn't dumb. I would merge with the male in the proper setting. The lacrosse player, oboe player, Eagle Scout. I would merge for a year or so. Then, on to Hollywood, where I could begin the major phase — taking my place among the world's screen legends. Of course, Metro would wait until I'd finished college. That was smart of them. I would grow older, handsomer. I would become heterosexual. Sure. Let's do college.

Williams enchanted us in spring and fall. After dinner, my roommates and I walked around the campus. Every year was the same. Students with books. A handball game, feverish and shouting, next to the frat house wall on our left. Down the walk, a three-on-three basketball game threatening to outshout the handballers. The sun made everybody orange and the trees rocked gently in the sweet late-day air. Short-sleeved shirts torn but still worn. Someone had a cowlick — some straw-haired Nebraskan with an aptitude for vectors and Hemingway. Nice school.

One such evening, a jogger approaches from the west. He lopes his way closer. A rangy, shirtless boy. A boy who is tall, smooth, and has nipples as large as poker chips. He says, "Hey, Bob," pats me on the shoulder and goes by us. I say, "Hello, John," I wave, and I notice that I have stopped moving. "That is the most attractive man I've ever seen," I say. My roommates stiffen and look grimly at each other.

Sure, I could notice a half-naked man. To talk about it was an act of social filth. They were embarrassed for themselves, for me. I was ruining the plan. We walked faster. All I could think of that evening was John Rawlings.

By sophomore year, I'd started to provoke challenge matches with people I scarcely knew. These weren't fights, they were invitations to play. "Nick, you're on the wrestling team," I would say. "How about showing me a few moves?" He would laugh, grab me, and I'd probe. It was fast but it was skin, my first taste of the hard flesh of the male. Afterwards, I had to return to the desk in the dorm, where I wrote about *The Tempest* and clear, distinct ideas like ontology, justice, and John Rawlings' smile.

On second thought, fuck the plan.

But I couldn't pretend girls didn't exist — everybody else was obsessed with them. To meet them, they took long road trips to Vassar and Smith. Young men piled into cars, screaming for pussy and popping beer cans all the way to Poughkeepsie. Sometimes I went. I wanted their respect. I wanted to pass for straight. If I made it through the date (an awkward, verbally busy affair capped by a goodnight kiss at the dorm), I got what I really came for: the back seat on the way home. The radio played Randy and the Tamburlaines and early Beatles. My friends poked each other, told dirty stories, or slept. Just to be with them was a good reason to spend four years in New England.

Chad Brinker had wire frame glasses, thick blond hair, and a deep bass laugh. He was sleepy. I was leaning against him, feigning drowsiness. I took a chance and let my hand brush ever so lightly across his crotch. Would I die? There was silence. Seconds passed. I leaned against him some more. His arm adjusted to me; his hand went across my back. We both fell asleep, sort of. (Him, really; me, not at all.) Sure, car rides were enough.

No, they weren't. Car rides were a fragment of bliss, not its substance. College continued. I still felt left out. Whatever miracle life contained was taking place on another balcony, the chalice held aloft before another crowd. Wrestling with guys for thirty seconds was not taking me close enough. I would do more.

Brad Heller was my closest friend. I told him about my yearnings, but I tried to keep them vague. "Why do you need to get closer?" he asked. "And what do you mean, by the way — closer?" Heller was a *very* smart guy, but he scorned my wish to play in an intramural softball game. "If somebody threw *me* a ball, or even a frisbee," he said, "I would promptly step to the side." Brad wasn't speaking about mechanics — to catch or not to catch — but of esthetics. It was unseemly to run around on a field shouting "Way to throw!" and "Wheeler, you dork, bat *lefty* the next time!" Unseemly for a person who wasn't *one of them.* "You may be coordinated, but you're no jock," he warned me.

"Don't be too sure," I growled, pulling on my t-shirt. I waved him away and marched down West College Hill toward the field. Toward the field and away from the library, Brad Heller, and a life of contemplative hunger. I left the dorms, houses, and halls behind. My walk took me into the vast playing fields at the campus's northern end. Softball games occupied the several diamonds that made up part of this acreage. From beyond these games came the pungent shouts of lacrosse. Some runners from the track team were jogging in the distance. The mountains were greening almost by the minute; the sky was deeply blue, with high fleecy clouds, and someone's radio played "Monday, Monday, so good to me!" I saw some people from my house and ran over to get included in the batting order.

"Trent! I don't believe it." Danny Mott was wearing his house t-shirt: *Brooks Brother.* I wasn't wearing mine but he grabbed my hand anyway. I was in the game — Brooks House vs. Hopkins House. I looked out on the field, looking for someone on the other team. Yes, he was there all right: the real reason I came to play.

Don Hauptmann wasn't popular, exactly. Certainly he wasn't well-liked. He was loved, hated, feared, mocked, and adored. He was hymned, feted, shunned, an object of perpetual editorials in the mouths of the intelligentsia. They felt he was dangerous.

Dangerous? He came from Chicago and some midwestern military academy that nurtured his patriotic notions and his posture, which was as straight as an iron cross. Likewise his teeth. He had a little blond crew cut, blue-gray eyes that kept looking at you, jutting jaw. Big hands and feet, tra la. In 1966, the whole world saw his legs. He was wearing sneakers and a pair of shorts so slight you had to blink to see whether you had dreamed or perceived them. The t-shirt suggested more muscles than medical students memorize. He was walking around in the outfield, carefully examining a dandelion he held close to his face. It was okay for him to go slumming: his real sport was soccer, in the fall.

"All right," I shouted, "let's play to win!" I was boisterous, possessed. I grinned. My fellow Brooks Brothers had never seen me like this. They laughed. They encouraged me. "You should play in more games, Trent. We like you this way." What they did *not* like was my grousing about being in the wrong house, my refusal to hang out with them. If I played hard, maybe they'd forgive me.

But I didn't really play for Brooks House. I didn't really shout to galvanize my team. When I ran the bases, I didn't care about scoring for us. I did it for *him.* During the first inning changeover, I thought I saw him look me over, like a car he thought he might buy. One of his roommates stood next to him. Hauptmann threw his dandelion away; then he almost smiled at me. Would his "America First" personality accept me because I sounded as if I wanted to win the game? I knew who *he* was but had no idea whether he recognized me. I wasn't dangerous. The boys played on.

When the game ended, everybody began the long uphill walk to the main campus. Hauptmann's roommate, Rick Mason, called out to me: "Hey, Trent! Why not walk with the real men?"

"Maybe just this once," I said, stunned but still casual. Don Hauptmann didn't have roommates, exactly; he had fans and press agents. I went over to them and we all shook hands. "How are ya, Don?" I said. Predictably, his grip was the strongest I'd ever tried. His biceps jumped for an instant. I looked at the vein running down the smooth, smooth arm, at the trunk suspended above the long, strong, hairless legs. His smile saw me watching him. Something was working behind the eyes. A plan, perhaps.

"I like your intensity, Bob," he said; a soft, low voice. "America could use an attitude like that." I gulped and we walked. After paying me a few compliments, Don Hauptmann told me about a little get-together in his room the next night. A few close friends. Would I like to. . .? I grinned, nodded, and counted to one. I was about to join a group whose entrance requirement was not literary skill but personal zeal. This wasn't Bloomsbury; it was Boystown. Would I *like* to? Would Nixon run again?

Brad Heller was logical, severe, a realist. He did not approve of Don Hauptmann. "He has those roommates in a trance," he said. "He's got them waiting on him, agreeing with whatever he says. They tell him he's better than the rest of the school." He was fuming. I said that *I* could use roommates like that. He didn't crack a smile.

"He has no sense of humor, either," Brad said. "He manages to be both dull *and* dangerous. And he says such goopy things. Maple syrup!" He shrugged off his crescendo of irritation and walked around in a little circle. Suddenly he pointed at me. "He'll look you in the eye. He'll tell you you're his friend, and then he's got you. I don't trust him. I don't. And I don't like seeing you fall under his spell . . . What is this meeting, anyway? A seance?"

It was. I wasn't "dangerous," but I was moderately well-known on campus. Because I sang with a group of eight or nine friends at parties, concerts and games — a sort of barbershop octet — I was almost a campus face. Perhaps this minor celebrity helped explain Don Hauptmann's interest in me. I believed he was deeply impressed by performers, people in the public eye.

I was studying Shelley, thinking about rock-and-roll or masturbation. Alone, dreamy. But the knock brought me back to earth.

I opened the door for my guest: Kenny Ross, most intense of Don Hauptmann's roommates. Kenny was gawky, cross-eyed, and somehow sexy. A deep voice complemented the virile yet nerdy impression he always made on me. "If this is a bad time, I can come back later, Trent." He smiled weakly, exuding deference.

"Sit," I said, encouraging him in it. He sat on the edge of the sofa, as if he didn't want the slipcover to know he was there. "You're coming to see Haupie tonight. Right?" I nodded. "Well, there are some things . . . I don't know. . . ." He pulled on an ear and scratched his neck. "It's great — you and him. I've always wanted him to have a friend of similar caliber. The trouble is," he laughed, "it's hard for him." Pause. "Nobody's good enough. The friends he makes turn against him. Even on the soccer team. They know he's the better man, so they. . ." His hands groped the air.

"Hate him?" I offered.

"That's it, Trent. They hate him. Envy, I guess you'd call it. Would you call it envy, Trent?" He smiled grimly.

I got a little annoyed. "What is this, a quiz? Yes, I'd call it envy."

"Well, you see, maybe that's where you come in. Maybe with you he's got someone smart. Someone who cares. About America and things . . . Someone. . ." He groped again.

"Good enough for him?" I said.

He laughed again. "That's it, Trent," he said. "Be a straight shooter." He stood up and put out his hand. I shook it, inferring that the interview was over. I couldn't figure out if I'd just been admired by him or measured for a noose.

I was excited. Who would be there? What *was* the meeting, anyway — Shriners, Masons, Hitler Youth? I wore shorts and a t-shirt. No way I was going to look serious walking in there. His door opened immediately when I knocked — by magic, I guess. "Come in, Bob," sounded from an inner bedroom. The entire suite was dark except for a faint glow coming from the inner room. I walked in.

His three roommates sat in chairs around the bed. He was sitting on it, cross-legged. There were a dozen candles lined up in front of him, making an altar out of him. The others were dressed in shorts, like me. He wore a bathrobe open enough to reveal — yes —

the most perfect body in the world. Was that incense? Because, oh, the sweetness of the air!

"Welcome to our group, Bob," he said. He smiled and untied his robe. He wore underpants but I could see a massive genital shift anyway. The whole building lurched to the right when he moved. I looked at his skin. I didn't try not to.

"Kenny, Ricky, and Frank care about what's happening to the country, Bob. The anti-war types. You care, too, Bob. I know you do. You care about people and beauty and doing what's right. You care about a strong defense. I've been watching you. You're looking for something. Something that won't let you down." He grinned. Flamelight bounced off his skin, the robe, the gray dorm walls, the abject heads of the three altar boys. He patted the bed. I came over and sat next to him. It was my entry into the group and something more: I was on *his* side of the candles. I was invited in, but not merely to worship. I, too, was expected to lead.

"I believe in friendship," I said. He nodded and shook my hand. He had finally heard what he'd come to Williams to live and to prove. He said they all gathered with the candles once a month. The meetings had an obvious purpose: worship of him. Was there any more to it than that? Nobody sang, imitated a funny animal, read minutes of the previous meeting, or made any motions. Motions, my ass. Nobody moved at all. It was a thrill, vulgar and silly as a flavor straw.

The next day, Brad Heller demanded an accounting. When I mentioned the candles, he slapped his forehead. "Don't you see how sick that whole situation is?" he asked. "They're like drugged zombies, programmed to do his will." He made the sign of the cross, blessing the hot dog I was eating. I smiled out into the snack bar. "Is it sexual, do you think?" he asked.

"Oh, not at all," I said airily. "He spoke about some girl at Smith, I think. Girls in general." This was true. The meeting had ended with his eulogy to this girl, someone he had dated a couple of times. "Besides," I added, "you know he's always taking girls to bed." Hauptmann's weekends were a campus legend. Even Brad Heller couldn't deny his prowess as a seducer.

I didn't bother to mention the ripening friendship to my roommates. They were so ironic to begin with, I figured, why give them ammunition? One night about then, I saw my first shooting star.

The trees got greener. The radio played away, and the songs seemed gaudier, richer than the spring before. I was a pulsating, breathing Anticipation. Great outcomes were mine to embrace. Schoolwork was easy, texts lucid and rewarding. I sang better, spoke better, wrote better, lived better. I was probably hard to stand. Nobody wants an ecstatic roommate.

Don Hauptmann told me his roommates would be away the last weekend before exams. Maybe I'd come over, share a bottle of wine, and talk about God, who was in, who was foolish. "We'll just relax, Bob," he said and smiled. Again, I saw wheels grinding behind his serenity. I said I'd be there at eight. I told nobody. Not Heller, my roommates, my mother, the dean, or my draft board. It was a secret — mine, and maybe it would stay that way.

Maybe there would be nothing to hide. Wine. Discussion. Another Saturday night in the dorm. Big fucking deal. I bathed in deodorant, put on the usual shorts and t-shirt, and combed my hair for five minutes. I headed toward his dorm — the legendary (in my mind) Hopkins House — and realized I'd never been alone with him. I'd never *seen* him alone. Always there were roommates, fans, and slaves for life. I counted to two.

"Hey, Trent. What are you doing?" Two fellow singers passed me on "his" stair. My heart raced. *What's to hide?*

"Hi, guys," I said. "Running an errand." And I marched upstairs, concluding discussion.

His door was open, so I went right in. *Rubber Soul* was singing from the living room. His legs were gleaming at me from a chair. "Bob, come on in," he said.

"Hi, Don." I smiled, shook his iron hand (dazzled again by shorts, the great teeth, the little shirt) and collapsed on the sofa, four feet from the chair he sat in. Already he was pouring glasses of wine. "A fine wine. . ." he was saying, "a great girl. . ." He stretched slowly. "If I found the right girl, I would work in garbage all day, as long as I knew I'd be seeing her when I got home at night. All tired and dirty." He smiled. "I think you're a romantic, too, Bob."

"I've met a girl or two," I said, also smiling. "I mean, a girl or two I thought was worth making a religion out of." I suspected that all this talk of girls was the circuitous but very real, route to paradise.

He frowned. "No, no. I don't want a religion, Bob." But he paused to consider. "That's a very romantic idea: to make a religion out of somebody." He was in front of me, his hands on my knees. "We have something special, Bob," he said. "Very few people feel the world as intensely as you do. You have a special kind of intensity about you, don't you, Bob?" At this question, his hands opened out to me.

"I believe things should matter," I said, having some wine. "People matter." I heard my heart and told it to shut up. I was aware of trying to speak slowly, evenly.

"I think it's important that we met, Bob." He refilled my glass and put a hand back on my knee. I felt the lightning this time. A modest lurch in the loins.

A little wine. A little giggle. A strategic slump to the floor. Much less drunk, he also sat on the floor. Our legs and feet entwined. "Don't pass out now, Bob," he said, and grabbed my head with both hands. Now he was whispering, "You haven't had much wine before." He smiled.

"That's not true," I said. Wine dribbled down my chin. He blocked this cascade with his own chin. We rubbed chins. Laughed. I felt his full lips on my face. He felt mine. We didn't kiss on the lips but we sure came close.

I wish we had kissed on the lips. At the time, I'm sure I thought I was keeping my cool. (Men don't kiss — they just get hard.) I was drunk, but that didn't matter at all. I felt it was he, rather, who needed the excuse of liquor. We reached for each other and fell back onto the rug.

What follows is a tantalizing sequence of movie stills. No narrative, no action connects them. His muscular thigh, smooth, exquisite. Me, stroking it — amazed at my good fortune. Me, watching his bullet head as he placed his lips on my erect cock. Me, falling on the floor and smiling up at him. Me, not caring that, as I fell, I was landing on broken glass from a little accident we'd had. Him, stretched out on the floor with my legs around his head.

I know I drank more than just wine. Vodka. Beer. Blood of the gods. He was, it seemed, a health nut, boy scout, and major drinker. I got sick and staggered into the bathroom, threw up madly, then lunged back to his living room floor and woke up a few hours later under a shaft of sun. I was blissful. I didn't know or care where he was. I looked out the window. The campus bloomed some more for me. It was time to go home.

The hangover was easy; the passion, terrifying. At first, things were fine. We had exams. I saw him, I think, twice. Some of this was heaven. Heaven to know that around the next old building, he — shiny and new — might walk, smiling at me. He was gracious, not different. But I wanted more. I wanted to *talk about it*. He, ever cordial, obviously did not. The day he left he told me to "Be strong," and have a good summer.

Have a good summer? He was leaving for Chicago and I couldn't spot any grief on him. He said he'd write and call. I knew *I* would. I knew death.

And my other friends? I was polite to everyone, grinned for the world, and slow-danced the semester away. I was expected to go on with that marvelous nothing, the rest of my life. My peers scattered back to their homes, jobs, girlfriends, classical discs. Brad Heller — upscale, principled — went to Washington to work for Mo Udall. Bobby Kennedy. Somebody. I had no summer plans. I wanted none.

All I wanted was him. To look at him and find him true. His eyes. His chin. His fingers. I arrived back in suburban Long Island with my splendid secret, good grades, and a readiness to weep if the radio played "Softly as I leave you."

You can get away with this for a couple of weeks. TV. Moping. Walking the dog. My mother didn't like to push. "Uh, Bob," she said, "is there something you might like to *do* this summer?" Do, mother? I smiled stoically. Deluded woman. I decided to go to Washington to visit Brad Heller.

"It's simple," he said, as we looked into the gorilla cage at the zoo. "You love him."

"Yes," I said, pulling him toward the big cats. "I suppose I do. But you haven't heard everything." He stopped. He looked me right in the secret. "Tell me something new," he said.

"The night I went to see him . . . No roommates. No candles.

We got drunk. We had sex." I looked down at the gravel walk. So did he.

"I was afraid that would happen," he said, sounding far away and impossibly sad.

"Don't be upset," I said. "Nobody ever wanted it more."

"More than you did or more than he did?" He faced me, hard and sharp. "Look, I said he was dangerous. Now that he's hooked you, I'm genuinely worried about you. Are you gay, or what?" Was *I* gay? What about the rest of Hopkins House, for starters? What *was* the danger here?

"I understand those feelings," Brad said. "I've had them. But listen: have them for someone else." He looked angry. "Don Hauptmann is an abusive person. He likes having power over people."

Heller had felt these things? But I *knew* he was straight. For whom had he felt them? For Don Hauptmann? Perry Como? Me? What had my little experiment revealed about the world? Obviously, I wasn't the only one with secrets. But Brad was on a roll: "Enjoys it, I tell you ... those liquid eyes, the deep stares. The touch of the hand on your chest. That's one of his best." He paused. "No," he went on, "I see what you're thinking. No. He didn't seduce me too! I'm worried about you. Shouldn't I be?" There was such alarm in his face, in his voice, that I, too, began to feel that I had blundered into a world I couldn't face, and attachment too intense to control. For Brad Heller, there was also the problem of taste. He disapproved of Don Hauptmann and intramural sports. It was poor style to fall for a grim boy scout.

"He hasn't called you or written, has he?" Brad asked. I admitted that I hadn't heard from Hauptmann, and for a minute I absolutely hated Brad Heller — hated him by displacement, instead of hating Hauptmann. But I was in crazy love and the smile came back to me. I couldn't stop smiling, in fact. We were standing in front of the crocodiles.

* * *

Have a good summer. I charted no vistas. I made no new friends. My interest in girls, heretofore slight to the verge of mere notionhood, was nonexistent now. At the end of August, I decided to go to

Chicago to see Don. He had left school with such tranquility. He hadn't written (Heller was right), hadn't called. How could he be so well-adjusted? I wanted to work in garbage, come home to him. Hold him. Watch him. He wanted to go to Europe for the summer. And to Europe he went. Or so I found out when I finally got to see him. He was back — contented, soft-voiced, and still gorgeous.

"Bob, I think you'd love Europe," he said. He told me a charming story about taking some woman away from her husband. "She knew I was only nineteen," he purred, "so she didn't try to keep me with her. I told her she should go back to him. Her tears were beautiful, Bob." There were other women. Young girls. He had been Don Juan that summer. With the recounting of each triumph, I felt a little smaller. I felt that he was trying to erase me.

And something else. He took me to the beach. Girls on blankets stared at his gleaming, laughably beautiful legs, his angular, hot face, and I began to feel something other than mere desire. I felt envy. How could I expect him to continue wanting me if the girls didn't stare at *me* too? I was there, but they saw only him. I had to take it. I had to realize that he also knew it. He knew he had the power. Would living without him from now on be easier if I felt hate instead of lust?

It would not. I returned to school in the fall hating and loving him, afraid I would be too obsessed to study. I was a senior. The wider world would soon replace college. It was time to put away the pastoral dreams of wrestling, fellatio, and music. Time to apply to grad school, wake up, smell the coffee; to see a psychiatrist or blow my brains out.

Envy is the most painful feeling of them all. Grief? Loneliness? The stuff of mere *adagios*. Mourning is a little flower and rejected love the tender self-soothing of a quiet weekend. Envy is the green monster, all right. The monster was me.

A lusting monster, too. Oh yes, I still wanted him. A scalding half-taste in my mouth. And that skin. That skin. But the progress of history was achingly clear. He was burying me with his heterosexuality. His girls continued through the fall, so I told him I had decided to stay away from him for the rest of the year. Since I was a senior, that meant forever.

"Whatever you think is best, Bob," he said, stoic or simply glad

I was going. I walked out of his room and burst into a manly spasm of tears. I hated him. I wanted him.

I hated the girls who looked at him with the kind of hunger not usually seen at a college mixer. One of them was as helpless as I was. Chrissie Haldane had tasted him one trashy weekend when he'd decided to forget his ideal love and console himself with the fleshpots. Like me before her, Chrissie wanted nothing of her old life after this. She left Aurora for days at a time, coming to Williams and staying in his room. When he was sick of her, she stayed in a motel. I knew this feeling — once you've licked Paris, to hell with Flushing.

I recovered some. I was able to study again, apply to grad school, wrestle with new recruits. Spring came back, tentative and chilly, then blooming its buds off. Nobody was going to replace him but I sang, I laughed, I lied. I held on to some friends. I felt as if I had been stuffed with straw.

His roommates were cool to me: I had deserted the leader. One night, I huddled against walls and trees in the rain, running from landmark to puddle to get home from the library. "Trent, you shouldn't care about the weather." Kenny Ross stood on a stretch of grass between two big elm trees. Water was pouring off him but he was smiling.

"I don't care about it," I said, not slowing down.

"Too bad nobody's as good a man as Don Hauptmann," he called after me as I reached for the dorm door.

All right, fuck the weather! I turned around, marched over to where he was still standing, and said, "You're an asshole. A major asshole. You don't know anything about him. Some day, when you're ready, come ask me. I might tell you something about your 'Haupie,' something that might make you want to leave the play-pen." I walked away, full of injured glory.

On the last day of finals, I came back to my room and found Ross sitting at my desk. "Hey, Trent," he said, leaning back to show me he felt at home, "tell me something about Don Hauptmann."

"One night last spring," I said, sitting down immediately, "your saintly friend and I had sex. Haupie and I had sex." I wanted to make sure he got it.

His grin vanished. "No, you didn't . . . That doesn't compute, Trent . . . Haupie wouldn't do that . . . He's straight." But his voice was fading as he spoke.

"Yes, Kenny." I spoke softly, cruelly. "It happened. And I don't think he'll deny it if you ask him." I was a rock. A traitor, sure, but a rock. He ran from the room.

I tried to read but a half-hour passed and I was still on page fifty-seven. I got up to put the book away. The front door was open. When I looked toward it, Hauptmann was standing there, both hands in front of him like a karate champion. He looked very grim and his head bobbed up and down a few times, mere matter incapable of expressing his torment. I felt a sickening fear. "Don," I began, moving toward him. He held up a hand to stop me. His eyes burned into me.

"I thought you were a better man than you are," he said. "Some friend." He whispered these last two words fiercely, stared balefully at me a few seconds more, then dropped his head to look at the floor between us. I wondered if he was meditating some violence. Instead, he left.

Brad Heller told me quite succinctly that I had probably ruined Kenny Ross's life. Two weeks later, I was graduated from college.

* * *

I went to grad school forever in New York. There I discovered this amazing thing called the baths. Sometimes, though, I felt keenly that nobody in the world could be as attractive as Don Hauptmann. I wondered what it would be like to see him in a towel.

I don't go back to Williams for fall football reunions or spring blossoms. Even Christopher Reeve doesn't get me to its Adams Memorial Theater in summer. In 1975, though, I went up to Westchester for the wedding of a fellow singer from the old group. Many of us were there. We sang "Soft Summer Breeze" and "How High the Moon." Some were married and showed up with little versions of themselves who hung around and stuck their fingers in the food. The bride was lovely, the whole event graceful and chock-full of smiles. As we stood around the punch bowl telling our new tales of life, a few reminders of the past cropped up.

"Chad Brinker couldn't come," someone said. "He's a doctor, down in Charlottesville, and I don't think he *ever* gets away."

"Yeah, well, good for Chad," another offered. "You know — Clay Henderson is paralyzed in a hospital in Denver."

"What?" Glasses stopped moving.

"Yeah. He was climbing again. You remember how he was always scaling walls? Well, this time it was a genuine rock face. His wife comes and reads to him." This news dispirited the group into silence for a moment. Then Dick Holt, someone I knew only slightly, added more news.

"You'll never guess who I saw," he said. "Don Hauptmann. Just walking down the street in Cincinnati. Same posture. Same stare. The old military strut."

Everybody laughed. For them, Hauptmann was a slightly absurd figure. Everybody laughed but me. I felt my feet rise in my shoes. Holt continued.

"He dropped out of Chicago, gave up his law practice. I can't believe a guy doing that. He said he had disappeared for a while — bummed around the Midwest. And get this..." Pause. "It seems he's joined a commune." He leaned forward and whispered, "A gay commune!" They really had a good laugh over that one. Don Hauptmann in a gay commune? Mr. Straight Arrow? Mr. American Leader?

"Oh yeah, Trent," Holt added. "He said that if I saw you, I should say *hello.*"

I looked around at them, wondering if my case of leprosy was starting to show. I guess I always suspected that Hauptmann would never let me sleep comfortably again. I raised my glass.

"To the new couple," I said.

Feedbag Blues

What in fuck-all he was doing in Dubuque he didn't know. Dubuque, Anything would have been a valid question. Dubuque, Iowa was a *good* question. *Good question,* like you say when you scratch your head at the imponderable.

It was a question Shelley felt he couldn't answer; even though he already had, twice before breakfast even. He'd answered it to the waitress and to the cab driver. He would no doubt answer it many times more. With the same sort of non-information: "Oh, I don't know..." (Which he didn't.) "I guess it just looked like a place to get off the bus," (which it had) "and so I got off." Which just went to prove that the truth doesn't necessarily make for a good answer.

There was more to it, naturally, as there is more to anything; even to ordering scrambled eggs, which Shelley was doing at that moment. He could have voiced his thoughts on the red splotch decorating the waitress's neck. "A real King Kong hickey you've got there," he thought about saying, as he said, "Scrambled, please." But he didn't. He gave his order and let eggs be eggs, and thought about other things.

He got off in Dubuque at least partially because he hadn't wanted to get off in Waterloo. He'd been asleep, on the last of the pills — which he'd taken too often, blowing the whole prescription in less than two thousand miles — and he woke up as they came through Waterloo. He knew this had to be his last stop, or the next one did. He wasn't going to stay on the bus without pills.

He dug out his map and saw that the town called Waterloo was just about the last bend in the road before they ran out of Iowa. But he didn't like the sound of it. He had little in common with Napoleon, other than being at war in a strange land. The map offered a little more Highway 20: there was a twist upwards and a long elbow back down to the Mississippi. At the wrist was a burg called Dubuque.

He was out of pills and he didn't want to go on to Illinois or Wisconsin or wherever the bus went next, so he got his stuff fished out from under the seat and above the rail, from the crevices in the cushions and all the other places things end up hiding. The sun was coming up, a blue-bright day for autumn. He gathered up his things, watched the passing horizon turn from flat to hilly, watched corn turn to trees, and knew it was hardly Iowa any more. At mid-morning he got off, still in the state: he got off in Dubuque.

"Not much work here," she said, the waitress. She poured his coffee too full, splashing the table with a faint hint of unwelcome. "Plenty of people out of work already." You could imagine that she saw right into his pocket, saw the typical quarters and pennies, end-of-the-road money, lonely for the last precious twenty folded in his sock. A motel waitress could see most of that and figure on serving no more coffee and eggs to this character, at least not after the twenty ran out. Not to mention figure that he wasn't going to be breaking that bill for a tip. She didn't apologize for the splashed coffee.

As it was, actually, she was not only rude but wrong: Shelley had a whole fistful of twenties, plus traveler's checks. Jeremy hadn't left him badly. Jeremy had left, which was bad enough, but the details had been dealt with properly — the checking account split, the bills paid, the car sold and those proceeds split as well. Shelley had more than four thousand dollars for Dubuque to welcome.

It would no doubt go further here than it would have at home. That was another bad answer to the good question, but why bother looking for more? There was the true answer he'd given the waitress and the other true answer, that he'd run out of pills. Then there was the ironic answer, the one he was holding at arm's length; the one that had made Iowa stand out on the map. Jeremy was from Iowa.

Not a short time ago, to be sure, so it wasn't something he talked about much. But it was something; it did a lot for a name on a map. All things considered, it might be the truest answer of all, which made it doubly unlikely to be a very good one.

And so, eating eggs and looking out at a cold day, he kept the question on hand: what in fuck-all was he doing here?

* * *

For the past four years in San Francisco, he had worked at Transamerica, so the waitress was wrong about his chances of a job, too. The work he'd done wasn't high-tech or high-education, but it was modern — filling computers with insurance numbers, making the numbers turn over and do tricks. It was the coming thing. Insurance companies everywhere wanted it done. The Radley Group on River Street was a perfect example and hired Shelley the third day. There, he had to answer the question countless more times, under more official circumstances; even on paper, twice. He wrote variations. "I wanted to get away from the city," he said in one interview. "The traffic, the noise, the crowds..." The interviewer looked sympathetic.

"No place to raise a family," he agreed. "Something you're probably thinking about," he added, "at your age." The law didn't allow the man to ask Shelley directly if he was married and the Radley Group was a big enough and careful enough company that it obeyed the law. But they had nudges. "Lots of nice girls around here looking for husbands," the interviewer nudged cheerfully.

Shelley gave a rehearsed smile and a practiced blush. Then he allowed the nearest computer terminal to engage his attention. "Is that a PMS-6000 system?" he asked. "I've always wanted to get to know that set-up." He played the intense specialist throughout the rest of the interview, stepping lightly past the fact that the PMS-6000 was a notorious piece of shit. He admired the wisdom of its acquisition and stroked ego. He got the job, and there was no more mention of marriage.

* * *

Pamela worked at the next desk. She was a game nut who did the "Riddler" questions in the Des Moines *Register* out loud every morning. In the afternoon, she thought up riddles of her own and flashed them onto other people's terminals, in the middle of their work. Shelley thought he was cracking up the first time. Then he saw her grinning at him.

"Do you know?" she asked. The riddle intruding among his mileage statistics was, *What makes the judge at an art contest fall in love?* "I don't know," he told her. She grinned again and tapped keys. The mileage statistics moved out of the way and his terminal said, *An art-official heart!!!*

Shelley said "Ha-ha!" for her. She looked pleased and tapped some more and the joke went away. It took its three exclamation points with it, possibly to be saved for her next creation. Pamela was a three exclamation point sort. She had rainbow stickers plastered on her desk and she identified herself on inter-office mail with a drawing of a happy face. She undoubtedly kept stuffed dogs at home, three little ones to scatter about the bed and a huge, floppy-eared St. Bernard in the corner. Jeremy would have had a priceless name for her. He would have done her hair, probably a special lark for her since he wasn't inexpensive. Then at night, at home, he would have had her number and given it out flawlessly.

"Simply the *tamest* little thing in the chair today, Shel . . . A pet precious hand-fed on *People* magazine with a dash of Garfield calendars . . . I've no doubt her cunt smelled *naturally* of Spring Rose . . ."

And Shelley would have come back with the sort of repartee Jeremy loved, or at least used to: something short and nasty, something about the latest scent being organic sturgeon. Jeremy would have tossed his head back and howled, expensive dark curls shaking. His friends, if they were around — and when the hell weren't they towards the end? — would probably have laughed too. At least they would have smiled, and one would've given Jeremy that indulgent look: *You do put up with a lot, don't you, dear? . . .*

Shelley stopped and mashed the RETURN key, which flushed his carefully listed numbers back into the circuitry. It would take an hour to retrieve them. In that time, with any luck, he could manage to quit thinking about Jeremy.

* * *

Shelley took walks and found the supermarkets and the laundromat. He had cable installed in his apartment and bought a TV. Jeremy had kept the records — they could hardly have been carried on a bus, anyway — so Shelley didn't bother with a stereo. He picked up a radio at a cheap shopping mall store.

A new coffee pot was the first thing that made for a feeling of home. Shelley sat on Sunday morning, his first day off, and looked out the glass doors of the terrace at the town of Dubuque, big bully hills, and smoky sky. He sipped coffee and watched the puffs from the brewery chimneys.

Life turns a lot, he told himself. You wouldn't have thought to end up here, even as a joke. But here you are. It's a stop-off, a place to remember someday, a time to look back on. Remember when I . . . oh, yeah. That was after I broke up with Jeremy. I took that silly bus ride, got off because I was out of pills. I stayed in that hick town for . . . oh God, how long was it? Seemed like forever.

He thought, then, how scary it would be if it *was* forever; if he was still here when it was time to remember the bus ride, when it was all nostalgia. *What are you doing here?* It wouldn't be a good question then. It would be an awful one.

He made breakfast in his rented kitchen. He enjoyed fixing pancakes his own way. (Jeremy and his goddamn blueberry glaze!) He sat at the round formica counter on a plastic leather stool and ate. Then he turned on the new TV, made more coffee, and watched football.

It was a peaceful morning.

* * *

Pamela surprised him a few weeks later by admitting that she smoked pot. She whispered, because Mrs. Morimer, the secretary of the man who did interviews, was in the next room. Mrs. Morimer hadn't learned the art of cheerful nudges; those subtleties were ahead of her time. She stood at the desks of lesser employees and tremulously urged proper lifestyles. Yet she knew she could say only so much — there were New Rules these days.

"A single girl has to be careful," she told Pamela. Mrs. Morimer often quoted the *Register*, and she did so now. "Cancer

Risk Higher for Singles," she read. "It's a new study."

Pamela didn't much care for the mention of cancer on a Monday morning, and looked down at her rainbow stickers. Mrs. Morimer said, "Shelley, you've lived in the city. You know how it is."

"Yes," agreed Shelley, without the vaguest idea of which *it* she was referring to. He knew the *it* of living in a Castro Street loft with a hairdresser for a lover.

"You don't miss it a bit, do you?" she went on. "Of course you don't. All that fast stuff. But we're getting big here. It's just not the same any more. All those problems are filtering down to us . . . drugs, diseases."

"Terrible," Pamela said, wishing Mrs. Morimer would go in and take dictation.

"The thing that's nice here," Mrs. Morimer said, "is that you can settle down."

Shelley keyed his terminal, made numbers appear. There *was* work to be done. Mrs. Morimer stood a moment longer and wished she knew how to nudge. Then Pamela keyed her terminal, and two hints were enough. Mrs. Morimer sighed and went on with her day.

Pamela shook her head. "Old Mary Worth," she said under her breath. Secretly she appreciated it. A Mrs. Morimer, at the right time, could give even stuffed dogs a touch of panache. And Monday morning was the right time, a time when drawing happy faces could begin to seem just the teensiest bit boring. Pamela had a comfortableness with who she was that comes only to those who never think of being anyone else; but these days she was sitting next to this Shelley fellow who was from the Coast, and God knew what he thought of Mrs. Morimer and Dubuque. He was handsome enough that Pamela cared about his opinion, at least a little bit.

So she told him, in roundabout ways, that she did a few "fast" things herself. She let him know that she went out dancing, sometimes two or three times a month, and that she was no virgin to bottled beer. She didn't say anything about being a virgin in other respects, or not; but she did say that she smoked pot. "My brother is in a band. Me and my girlfriend get it from him. My mom and dad would just *die* if they knew."

"We could bury them next to Mrs. Morimer," Shelley suggested, "who would have given up the ghost on the same schedule." He surprised himself with the comment. It was like something he would have said to Jeremy.

He surprised Pamela, too, and upset her. It was one thing to say your parents would just *die,* and quite another to joke about burying them. There was more Mrs. Morimer in her than she knew, and she didn't send Shelley any riddles that day.

* * *

The fast life in Dubuque was high school football and a few taverns on the edge of downtown. If one wanted to get really reckless, there was East Dubuque, across the river in Wisconsin, with its hell-bent-for-leather drinking laws and people boozing on Sunday.

Shelley went to a football game on a Sunday afternoon when the TV cable had gone down in high winds and there wasn't a blessed other thing to do. He watched the game only intermittently, spending more time analyzing the gathering. The boys on the field were cute — helmets with longish hair curling out the back, pads on their shoulders and around their bulging protected crotches. Their parents in the bleachers were less cute. They had bulges in all the wrong places, in their brows and jowls and guts. They cheered lustily and seemed highly conscious of themselves, of feeling good about football and manliness, and of having done some protecting of their sons' crotches themselves. Shelley sat among the coats and scarves and ate peanuts, feeling extremely homosexual.

The home team won in a walk, 48-14. The crowd shouted and whooped, elbowing out of the field, lining up in their cars, honking horns. Night was falling, dark cloudy skies closing in. The lights on all the hills, the lights of the place they called "The City on the Bluff," were twinkling on. The cute football players and their parents were heading for home. Shelley felt excruciatingly lonely. He walked down Highway 66, wandered into downtown and found a cab. "East Dubuque," he said.

* * *

By the next Monday, Pamela had forgiven him. She had good advice for a hangover. Then she fussed with her desktop collections and invited him for Thanksgiving. "If you've nothing planned," she added. "It'll just be me and my folks, and my grandmother and my brother."

"The one in the band?" Shelley asked. Hangovers came with a strange kind of gritty lust. He'd masturbated twice already, once with coffee, once in the shower. He was still horny. He wondered if her brother was a football player.

"Mm-hmm." She poked in her purse for an accordion of pictures. "His name is Tom." She found what she wanted and held it up. The photos cascaded down. "Here's my family."

He was able to find her parents immediately; then her, and her again, and her in high school graduation robes. There was her grandmother and her cat. But no brother.

The hell with it. He asked outright: "Your brother? Tom?"

She took the pictures back. "Oh, he's probably not in there." She wrinkled her nose, dismissing silly old brothers. "He'd think it was sissy for his sister to carry his picture around."

"Couldn't have that," Shelley muttered.

She folded the accordion back into her purse. "Anyway, he probably won't be there. He never shows up for family any more — he's always with his girlfriend. But like I say, you're welcome. Let me know, so I can tell Mom."

He didn't answer and she was suddenly embarrassed. "I'm not being . . . well, you know, pushy," she said defensively. "It was just a thought. I thought you might not want to be, you know, alone. On a holiday."

He still didn't answer and Pamela looked back to her work. Well, there, Mrs. Morimer, she thought, I gave it a try. I think he's just a strange one, that's all.

Shelley thought about the cute football brother who wouldn't show up for family. He decided there was no worse idea on earth than the one of spending a slow Thanksgiving afternoon with Pamela and Pamela's grandmother and Pamela's mother and Pamela's mother's turkey and dressing, watching football and drinking warm wine and waiting to see if the brother would arrive, with or without his girlfriend.

He found he had hit the RETURN key, and all his numbers had disappeared.

* * *

On Thanksgiving, he ate at the bus station diner, which had a sliced turkey special. He was folding whipped potatoes around his fork and reading the paper. In it was startling news: there was a gay bar in Dubuque. The paper only acknowledged this in the course of explaining why a brick might have been thrown through the bar's window. It was only mentioning the brick because it was the origin of the glass in the street, which had posed an inconvenience to motorists. There were two flat tires involved and these got most of the story.

Shelley finished his turkey slices and the pumpkin pie that came with them. Then he folded his paper and left, walking down the street with an eye out for the address of the bar. He found it after a few blocks and one or two random turns. He went in and ordered a beer. There were three older men in the bar, and one came and sat next to him. After some beers, they had a few words. Shelley ended up talking about the Radley Group office, with its Pamela and its Mrs. Morimer and its cheerful nudges. He told the story about seeing Pamela's pictures and not finding the one he wanted; told it in a way that would have had Jeremy in stitches.

But the middle-aged Dubuque homosexual only nodded, as though the same thing had happened to him twice that morning. He was a caretaker at a theater. As a young man, he said, he had been an actor, but nothing had come of it except an affair with a producer and a wink once from Troy Donahue. Shelley imagined Jeremy retelling the story. It was too cruel, like seeing the old man pounded with snowballs by ruthless kids, watching him fall in the street and lose his hat. Shelley heard Jeremy and giggled anyway. The ex-actor stopped, lost the thread of his tale, shrugged and looked away.

No one young came in. The jukebox played quietly, old Streisand and Paul Anka. The bartender walked to the front and switched on the beer signs in the windows. One was boarded up. The bartender sat back down with a magazine. Shelley stood by the jukebox and pretended for a while that he was slumming with Jeremy — they searched together for Johnny Ray classics.

He came back to the bar and sat down. Out the high, narrow windows, he could see that a light snowfall had begun. The flakes shimmered in the street lights.

"Snow," the old man said.

I commend your powers of observation, Shelley thought. My God! Is this all there is to talk about? The weather? What about art, or gossip? What about Troy Donahue, even? Shelley was getting hazy and bemused from too many beers, too much sitting. Every now and then the door opened and another gray Dubuque homosexual came in; all the same, all quiet and cautious, cautious and fragile. Now and then they left, singly or in lonely pairs. Some talked. Some watched the snow falling beyond the beer signs. Shelley said thickly, "In San Francisco, there would be a crotch at every knee by now."

"Hm?" the old man said. He sipped at his beer and seemed to notice Shelley as though he'd just come in. "Why are you here, anyway?"

"I ran out of pills," Shelley said. Then he thumped the bar with his bottle. "No. I got off here because my lover was from here."

"Dubuque? What was his name?"

"Not here. Around here. Ottumwa, I think."

"Oh, down there." Down there wasn't up here. That was apparently all the man had to say of Ottumwa.

"He left when he was seventeen," Shelley said. "He was on the basketball team. He always said that he knew he and Ottumwa were through the day he got a hard-on in the shower. He told the other guys he was thinking about a girl. And they believed him." Shelley did Jeremy: *They believed me, heaven knows why, and I found that I was entirely infuriated by it. The anger was an awkwardly sincere emotion in my adolescent panoply of feelings ... possibly the first brush I'd had with true passion.*

"You?" the man interrupted. "I thought you were talking. . ."

"I was doing Jeremy," Shelley said. "My lover. He's an exceptional talker. As a conversationalist, he could hold his own with Truman Capote and Gore Vidal."

"Capote's dead," the man said. "Now that Gore Vidal, he's pretty good. You ever read *Myra Breckenridge?*"

"So Jeremy," Shelley went on impatiently, "waited until the next home game. He deliberately got there late, so he was alone when he changed into his uniform. The rest of the team was already out on the court. He came out of the locker room and, bit by bit, row by row, a hush fell as people noticed the enormous bulge in Jeremy's shorts. He was showing a basket the size of a pumpkin. But the shot went off and the game began, with Jeremy starting at guard."

Others were listening now, casually inclining their heads. Shelley was enjoying himself. "Three minutes into the game, Jeremy's naughty protrusion began to come unraveled. First it poked at the leg of his shorts and then, as he took a jump shot, it began to slip down. He was. . ." Shelley started to laugh. ". . .he was wearing a huge, I mean simply enormous, rubber dildo. One end was tied around his waist and the other was hanging down to his knees, and still descending. The home team made four straight shots on shock alone because the other players couldn't remember to look at the ball. But when people started tripping over the thing, they stopped the game." Shelley laughed harder and wiped his eyes. "Jeremy was summarily dismissed from the team, the school, and, by his own additional choice, from the community. He ended up in San Francisco, where I met him and. . ." Shelley noticed his beer was empty and ordered another.

"You met him. . ." the man prompted.

"Yes, I certainly did." He felt a sudden fading of the laughter. Here he was, telling Jeremy's stories in Dubuque, and they were believing him. He gulped beer, poured alcohol on it. He turned to the gray old man. "Have you ever *met* anyone?" he asked, plaintive and drunk.

The old man was still sensitive to mockery; he wasn't about to get into Troy Donahue again. "Time to time," he said. "Every now and then there's a new face." He tipped his beer bottle at Shelley meaningfully.

Shelley snorted and said, "If you've been waiting for me, you've waited at the wrong stop." He realized what a putdown it was after he said it, when the man turned away. He started to phrase an apology.

The Dubuque man slid off his stool and buttoned his coat, a dark, tired look on his face. "Happy Thanksgiving," he said, and he walked out of the bar. Shelley raised his bottle to the man's back. The apology, too late on his lips, wandered around and was lost.

No one else came to sit by him. He felt that his great story, his Jeremy story, had only upset them. Cold air crept into the bar through the boarded window. Shelley moved to a table. It felt solid, so he leaned on it. He rested on his elbows and drank until dawn.

* * *

Pamela had discovered Trivia over the weekend. "It's too bad you didn't come," she said. "We had a neat time. And you know who did show up? Mrs. Morimer! She brought a ham."

Shelley looked up. "She brought a ham to Thanksgiving dinner?"

"Well, she didn't come for dinner. She came afterwards. She wanted to see my parents, and. . ." Pamela's voice trailed off. "Well, we had a little problem. Mrs. Morimer has been Mom and Dad's friend *forever*, so she came by." Pamela shifted subjects quickly, with determined perk. "We must have played that silly game until three in the morning. It's really fun, remembering movie stars and old headlines and things. My father was the best at it, but I got a few." She turned and tapped at her keys. "Hold on. Now — look at your screen."

Shelley looked. In the midst of actuarials, it said: *What was the name of the hit song written by Mr. Ed?* "Mr. Ed?" he mused aloud. "Mr. Ed?"

Pamela wrinkled her nose at him. "You know. Mr. Ed! The horse that talked. On TV."

"Oh." He didn't remember at all. Jeremy would have. He was a nut on old television. He did an Ethel Mertz that drew crowds. "I don't know," he told Pamela. "What was the name of the song?"

"I don't know either," she shrugged brightly. "That was the one question no one could answer . . . Mrs. Morimer didn't even know, old as she is." Pamela giggled.

"Couldn't you have looked it up?" Shelley asked. "The game comes with answers, doesn't it?"

Pamela shook her head. "That would be cheating. We're going to make it a project to find out." A project! Something to do for the winter in Dubuque! Shelley felt tired, and irritated at the question on his screen.

"Well, you needn't leave it there," he said. "It's not going to suddenly come to me, because I don't know." He watched the words disappear from his terminal. "Maybe Mrs. Morimer will find out for you," he added. "She can ask Mr. Ed, one old horse to another."

Now Pamela was upset again and she went back to work with a bright pink flush on her face. Shelley couldn't really begin to give a shit, but he said: "I didn't mean to sound snotty."

"It's all right. I'm just on edge. I never have anyone to talk to, and when I try to talk to you it's like . . . oh, like everything's just a joke to you. All of us. I know you've been better places and all, but. . ."

"I'm sorry, honest. I don't mean to be . . . whatever." The odd part was, he really didn't. He didn't know why he disliked her so much. All she was doing was showing him her life, in honest pieces, a day at a time. Why puncture it?

"It's my brother," she went on. "That was the trouble. He was arrested. He's such a nice kid, real upstanding. My parents could just die."

"What did he do?"

"Nothing so much. He threw a brick through a window. He was. . ."

Shelley sat up. "He threw a brick? Downtown?"

"Uh-huh. He was just drunk, I think. And awful upset. His girlfriend . . . well, she kind of dumped him, I think."

Shelley looked back at his screen and the Radley Group's numbers and he hit RETURN to make them go away. Then he got up, retrieved his coat and his lunch, and made himself go away as well.

* * *

He got hold of Jeremy on the second call. Right away, the signs were encouraging: Jeremy wanted to talk and talk. Through a handful of quarters and then a pocketful, Shelley stood at the pay phone and listened gratefully to a voice a thousand miles and more from The City on the Bluff.

"I cannot *imagine* you in such a place," Jeremy said for the fifth time. "Are you trying to prove your courage, love? Slay a redneck and bring it home on your spear?"

"I didn't know I had a home," Shelley said. "All I left was an apartment, with no one in it but me. Home is what I went looking for."

"Well, you're sure as *hell* looking in the wrong place, sister dear. You're being a bore about the whole thing. We were still seeing each other, weren't we? And then suddenly you're gone. The bus in the middle of the night! How Holden Caulfield of you."

Shelley couldn't help laughing. No one else would have said that. Nobody. He only held out a little: "But didn't you tell David you were . . . what was the word? *Chafing,* I think. Chafing under the bridle. I heard that, you know. I was standing right there."

Jeremy sighed impatiently. "Shelley, love, learn not to eavesdrop unless you know what to ignore. I am apt to say anything to David when he's buying the drinks. We have a long-standing relationship on that basis. We never listen to a word from each other. It's how we get on so well."

No one else could have said that, either. Shelley gave up and smiled into the phone. "Do you want me to come back, Jeremy?"

"I really couldn't give a flying Neanderthal fuck, but if you're not here by the time I count to ten I shall hack off a random limb in anguish. Then I'll count to ten again and do another one. Please try to make it home before I become a quadriplegic." There was a pause and Jeremy's voice came again, softly: "Come on, Shel. I need you here, I really do. Because you know something? It isn't really all that much better than there."

"There's a bus at nine," Shelley said. They had a moment of silence, a moment together. Then Shelley said, "Jeremy, there's one thing I must know. It's very important."

"If it's about that boy at the beach, nothing happened. You have my word."

"It's not about that. Jeremy, what was name of the hit song that Mr. Ed wrote?"

Jeremy was not one for missing beats. He gave the answer instantly. "Does that help with your decision?" he inquired.

"A lot," Shelley replied. "I have to go now, Jeremy. I need to pack."

* * *

He packed. He pulled up shallow roots, giving the key back to the building manager and selling him the TV and the coffee pot. Then he walked downtown to the Radley Group just before they closed. Pamela sat at her terminal with a harassed air, terminating for two. Mrs. Morimer came out of her office and regarded him coldly.

"A long lunch, Shelley?"

"I'm afraid I'm leaving you, Mrs. Morimer. I've decided to go back home." Pamela looked up at him with distant curiosity, not understanding, not sure she wanted to.

"It's rather a sudden decision, isn't it?" Mrs. Morimer sniffed.

"Not really. Actually, it took an awfully long time to make. May I have my check?"

"I'll have to make it out. Please wait." She went back to her office, leaving him alone with Pamela. Pamela pretended to be busy but after a minute she looked up at him.

"I guess we're not exciting enough for you around here. Is that it?"

He shrugged. Then he said, "Do you remember the question?" She looked blank. He sat down at his former terminal and tapped it out. She looked at her screen.

"Mr. Ed?" She looked at him oddly. "What about it?"

Mrs. Morimer came back with his check. "I know the answer," he said. Mrs. Morimer raised her eyebrows. "I know the answer, Mrs. Morimer."

Pamela spoke up: "He means to the trivia question — Mr. Ed's song."

"I see," said Mrs. Morimer. An awkward silence fell; they felt each other's presences in the room. Mrs. Morimer's middle-aged dignity started to go askew. Quickly she asked: "Well, what is it?"

Shelley walked to the door and opened it, then turned back to them. "I'm not going to tell you," he said.

Pamela reddened. The corners of Mrs. Morimer's mouth turned down. "That's certainly a strange way to say goodbye," she said.

"It's the best I can do," said Shelley. "I don't have a dildo." And he stepped out into Dubuque's snow, closing the door on the two of them.

Tomás Vallejos

Piñons

I remember, when I was in grade school, the nuns made it all seem so simple. God is up in heaven, they said, watching over all His creatures. It's all part of an intricate plan, they would tell us, like a gigantic patchwork quilt. And everything, every little stitch, has its place in this grand quilt He designed. No matter what color you are, no matter what size or shape, there's a place for everyone.

Sure. So they said. But they forgot to mention anything about people like me. I don't seem to belong in anybody's patchwork quilt. Even my own family treats me like a misfit.

Don't get me wrong. I love my family, you know? But they can be so pigheaded sometimes. Such brutes. They just don't understand. Dad says I'm too sensitive. "Delicado," he says. And Mama doesn't say anything. She just acts as if nothing is happening. She probably prays to God every night that it's only a phase I'm going through.

Maybe Dad's right. I don't know. Why else would all the kids call me names? Even my own brothers. I remember the time my brother Eddie made fun of the way I walk. I was twelve then. I can still see all the kids laughing as he sashayed down the sidewalk, holding his arms tight against his sides, flipping his hands back and forth and wiggling his butt from side to side. I felt like sinking right out of sight into the grass, like a worm. Even Mama once mentioned that I walk as if I'm tiptoeing over eggshells.

And now, here I am, almost seventeen. I'm doing great in school, but out on the street I don't know where to put my hands or how to move my shoulders when I walk. I feel as if everyone is watching me. More and more, I'd rather be alone than have all those people looking at me with that terrible look in their eyes, like I'm beneath contempt.

But here it is. Piñon season. No one wants to be alone during piñon season. At least I don't. That would be like being all alone on Christmas. But things are so different since the last one. Seven years ago I was a little kid, picking piñons with the rest of the family. You know, just another family outing. Well, I guess I shouldn't say just another outing. It was special, because piñons only bear fruit about every five to seven years. So we look forward to piñon season. Last time, we took all the empty flour sacks and buckets we had and tried to fill every single one of them. The whole idea was to gather enough to last until the next harvest.

Of course, they didn't even last until the following summer because they taste so good, who could possibly keep from eating them? Just the aroma that fills the house when they're roasting makes you want to eat them all that same night.

Last piñon season I was only ten and all I thought about then was getting as many piñons as I could. The whole family went and we spread tarps under the trees. Then we shook the branches till the piñons fell from the cones. And the little kids like me would hang from the branches and swing, sometimes until they snapped. The grownups and my older brothers and sisters shook the trees so hard it's a wonder they didn't destroy them all.

That's what I mean about my family. I know they don't mean to be that way, but God! They claim to be so religious, but it never occurs to them that trees are part of Creation, too. We should have a little respect. But try saying that to my Dad. Forget it. He just tells you to grow up and start acting like a man.

Tomorrow they'll go out and spread the tarps again. Then they'll shake the trees until they force the piñons out. I don't even know if I want to go this time. If I do, I just know what they'll say when I rock the branches like the autumn breeze instead of twisting them out of shape the way the rest of them do. The pendejos! They should know the tree won't give its fruit until it's ready. They just don't understand. It's a gift. You don't have to tear it from the tree.

You know, I've discovered something about piñons. They're hermits. Kind of like those cloistered monks the nuns tell us about at school. Kind of strange. And very shy. Their seeds are like that, too. You don't barge in on them. You coax them from their little cells. Quietly. And gently. Don Mateo taught me that. He's the old man who lives a couple of blocks away from us, in the projects. "Piñones," he told me, "are the soul of the people who live here on these mountain slopes. They are rough and enduring, but sweet and delicate at the same time."

"And most of all," he said to me, with a look of reverence I will never forget, "they are rare. Always remember, son, those things that are most unusual in this world are miracles. They are special gifts to us. We shouldn't abuse them." That's why Don Mateo says you should shake the branches gently. That way, you don't get any green piñons. Just the ripe ones that taste the best. Then you move on to the next tree. Leave the rest to ripen, he says, and come back another day. Or leave them for someone else. It makes more sense than tearing up the canyon the way my people do. But try telling Dad that.

There *is* one thing I really like about piñon season. That's the way the families get together in the evening to roast the piñons. I love the way the house fills with friends and relatives, all the kids playing and running around in the back yard. And out there in the cool darkness, the air crackles with the sound of breaking shells. They crack between your teeth and you pop that warm little nut into your mouth, savoring the subtle sweet taste. And everywhere you walk, you hear the thin crunch of broken shells underfoot. It's a big party that lasts until you get so sleepy your head is ready to slip down into your shoulders.

But you know what? My Dad and his compadres end up spoiling that, too. I didn't notice it when I was real little because we fell asleep before they started acting like brutes. But last time I got to stay up late and I learned one thing — tomorrow, I'm leaving before they start getting drunk and acting like a bunch of pigs.

I almost ended up crying right in front of them that time. It was bad enough the way they were acting, bragging about all the women they'd done it with and having arm wrestling contests to prove who's the strongest. But then they tried to make me and my brothers and cousins do the same thing. They even got my brother Eddie and my cousin Abe into a boxing match. And to top it all off, they made bets on who would win, as if Eddie and Abe were dogs or fighting cocks. They didn't mind, but I hate that. So, because I wouldn't do it, they started calling me names. And my Dad was just as bad as all the rest.

Well, not me. I don't like getting my head knocked in. You know what I do like? I like to walk way out into the canyons and just watch. And listen. Out there, I don't have to listen to the priest and his stupid answers when I ask questions about God's justice and mercy. I don't understand how God, if He really exists, can condemn anyone on this earth when He's the one who made us imperfect in the first place. But the priest always ends up telling me the same old thing. "That's the mystery," he says. "You have to have faith."

And out there in the canyons, I don't have to hear Mama, mumbling on and on, rosary after rosary. And Dad, telling me how God made men to be this way and women to be that way. I'm supposed to feel like some kind of freak because he says I'm too delicate. He calls me a weakling. But when things go wrong, he's on his knees in church, begging God to make them right.

What I like most of all about the canyons is being among the piñons when there's no one else around. Not that they're the most beautiful trees in the world. Far from it. They're squatty and gnarled, kind of like old hunchbacks. Not like regular pines that stand so tall and stately.

Still, there's something brave about them. I don't know if I can explain it. It's not like being brave the way my Dad tells me to be, swinging blindly while someone is cracking your nose with a boxing glove. Feeling it burn and tasting the salty blood dripping down into your mouth. No. It's something deeper than that. Something those pendejos wouldn't understand.

I go out to the canyons in summer and see the piñons almost writhing in the heat. I'm especially fascinated by the ones on the steep canyon walls. They remind me of some fierce bird, like a hawk, with knotted talons clenched tightly in the soil. There's something lonely about those trees, something lonely and tense. Like the shrill whistling of the dry wind. Or those almost electric screams of the cicadas looking for mates.

In the fall it's even sadder. The cicadas are gone. All that's left of them are empty shells that you can see through, and wonder where the life went. I stand on the edge of the canyon and listen to my echo bouncing off the walls, repeating itself until it fades away. The trees there are windswept, as if they've been beaten low through more lifetimes than you can imagine. Some are huddled and lopsided. Others have their branches splayed. They are frozen in that awkward position, like an animal fighting for its life; locked forever in a struggle against some brute force.

But how could I ever explain that to my folks? Mama would probably think I'm possessed by the Devil. She'd make the sign of the cross all the way to church and light twenty candles to the Virgin. And Dad would just say something like, "Why do you waste your time thinkin' such stupid things? . . . If you ain't gonna go out for football, why don't you get a job?"

I do love my folks. And sometimes I wish I could be the kind of man they'd like. But I think maybe those nuns were right after all. Just because people don't appreciate something doesn't mean it has no place in the world.

Let them think what they want. I'm going out tomorrow to pick piñons the way Don Mateo told me to. Nice and gentle. The only way I know.

Patrick Franklin

Sea Gift

Once I loved the sea. I can remember images that were exciting to me then: the sea churning itself into a foam of frenzy, the waves beating into my consciousness from a depth that I could not begin to imagine. I walked its shores, finding joy in the gifts it brought up, believing its magic to be kind. I still look for what it might bring me.

How long has it been since I came to know its real nature? I can no longer put a date to it, or even a year. There was a time, though, a specific one that came at the end of a long summer. Was it called Labor Day? Holidays seem hard to understand, and any change from my day-to-day existence does not come. A holiday? They were all holidays then.

Say it was Labor Day for a point from which to begin. I know that the sun had turned my skin brown and brought red lights to my hair. I could smile at my neighbors, appreciating their admiration in return. They loved me then, and I loved the chance to live among them, those simple people who easily understood my simple needs.

Not much: a cabin far away from most of them on the shore; a big room with a fireplace I soon learned to abandon for the wood-stove that was uglier but more efficient; a small, always cold bed-room. To that cabin I brought back kerosene and flour from my hikes to town, happy when I was lucky enough to catch a ride in

Fred Towner's new Ford, riding in style with the supplies stuck in the rumbleseat.

There was always fresh fish, or shrimp with some luck. There was a clean well and indoor plumbing, even if it piped only cold water. Cleaned and oiled, my trusty L.C. Smith typewriter was a good companion that hit the paper with satisfying clunks, forming words that made sense to me.

If there had been a deadline, I might not have felt so free. I had an excuse for independence: I had written a book, a modest seller that provided me with a passport to a summer of what I thought of as productive indolence, a time to relish the happiness of nothing to do and everything to express. Maybe such a time has been your dream. Nothing that I needed was beyond my means. Food and housing were cheaply paid for, and Fred could even come up with a pint of brown liquid that claimed to be brandy for those times when I needed to dull myself into dreamy oblivion. Depression and Prohibition were meaningless concepts, for the concern of others far, far away.

I had no need to join them, and certainly no desire to do so. My summer world was bounded by the flight of gulls and defined by the regular progress of the sea. Sometimes it gave me broad room when it lay low and sometimes it cramped my lawn when the moon whipped it high toward my small house. I enjoyed an agreement of life and nature that summer's end had begun to cause me to mourn.

Sarah Constance was my landlady and even she saw the growing sadness with which I matched the waning of the sun. It was she who sold me kerosene and flour, she who measured my unhappiness as my orders dwindled from gallons to pints and pounds to ounces. Sarah's shrewd storekeeper's eyes had amassed experience over the years. She knew that needs would be told to her, but dreams were something she could read without words and exploit for herself.

"Clearin' things out?" she asked that day. "I can let you buy eggs by the each, if you want. No need lettin' them spoil."

"Thanks, Sarah, but I've got plenty of eggs," I must have whimpered. "More than I need, in fact. How about selling me a bit of butter and cream? Maybe I can finish it all off in something good."

"Lotsa leftovers? You been buyin' fairly regular, payin' better'n most, too. Whyn't you just stay over?"

"You know why, Sarah. My rent's paid through the weekend, no more. It's time to leave."

"Not unless you want it to be," she rejoined, looking away from me. "Good renters like you ought to be encouraged. Ya interested?"

I heard the gentle rush of the surf while the noise of els and traffic engorged my mind. Visions of friends who disturbed my work beset me. Cocktail parties and visits to speakeasies seemed to stretch to a long and pointless vista. Against that, I found myself weighing the flight of birds against gray days, a cold wind fighting my small fire, and the possibility of snow falling on a boundless ocean.

"Yeah," I answered. "What's your price?"

What she named was a ridiculous amount for a ticket to tranquility. I decided then and there to stay until the change of season once more. "Winter," I said, but Rimbaud's words came to my mind — "the season of comfort."

"It's a hard time," Sarah offered, "but it's a quiet one, too, and that's what you're after, I think. You'll get plenty out of it," she added cryptically.

"Thanks, Sarah," I replied, trying to keep the excitement out of my voice. "I don't think I'll need much more than what you've been giving me."

"You may just be right," was all she said.

The weeks that followed were more glorious than summer. No tourist, no invader broke my solitude, and the season set the trees afire with color and brought choirs of passing birds whose songs faded south, only to be replaced with others as brilliant and even swifter in their flight. My routine fixed itself as I learned the appetite of my lamps and my need for staples. From a weekly venture, my trips to town slowed to twice a month, then less. In late November, Fred Towner stopped by of his own accord.

"Thought I'd bring you the mail," he mumbled, shy as always.

I shuffled through the slight assembly of bills and notices, finding nothing of any importance. "Hardly worth your trouble, Fred," I observed. "Thanks anyhow."

"Ever see much out here?" he suddenly inquired.

"Oh, plenty — as much as I had hoped." My gratitude for being where I was didn't seem to be the response Fred sought, however. "What do you mean?" I finally asked when I read his face.

"Never mind," he said, in a manner that insinuated there was much to mind.

"Come on, Fred, what should I see?"

"What you should see is what you do see. I was just wonderin' if you seen anything else."

"And what might that be?"

"Just crap. Just a lot of tall tales old women tell."

"Fred, did you bring any of that hooch with you?"

"Never miss. Sure I did."

"Well, sell me a bottle of it, and let's sit down and test some."

Fred's liquor had a hard edge to it, and so did his story. It was about a captain whose ship had struck the reef just offshore from my beach, within sight of home. "Buford Tillson was his name," Fred whispered, reaching for the bottle, "but I can tell you more that the old ladies don't know at all."

"Another snort of the alcohol you sell and nothing will faze me," I joked. "Give it to me straight."

"They killed Buford Tillson because he liked his men too much," he leered, pouring himself a shot. "If you get my meaning. All that was fine with the men as long as the sailors needed him for a way home — and for a sweet moment of pleasure, if you get what I mean." He looked at his glass and decided to take the easier course, hitting the bottle as he continued.

"But he had one of them right in sight of shore." Fred looked out at the sea. "The men rebelled. They figured what was all right at sea was something to be forgot when they got home. They rebelled against him — lifted him right off his catamite, I hear. They didn't quite kill him. They made him suffer, and they made him hurt. He was bleeding to death as they threw him overboard and hove to home. They just threw him into the waves and left him to drift up as they limped into port."

"Did they ever find his body?"

"Tillson? Not ever. And here's the bad part," Fred continued, giving me a warning in his drunken way. "They say that you still see him walking the beach and searching. That's what I wanted to know if you ever seen."

"Well, Fred, not yet," I began, figuring that it was time to let him feel some sophisticated scorn for such a naive notion.

Fred only heard my words, not my tone. "When you do," he replied deliberately, "tell me first. Maybe I can help you."

I held my laughter until he left. It was a good joke, a spark that lifted the gloom of the first fog of the winter drifting in behind him. It was too good a story for a writer to forget, one that begged consideration and treatment. I found it piquant in several respects. Buford Tillson was a perfect name, one too genuine to be called up by even the most inflamed imagination. Death in sight of home was a fine touch; and maybe it was not even death, but something else. I decided to do some research on the story.

Sarah was the logical place to begin. As the quartermistress, supply mistress, postmistress and general factotum of the town, she kept all the records of the place, from marriage licenses to death certificates. When I told her the story, I was surprised to hear her answer.

"Buford Tillson? Never heard of him."

It was strange that Fred had been so certain of a local legend and Sarah so definite in denial. Stranger that it affected me so directly. Strange enough to send me miles away to the nearest library. It didn't take too long to find a listing for Buford Tillson, nor far more than that.

Fred's story might well have been based on fact. Two seamen had been charged with mutiny in 1888 when an incident much like he had described occurred. The details were not as racy as the ones he had recounted. A sea captain from a nearby port had been overpowered within sight of land and cast off his ship, while the crew sailed on home. The two men claimed that the captain had been swept from the ship by a huge wave and were eventually exonerated. Strangely, only they had testified; none of the rest of the crew was questioned.

The newspaper account provided me with one lucky stroke. There was a picture of the captain himself in the clipping, an old engraving that showed a man with dark brows hovering over saturnine features. A boldly flaring nose lent authority to the sensuousness of his thick lips but the details of the face were lost in the haze of the engraving. In any event, it was a memorable face, one not easily forgotten.

Troubled, I returned to my solitary cabin. Winter hung heavy over its roof and the fire in the small stove felt smaller and smaller with the growing length of the nights. Fog brought dampness that clung to the walls and furnishings. My typewriter developed a rusty spot, making the "n" stick each time it was struck. No amount of polishing with steel wool could make it bright again.

There was a full moon at the solstice, an astronomical rarity that I had no way to appreciate. It brought waves farther up the shore than I had ever seen, where they crashed bright silver on the sands in the light of a sometimes brilliant moon. The surf was threatening, almost vicious in its forays to the shore. Clouds made the scene's illumination unsteady, as if what was happening were shameful, something secret that should still be recorded.

The sound of a startled bird pierced the roar of the surf, seizing my attention. I turned to see a figure that chilled me. It plainly made its way from the high line of the ocean's reach, laboriously climbing the sand and marking it with heavy footprints that showed its progress. The form was human, struggling, apparently in pain. Never quite falling to a crawl, it teetered on the edge of balance, determined somehow to achieve its goal. Judging from its emergence on the beach, its betraying footprints, and its dogged path, it aimed directly for me.

I could not move. What frightened me simultaneously fascinated me with a terror that wanted sureness. So many times had I read of, dreamed about, pondered and wished for a contact with a revenant, a visitor from the other side of death, that this chance, this moment of knowing, gave me a bravery that made my blood run cold even as my heart beat faster.

As he approached, his lines became more distinct. It was a man wearing a coarse seaman's shirt and pants, a pea jacket and a billed cap. He was sodden with water, but the sea had left its marks on him in more troubling display: he was draped with long strands of kelp, like some denizen of the dark ocean's garden. His face evaded the light. I could not make out his features. What I had felt as a chill of the night I began to realize was a shiver of fear. I peered closely but the collar of his coat, the bill of his cap, or the shadow of a scudding cloud occluded his eyes, his nose. He fell face down against my steps, motionless.

The sea rose to a great roar as I looked at his back. The hair that edged below his cap might have been any color; it was wet through and through, dripping with salt water. His breathing was barely apparent, made hideously perceptible only by the tremors of the dank sea fronds that trussed him. Cold as I was, I dreaded touching the cold I knew his body held. Then the screech of another sea bird sent a further chill through my frame. I was as cold as he. I reached out and turned his body over to face the pale and uncertain light of the moon.

The visage I saw frightened me as much as the one I expected to see. It was that of a young man, fine-featured and sensitive, whose chiseled nose should have dwelt between rosy cheeks. Instead, the face was livid with cold and exposure, its lips blue and oxygen-starved.

He was absolutely still. No motion indicated any hint of life in the form and I feared for the handsome youth who lay before me. I parted his jaws and almost automatically placed my mouth on his, exhaling roughly to force his respiration, intent on breathing life into him. I felt him stir, sensed a shudder in his pitifully bony body. Encouraged, I continued. I held his hand as I blew air into his lungs, and felt it tighten to clasp mine. A slight sigh against my mouth let me know that he had begun to breathe again.

Then I felt a more disturbing sensation. My mouth was still on his, trying to anticipate and assist his inhalations and speed his recovery. But a warm, moist invader answered me. His tongue touched mine, then began an amazing exploration of my teeth. I drew away.

He opened his eyes, brilliantly blue ones that I wondered at even then. All that sea water and still so clear. Then he spoke to me,

"You gave me life again," he whispered. "I will make you a like gift."
I thought he was delirious. "Are you awake?" I asked. When he nodded, I spoke to him gently, as if to a child. "I'm going to get you some dry clothing. Just stay there until I get back, and we'll get you into a warm bed."

"I'll see you again," he answered, but he made the words a statement, not a question.

"Of course," I assured him. "Everything is all right now."

That seemed to satisfy him and he smiled as he watched me turn to go into the house. I ran to load myself with blankets, towels, anything warm and dry I could find, rooting through cupboards and closets. Yet, though I was away from him for only a matter of minutes, I was not quick enough. When I hurried back to the steps, he was gone. The place where he had lain was bare, only fronds of kelp remaining to show me where he had been. There was no damp, no mark from his wet body; the wood was dry and unstained. Even the seaweed was dry, dessicated as if it had been thrown up on the land many years before.

I ran to the beach, searching for some sign of where he had fled, but the fog had crept in to obscure the moonlight and shroud the dunes. The thrusting surf had erased the tracks leading to my house, leaving only the last few hesitant marks he had made as he fell at my door. Already, the wind was at work scouring those away. Except for the relics of seaweed, there was no indication that my visitor had ever existed.

I sat awake that night, thinking that he had to reappear. I could not believe that, weak as he was, he could possibly survive the cold and wind. Twice more before dawn, I wrapped myself in heavy wool to go out and search for him in the dunes but I found no track, no trace to follow. I grew more agitated and distressed.

I attempted to find rational explanations for what had happened. I kept reminding myself that my anxiety was what any normal human being would have suffered; that such a strange and life-threatened apparition would have spurred the most phlegmatic man to high concern.

But something else gnawed at my conscience, and that was something I could neither understand nor rationalize. My self-imposed exile had been an easy choice, for I was a solitary. Marriage and family held no appeal for me, and I had long before abandoned the pursuit of women. Whatever it was that I lacked, none of the fair sex seemed to fulfill. It was simpler to live with an apparently undefinable need than to complicate my existence with what would at best only be pretense.

My mouth remembered the touch of his, though. My lips still smarted from the rasp of the whiskers that had rubbed them. No kiss had ever moved me to emotion before; yet his, the first of any man in my experience, had invaded me. I had to find him, if only to expunge that sensation.

At first light, I set out once more. I prowled in ever-widening circles, always returning to the cabin in case he had come back to it from a different direction. Neither dune nor marsh nor littoral yielded a clue. Exhausted, I stopped at dusk, returning home to light all my paltry collection of lamps to place in the windows, hoping to set a beacon for him to follow.

I sat beside the door, alert to the smallest sounds. A scrap of shell blown across the porch brought me to instant reaction, but neither lights nor my call into the dark brought any response. I dozed, only to be wakened by a crash. The rising wind had thrown a night bird against the window and again I fought to make myself heard above the gale. I prayed for him in the coming storm.

Sleep dropped heavy on me, unpreventable. As if drugged, I passed into unconsciousness, dreaming fitful dreams of yawning chasms, ocean depths, mouths. I do not think it was light or the curing of fatigue that woke me. Instead, a profound and pervading silence broke my sleep.

The wind had died, the ocean was calm. The quiet was such that it seemed as if all life was poised and waiting for a signal. I looked out my window to see a picture of glory. The cold wind had condensed fog on all the vegetation in the dunes. The night air had frozen the weeds into glassy lines, frosting each stalk of sea wheat and etching glittering diamonds on the mulberries. For a moment, possibly that very moment I saw them, they would be beautiful. Then, as sun melted the ice, they would blacken and die. The ephemeral display was magnificently appropriate. I suddenly realized the date; it was December 25, and this was nature's Christmas gift.

Excited, I threw open the door to rush out into the sparkling landscape, and nearly fell over a figure on my doorstep. It was he, the man whom the sea had washed ashore to me. His bright blond hair shone in the sun with almost as much intensity as the ice-crusted plants. He broke his scrutiny of the dead-calm water to look at me. "You're awake, then?"

"Yes, and for heaven's sake where have you been? I thought you had wandered off in the storm to die."

His clear blue eyes regarded me closely. "I did wander off, into the reeds. I wasn't what you would call in possession of myself. I've been sleeping out there."

"But what can I do? Come inside. Where were you? I looked all over for you. Is there anyone I can call? Are you hurt?" My babble went unheeded. I drew him up by his shoulders, feeling new strength beneath my hands. He accepted my aid, his hand lingering on mine as he rose. I know I must have reddened at his touch. "What can I get for you?" I hurried to offer.

"Some coffee, maybe," he suggested, watching me intently.

Even then, I doubted that he needed my help to move to the table. He walked easily, though his hands and face were dried and caked with salt, his clothing was ripped and shaggy. I felt pity for him. As I made the coffee, he chafed his hands, flaking the residue from them.

He accepted the mug, savoring the heat of it on his fingers. His movements were slow and measured, as if he was remembering long-forgotten things. He held the mug to his face, allowing the steam to warm him, sniffing the aroma of the brew. He watched me as I watched him, measuring my movements as I did his. I was embarrassed by his calm, unwavering gaze. "Can I get you anything else?" I asked, trying to break the hold of his riveting eyes.

He paused, setting the untasted coffee on the table. "May I have a bath?" he asked.

"Of course," I responded, glad to have some excuse to evade him for a moment. I drew water into the big kettle and hoisted it onto the stove. "It will take a few minutes to heat up, though."

"That's all right," he said to my back. "I've been waiting a long time for it. I can wait some more." I ignored the comment, busying myself by dragging in the zinc tub and pumping cold water into it.

When I turned to look at him again, he was standing. He had removed his jacket and folded it carefully on the back of the chair. He continued to remove his clothing with motions that were careful, almost studied, and their slow progress hypnotized me into inaction. I watched as he drew his shirt from his wiry chest, admiring the muscles that plated the still-visible ribs beneath them. He sat, pulling his boots from his feet, then his socks, which he folded neatly atop them.

His eyes forbade me to ignore him as he unlatched the clasp on a heavy belt buckle, once brass, now green with salt corrosion. The buttons on his trousers popped open and he slid them down long, slender legs. The trousers, too, he folded carefully, placing them on the chair seat. Then he stood before me, naked.

His body was hairless. No scars marked his flesh. They would have been apparent on the expanse of milk-white skin that only faintly tinted to rose. He seemed exquisitely vulnerable, except for his eyes, which glowed with some message I did not understand. There was pride, even surety, almost arrogance in his attitude. And then he shivered. His involuntary motion woke me from inaction and, I must admit, my frank inspection of his body. I hurried to get a blanket; but I had noticed with gratification that his lips had lost their unhealthy blue tinge.

When I returned, he was standing next to the stove, clasping his hands to his chest to conserve his body heat. The stark relief of his ribcage and its contrast with his rounded buttocks reminded me of the body of a child. He turned, smiling, as he heard my footsteps. I flared the blanket into the air, trying to settle it on his shoulders. He caught one end of it and turned, wrapping me in the covering as well, drawing me close to him and pulling my arms up so that I embraced him.

His cold was penetrating. It felt as if he drew the warmth from me into himself, but the heat of my suddenly rising emotion generously supplied both of us. I felt the bones against me; but in a far, far more affecting way, the roundness of his hips and their promising softness. The water on the stove was beginning to seethe. Only the tiny bubbles rising to its surface broke the stillness until he spoke. "Your clothes are cold," he complained. "Warm me with yourself."

He faced me and began to undo the buttons of my shirt. I could do little more than stand and allow him to undress me beneath the blanket. His hands were sure at their task, leaving his eyes free to taunt my modesty and tempt my increasing arousal. His cool, smooth flesh against my heated body stimulated me; I tried to hide that from him, but only increased his ardor. He drew me closer and I felt the tingling of the only hair on his body grinding against me. Then he turned.

My anxious flesh was both soothed and excited by that position. It found solace in the softness of the hemispheres that tried to surround it, but surged harder to explore the darkness that lay between them. He moved slightly, surely, and I was engulfed, swallowed, swept into a maelstrom of sensation that erased my will, transforming me into a machine of lust that knew but one aim. We fell to the floor, I barely sensible of the frailty of the youth who lay beneath me. I rode to a destination too ecstatic to be remembered and then lost myself in senselessness.

Some great power had passed between us, but it was the gentlest stroking that caused me to open my eyes. My cheek was on his shoulder, and he was gazing at me from a cramped position. He had disengaged one arm to caress my face with a hand that bloomed ruddy with blood and life. I hurried to separate myself from the shameful connection but an unusual lassitude slowed my movements. Still weighted with the fatigue of my shocking act, I found it hard to stir.

Not so with him. As soon as he was free of my encumbering bulk, he leapt up. The blanket fell to the floor as he dashed to the kettle to check the heat of the water. I groggily drew on my pants. Waiting, he showed every sign of energy; he stretched, expanding muscles I had not noticed before. His body was fuller, it seemed, heavy with strength and power. He snapped up a towel and poured the boiling water into the tub, testing it for temperature and drawing a bit more from the pump to cool it to his liking. "Soap?" he requested, watching me laboriously lace up my boots.

"In just a moment," I replied, and I could hear myself creak as

I stood and walked to the bedroom to fetch him a bar. My supplies had dwindled and it took me some time to locate a sliver of bath soap. I limped back to the kitchen, hardly prepared for what greeted me. Once again he was gone, this time leaving only the tepid tub of water and a limp, slightly stained blanket. I was alone.

I slumped into the chair that had held his things, my head aching with conflicting ideas, feelings, emotions. I had felt enough more than warmth to know he was real; indeed, what I had felt was too strong to name, too alarming to allow even the thought of that name to be spoken. I hated what I had discovered and I resented him for revealing something to me that I did not want to know. At the same time, I worried about his inexplicable disappearance and worried that he would not return. I dared not ask myself why I needed to meet him again.

I concealed those feelings within a cloak of anger. There was no coffee for me that night, only a pot of weak tea. My concern for the ungrateful stranger had made me forget my own needs. I had only enough kerosene to light one small lamp for myself, having burned so much in my attempt to attract or locate him. I resolved to make my way to Sarah's store the next morning and restock. I hoped to find Fred, too. His fund of information might lead me to some answers to the questions that plagued me.

My body would not let me wake the next day. My eyes opened several times, but I could not respond to daylight. When I did rise, it took every ounce of my energy to drag myself from the warm bed into the cold day.

The sun was already high in the sky when I set out to town. As I walked, I was newly aware of how many small hills and troughs there were on the path and I wondered at how I dreaded the rises and their demands on my legs, and how glad I was at the downhill slopes. My bleak mood slipped more when I saw Fred's coupe crushed against the bridge abutment at Elkhorn Slough. The odd angle of the wheels told me that its axle was broken, and even the lack of any evidence of injury to its passengers gave me little solace. All I could think was what that meant to me: I would certainly have to walk back all the miles from the store, carrying my purchases.

Sarah caught sight of me as I labored up the footpath to her store, coming out to greet me laconically at the entrance. "Buy small," she warned. "You got to carry it all yourself."

"Thanks, Sarah, I know. I saw Fred's car. He's not hurt, is he?"

"Naw, not a bit. Well, a little shooken yet, I guess, but no more'n that."

"What happened? A little too much to drink?"

"Jest silliness and damfoolery. Truth is, he was worried about you and went drivin' off in the fog, then bam! right into the bridge. It'll take a week or more to get a axle."

"Worried about me? What for?"

"No sense in it at all. He's jest got this idea about storms when they happen at the solstice, and he thought you was blown away, I guess." She moved away from me to the shelves, fingering coffee, sugar, flour. "Now, you're gonna want some kero for sure, and what else?"

"Like you say, I better keep it light. Small kerosene, a pound of bacon, some canned milk, beans, coffee..."

"Thank the Lord you're safe," shouted Fred, running into the store. His concern was evident, and it felt good to hear it. But then he stopped, looking closely into my face. "Lord sakes, what's wrong with you?" he asked. "You're pale as a ghost. What happened?"

"I think I must be coming down with something," I laughed. "I had a visitor, though."

"Jesus! Buford Tillson?"

"Now that's just crazy," Sarah cut in.

"I thought you never heard of Tillson."

"Fred told me about it," she explained. "Dumb ghost story."

"Wasn't so dumb for your brother Tom," Fred spat.

"Never mind Tom. This man don't want to hear none of that. He wants his supplies, and he wants to get home with 'em."

"No!" I objected. "I'd like to hear all about it."

"Tom used to say he seen Tillson outside your place."

"Fred!" Sarah's voice commanded. "Shut up! I don't want to hear no more myself. Now Tom's dead, and that's all there is to it, and I hate to hear it!"

Fred was cowed but he had more to offer, and I knew it. He tried to put a better face on things. "You're right, Sarah, and I'm sorry. Just give him what he wants, and I'll help him get it home."

"You'll do no such thing," she barked. "Not with all that stock settin' on the stoop and all your chores to do. Sorry as I am, we'll jest have to fix it so's he can tote his stuff as easy as possible."

She gathered my groceries and bound them into a tight bundle, enabling me to carry it under one arm and the kerosene can in the other hand. Fred watched her silently. As I left, he ran to my side, out of sight of the store. "Tom ain't dead for sure," he whispered as we walked. "We ain't seen him for more'n ten years, so he probably is. But he jest disappeared, so nobody knows fer sure."

"What does he look like?" I began, but Sarah's loud call from behind stopped Fred in his tracks.

"Fair," he cast back over a shoulder as he scooted to the store. "Strong, like his sister."

The walk home was endless. Tired when I began it, I was exhausted halfway back, and soon afterwards near to tears from fatigue. The early winter night was coming on and I anticipated the approach of the cold and darkness with dread. That alone kept me going, one step at a time, pausing only for brief rests that permitted me to shift the dead weight of my burdens from hand to hand.

The cabin looked small against the grey ocean when it finally fell into sight. The idea of an end to my journey and the spur of a sudden, cutting wind quickened my pace, but only at the cost of more pain.

I had no appetite or desire for food. Rest was the only need that filled my mind, but I knew the tiny bedroom would be cold with night's chill. I ignored the empty lamps, setting my kerosene beside them for the morning, and instead lit the fire laid months before in the inefficient fireplace. It soon roared and surged but its heat wafted up the chimney, bringing me little comfort. I edged closer and closer until my clothing began to smell of singed wool. Only when I ripped it from myself and stood as near to the flames as I could did my chilled body find any relief. My painful feet would not let me remain standing. I collapsed to the hearth, prostrate with weariness.

When it happened, or how long he had stood before me, I do not know. He had made no sound. I simply saw nothing one moment, and then realized he was there.

No longer was there any hint of the child in him. He was strong and sturdy, full-bodied and brawny. He smiled as he looked down on me. "Feelin' puny?" he asked. I attempted to rise, but I found I lacked even the slight energy that required. "Don't try. I know how it is." He was removing his jacket and shirt, still smiling as if he were amused by my impotence. I tried to mouth a word and he noticed my effort.

"Tom? That what you're tryin' to say?" He was undoing his belt, the buckle now shiny in the firelight. "So you found out my name, did you? Everybody else who ever seen me thought I was old Buford," he whispered as he reached down to caress my cold stomach. His hand was wonderfully warm there. "But then, they was all different, you know . . ."

His body was now completely bare and the flames shone on bronzed skin, under which muscles rippled too close and thick to allow any bones to show. He knelt at my feet, stroking my legs, still speaking to me in the tones of a lover. "I need you jest for that, jest because you're different. I need you because you're like me, and that's what old Buford needed." He extended himself to lie atop me, his weight nearly crushing out the little air I could pull into my lungs.

His face loomed only inches from mine and I smelled the sea on his breath. "A man is what you always wanted but you could never let yourself to admit it. And a man is what I need, to draw the strength from to let me live again." His hands were tender as they touched me and hot lips teased my cheek and shoulders. "Buford came back from the sea lookin' for that, and he found me here. Now, I've found you."

He kissed me full, his strong tongue probing my mouth. I was hungering for it. When he removed it, I felt as if the very water of my being left with it; and when it thrust again, it centered all of me in that one sensation.

"Once more," he said. "One more pleasure for me to draw from, and for you to lose yourself in." I saw nothing beyond his broad body as he knelt back, facing me, then raised himself on his heels. My last glow of bodily warmth gorged itself into my genitals. Freezing and shivering, I felt him accept me into his hot depths. I rose to an atmosphere of exquisite cold, soaring into winds that froze and bit my skin with pain. I was struck with a lightning bolt so frigid that it shocked me to my very soul.

An all-encompassing stupor robbed me of feeling; all my senses except one. I watched as he rose, gently, pityingly. He brushed aside the clothing he had dropped, picking up the shirt, jacket, pants and boots I had discarded. Miraculously, they stretched to fit his glistening frame.

When he had dressed, he placed his own gear carefully beside me. "These are yours now," he confided. "You may wear them for longer than I did, or maybe for less time, but they are yours to wear until you find someone like me or you to draw life from. Until that happens, you will walk this beach on the nights when the sun is weakest and the tides run high." He strode to the door but stopped to look back. "Perhaps my sister will remember you and try to send you a successor." Then he was gone. I lay watching the dying coals grow dimmer and less distinct. The moon did not shine. All light ebbed. Only the barest spark of something remained to me, a speck of life whose tiny contrast makes me aware of the great, painful cold that has been my world ever since.

I rose, picked up the clothing, and put it on. Then I walked through the wall to the shore, just as I knew I would be able to.

The house stands alone and forgotten, and I ask myself how long it has been. How long does it take for grass to grow through warped flooring and for blowing sand to etch window glass?

The dunes have shifted and the door hangs awry. Birds nest in the rusted chimney and field mice in the stove as I wait for the dark days of winter when some solitary person will come to set it right, seeking for a completion with an unknown name.

Don't you crave solitude and peace? Won't you come to spend a season of comfort, alone by the green waters of the sea?

MODERN
TIMES

Lee Rosario Kincaid

Coloring Inside the Lines

There were two Adams. The other one was the man, and he was the boy. The other one was his uncle, and he was the grandson or uncleson or something. The other one was the godfather and he was ... the godson. The other one cooked at the stove, inventing familiar and nameless clouds of food smell in the room, which steamed up the windows and played games of memory in his nose and on the insides of the friendly pocket of his mouth. He colored in a coloring book, Bugs Bunny.

There was something warm in the kitchen, something besides the smell of dinner. It was like a cat that came up and cold-nosed you first and then warm-backed itself into you for scratching. He looked under the table. "Uncle Adam, where's the cat?"

"I don't have a cat," said Uncle Adam. "You mean the cat at home?"

He shrugged. The crayons were all new and pointy. Uncle Adam had taken them out of the bag from the store without even trying them out himself. He started to say the colors to himself, from the top to the bottom. Orange, red, white, orange, brown, green, red ... "What's this color?" he said.

Uncle Adam came over with a spatula in his hand and sat down on the bench next to him. His arm came out and set itself on Adam's shoulders, and had the smells of grownup t-shirts and some bathroom-y soap powder and the dinner yet to be all around it. Adam hoped that the heart and voice that was attached to this arm would not be disappointed that he seemed to go outside the lines in so many loopy mistakes.

"What do you think it looks like?" said Uncle Adam. "You can make up the names of colors, you know."

"It isn't white and it isn't yellow."

"Does it look like anything you know?"

Adam withdrew the crayon from its place and held it up in the air. "It looks like a crayon."

"I mean, does the color remind you of anything?"

"I don't want to use it anyway." He put it back in, hard, and took out a familiar, earnest red.

"It's called silver," said Uncle Adam. "It looks like money, doesn't it?"

"It looks like a *cat.*" He checked underneath the table again to see if there was a silver cat there.

"You don't have a cat at home, do you, Adam? I don't remember that you do."

Remember . . . remember . . . That was a word that Adam didn't pay too much attention to. He had a cat in his mind and he didn't know where it was. He could look at his home in his mind, and see it with great exactness, scrutinize the very scratches in the paint of the back steps where he sometimes played, and as soon as he *saw* a cat on the porch stairs, there *was* a cat on the porch stairs, and when he said he remembered it sometimes the grownups said no. So he shrugged again.

The smell of the thing on the stove had turned from kind to mean, and Uncle Adam leaped up and swore, and then bandied the skillet across the room to the sink, where it hissed and threatened with puffs of silver. The phone rang and Uncle Adam said, "Don't touch the stove, now, it's hot," and twirled himself around the room like a dancer, tucking the phone under his ear and a leg under his rear end as he settled gracefully in a heap on a pile of telephone books on the floor.

His voice went on like smoke in the room, puffing and dismissing itself into the phone. Adam looked critically at Bugs

Bunny, who on this page was dressed up like a lady from the place where they had flying carpets and weaving, hypnotized snakes poking out of pots. Bugs Bunny had baggy pajama pants on and a veil over his nose, but you could tell it was him because of his funny eyes and the ears, too. There was a fat man behind him whose hands were clasped together as if he was in church, and whose heart was making a candy-heart shape coming right out of his chest and through his shirt. He had on a hat like a hospital bandage and shoes that curled up into points. His smile was scary, and, pointy as his shoes, a sword dangled from his belt. Bugs Bunny's tail stuck out through a hole in his pants, and Adam colored the tail the color of cats and money, and stayed carefully inside the lines. He made his pants red, the best color.

He took it over to Uncle Adam, whose face had turned away toward the closet with the peanut butter and the colorforms in it, and said softly, "See?" When Uncle Adam's arm came out in that sweeping way like the plastic arm that lifted to let his car go into the parking garage, his face turned too, and it was wet on both sides and his nose needed a good wipe. "Hold on, sweet," he said into the phone, "emergency cuddle break, one Adam to another, and I don't know which one of us relies on it more. Always a godfather, never a god, you know." He made a sound of paper tearing in his throat and said, "This is *very good,* Adam. When you're done with it, we can cut it out with a scissors and hang it up on the refrigerator."

"I am done."

"Why don't you color in the other guy?"

"I don't want to. I don't like him."

"How about the floor?"

Adam was doubtful, but went back to the table to consider it. He looked at the colors again, racked up like choirmembers in the choirloft, each row higher than the other so you could see all their faces. Only better colors than choirmembers, who were always blue with white collars. The song of crayons would be a Christmas carol. "Away in a manger, a crib for a bed, the little Lord Jesus laid down his sweet head." The song chased away the need to color the floor. He didn't know the rest so he sang that part again four or five times, until Uncle Adam said, "Adam, mercy, you're going to drive me to the nuthouse. Why don't you go play in the other room? I want to talk to my friend Michael."

He took the crayons with him, in their little portable choirloft, and the other room was silver and red, too, but in different ways than the kitchen, colder ways. There was a Christmas tree made of silver, with little shreds of shiny silver hair that looked as if they should be soft to touch but made you feel itchy inside. It had red ribbons and golden balls on it, and only white lights. Pretty boring tree, Adam had thought, no blue or green or purple or orange on it, but Uncle Adam had come in one day with a bag of candy canes which Adam himself had fixed onto the tree, on all the lower branches, and then it was a little better. Although the candy canes were red and silver, too, sort of.

He took one down and put it in his mouth. Today there was a new thing to play with again, Uncle Adam called it Lincoln Logs, and he'd already showed him how to draw out a house pattern on the floor and build up the sides. Adam couldn't think of how to do windows but he knew how to leave a space for the door, and he cleared a space on the rug far enough away so that the couch, which lunged capably into a double bed every night when it was time for them to go to sleep, wouldn't crash it down.

His own room at home didn't have a cat, at least not when he started thinking about it. It had a lamp made out of a clown puppet, and one of the legs of his big-boy bed didn't touch the floor. He'd stared and stared one day, while lying on the floor resting or thinking, and noticed that, and thought for a minute that maybe his eyes had suddenly gotten stronger and he was now able to see all the spaces that must be between things. But then Mommy had come in and sat on the bed to lace up her boots, and the space had disappeared.

The cat would have wanted to sleep on the bed. He would just move his legs a little, like this, if the cat wanted more room. He tried it now, and thought of the cat here. Would Uncle Adam let there be a cat in the bed *too?*

He went back to the house, and built up the walls, one log at a time, the way you were supposed to. He couldn't figure out how to get the roof pointy, though, and he didn't like the color of the green slats. Rain could go right through those slats, too. So Adam stood and looked around at the things that were his own height, and opened up some drawers. He found some checkbooks and some giant grownup underwear and, underneath that, a shiny magazine with naked grownups in it. They all looked like they were hurt somehow.

"Jesus, Mary and Joseph," said Uncle Adam, and took the magazine out of his hand before Adam even realized he'd gotten off the phone. "This is not for little boys, Adam. I forgot it was even in the place, things have been so crazy with the hospital and all. I'm going to throw it out right now." His face was dry, and now it was hard, like a burned cookie. "I don't have a fireplace, or we could burn it up for kindling."

"We could cook it in the stove."

"Enough out of you," said Uncle Adam. "I have to start dinner again. If we survive this thing in one piece," he began, leaving the room, and his voice caught in his throat again, like a bark of a dog or a sneeze turning into a bark. Adam hated when his uncle got so full of crying, but at the same time Uncle Adam had bought him a new toy just about every day since he'd arrived here, so he tried not to notice.

"Are you building a house for your cowboys and Indians?" called Uncle Adam from the kitchen, as cabinet doors slammed and a fresh frying pan whanged on the iron grate of the gas burner.

"I don't know," he answered. Again he went around the room, looking for a good roof. The newspaper would be too flimsy, and too big anyway, its overhang would sag to the rug. And the books in Uncle Adam's bookcase were too heavy, if they were hardcover, or too small, if they were paperback. Actually, that magazine would have made a good roof; it was the right size and the right weight. But he didn't have the nerve to ask for it back. On the desk he found a photograph of his parents, old dead Daddy, and Mommy in a white dress, although the black background made it look silver, a flood of silver snow from her head to her knees, which was where the picture ended. Carefully holding in place the triangular swinging piece which helped it stand up on a desk, Adam settled the portrait on the four walls of the house he had made. Its two happy faces stared up into the night sky of plaster ceiling and shiny white stars (all glowing from one side, the Christmas tree). The gold frame made a pretty roofedge.

The cowboys and Indians were jumbled in a friendly pile in a shoebox in the closet where Adam was keeping his other toys, too, and they fell out in an interlinked heap. He separated them and stood them up on the plastic puddles that joined their feet together, but they seemed too small to go into the new house. He lined them up on the cliff edge of the sofa instead, and every now and then pitched one of them off in satisfying slow motion into the tidal pool of the midnight blue carpet, providing the little faraway scream from his own mouth. But the problem of occupants for his new house continued to worry him. He thought about asking Uncle Adam to cut out Bugs Bunny from the book, but Uncle Adam had ruined one dinner already, and they'd probably have to go to the hospital *again* tonight and there wouldn't be time. He then thought of the silver cat, who, if sleek enough, could squeeze through the opening and have a nice cozy den all to itself in there.

In the end, when Uncle Adam came in to help him wash his hands before supper, whose smells were now formalized into the recognizable pattern of spaghetti and meatballs, he had thrown off the soldier-mean look on his face, and once again his arms came down around Adam like the boughs of a tree, like the big skirt of the lady in the Nutcracker that all the people came out of. They'd seen that together last night, Uncle Adam sighing and tapping his foot so often that Adam had thought he was angry at it. But that was Uncle Adam, back and forth between incredible ferociousness at — at something — and arms that could be cats, or trees, or Lincoln Logs, building a house around him.

"Who've you set up in there?" he said, sliding down onto the rug to peer through the doorway.

"I put in Mary and Joseph and Baby Jesus," said Adam. "I took them from the dresser. Also the cows and sheeps. The shepherds are up there with the cowboys and Indians, and the Three Kings, see, are in the shoebox on that patch of floor by the door. That's a boat."

"You made a stable," said Uncle Adam. "You made a stable for

Baby Jesus to sleep in."

"This is a *house,*" said Adam, affronted. "This time they have a real house."

"Do you like staying here? Don't you like it?" said Uncle Adam, making a cradle of his arms. "Am I being a good uncle to you?"

"There's just one thing," said Adam.

"Mmmm? What's that?"

"I *think* I need." He screwed his head around so he could look in his uncle's eyes. "I think I need—"

"You need—"

"A—"

"A—"

"CAT."

"Oh you do, do you?"

"I think so." Suddenly doubting a bit, he returned his gaze forward to the house. Underneath the roof of his parents the baby Jesus was sleeping. He could make the crayola crayon choir sing "Away in a Manger" to him later. "We could call it Adam," he suggested.

"You won't remember this time at all," said Uncle Adam softly. "You won't remember it and I'll never forget it. No matter what happens to both of us. Isn't that sad?"

But Adam knew about remembering. He knew about the silver cat, that it would always be there when he thought of it. It was only when he tried to talk about it that it would crumble into paste and cardboard, a picture of a thing with a heart pounding out of its chest instead of the thing itself. Like Daddy, dead and in Heaven with Baby Jesus, and now just a little silver face on the roof, the size of a nickel, the flatness of a drawing in a coloring book. Like Mommy, thin and cartoon-like in the snow drift of her bedsheets there. But outside of words, in the larger room of remembering, in a world far more thick, and tasty, their smell kept as strong as wood, their words shone as bright as wood burning.

And until he would try to say it, in five or six years, and then lose it for good from his memory, he could know the same of Uncle Adam. He leaned back into his arms as the spaghetti began to smell burned again, and remembered in advance the cat that would come to live in these rooms too. Adam to Adam to Adam, under the roof of his parents, all of them safe in the timber walls of their common name.

Stan Leventhal

The Bold Sailor

Time itself cannot touch you. It is the measurement, the containment, the stretching and contracting of the moments that leaves scars. My friends say that I will forget. Or that he will come back. As if the two were dependent. But something tells me he will never come back. And I know I will never forget him. I can count on this — on myself. Not that I am so remarkably reliable. It just seems that everything else is much less so.

I had noticed him sitting across from me on the subway. He smiled, and I imagined a terrific body beneath the loose-fitting designer jeans but I looked away. I never smile on the subway or in bars. The consequences could be dangerous.

That night, he walked over to me at the bar. Was it a coincidence that I'd seen him earlier, or had he been following me around? I'm still not certain. Blond and balding slightly, he had a tattoo on his right bicep: USN.

"What d'ya call that there you're drinkin'?" he asked.

"I don't call it anything, it's..."

"Vodka and cranberry juice."

"That's correct," I said. I was surprised but tried not to show it.

"I been watchin' them makin' your drinks for a few nights now. I wanted to buy you one but I didn't know what to call it."

"Vodka and cranberry juice."

"Right." He looked at me nervously, expecting me to say something, so I did."

"What's USN?"

"Huh?"

I touched his arm. "The tattoo."

"United States Navy."

"You used to be a sailor?"

"Still am. But I'm gettin' out soon. You?"

"I'm a painter."

"Pictures or houses?"

"Paintings. And I work at the library."

"The liberry?"

"No, the lib*rary.*"

I didn't make it easy for him. I never make it easy for anyone. A man's got to be careful. But I liked him and invited him to my loft. We spent the night together. I didn't find out his name until the following morning.

* * *

I'm always thinking about the time I spent with him. It's involuntary. I try to hold on to the good memories and not feel the pain. Difficult. Would I rather not have the memories at all? No, these are all I have to treasure, though the reminder of my present loneliness is the price. The sailor comes and goes, leaving behind a trace of salty sea air. I sniff and it stings my nostrils.

I know the songs of sailors. From before the steam engine. When ships sailed into the unknown on muscle power and sweat. Men sang songs to make the work go easier. And songs of home that lulled them to sleep at night. To dream about loved ones. Some were content living among all that manpower. Others dreamed that the captain's pretty cabin boy was a girl in disguise.

There among the barflies, so many hairdressers in cowboy drag, was what I'd been searching for. A man who loved men. I presumed he possessed all of the fine attributes of manhood: honesty, courage, ambition. Neither an intellectual nor a disco queen. He'd never seen a Broadway show or been to the opera. I was amazed.

The morning after our first night together he nudged me with his knees and asked if I was awake. I turned and looked at his cheery face. I offered to make some coffee and he finally introduced himself. "By the way, m'name's Wayne. Wayne Bedford."

We shook hands. The first time I'd ever done that in bed. He hugged me. We kissed. He started to tickle me but it was far too early for laughter. I jumped out of bed and boiled some water.

We got together again that night and the next morning I persuaded him to remove his belongings from the YMCA and spend the rest of his leave with me. There was so much I wanted to discover about sailors, and I figured he might learn a few things from me as well.

* * *

I know the songs of the sea. From before scientists started taping the sounds of whales and dolphins to be vivisected by musicologists. I have the records Wayne bought for me. *Whaling and Sailing Songs From the Days of Moby Dick, Blood Red Roses,* and one I found at the library called *We'll Go to Sea No More.* Tough songs about hard work, squalid lives and treacherous companions. Gentle songs about love and separation.

Perhaps Wayne joined the Navy because of some romantic dream about the old times. He knew that the days of piracy and adventure were over. But he'd been raised in a fishing town in New England, originally settled by Portuguese immigrants. The tales and songs had been passed down from father to son for generations.

Being out on the sea in the twentieth century was something different. The latest news, political and cultural, isn't foreign to the modern sailor unless he chooses isolation in order to escape it. I was never certain about Wayne's motives. Every time I asked him to tell me about the Navy, all he ever said was, "Drank a lot. More than you'd believe. Smoked a lot of hash. Had guys in every port. You can have an Eyetalian or an A-rab for a song." Then he'd wink and laugh. A deep, throaty chortle that would redden his cheeks and make his eyes shimmer. "But nothin' like you," he would add, and wrap his arms around me, kissing and squeezing, summoning something from within that would smolder and ignite until the two of us fell asleep, tangled together on damp, rumpled sheets.

* * *

I don't sell many paintings. That is, as many as I should. But I sell more than I did before I met Wayne. He taught me to be more aggressive. And that pleasing people is not sinful.

I remember the first time I showed him my work. My loft has stacks of canvases everywhere but I don't think he'd so much as glanced at one until I asked for his opinion. I selected four recent efforts and leaned them against the empty wall that serves that particular purpose. He lit a cigarette and carefully studied each one.

"I don't know what they mean but I like the colors."

"They don't *mean* anything."

"Then why paint 'em?"

"To create something that is appealing to the eye."

"I like paintin's of flowers and bowls of fruit. Oceans and hillsides. Y'know, stuff that's real."

"Well, my work is..."

"Work? You call this *work?*" He snuffed out the cigarette and asked if I wanted to go for a drink. I declined and spent the evening reading. He returned a few hours later and made love to me as though atoning for some horrible crime.

The next night, he insisted on taking me to dinner. He wanted to go to a semi-fashionable restaurant where the employees and clientele were gay males, and a Lacoste shirt and clean jeans were considered dressy enough. He said and did everything with great formality. I grasped that this was a big event for him and did not correct him when he mispronounced the wine he'd selected. I assumed his pose and acted as if we were at the captain's table.

Over coffee, he told me that he'd decided to terminate his naval career and look for a civilian job. "Could I stay with you and share the rent?" He reached for my hand, gallantly kissed it, and smiled. I felt like the one who catches the bouquet at the end of the wedding. He looked like he'd just won the lottery.

* * *

He called last night, the first time in about three months, but he was too drunk to communicate. I kept asking where he was calling from but I never got a coherent answer.

I couldn't sleep. I pictured him stripped to his jockey shorts and recalled the sensation of his skin against my own. I changed positions, stomach down, and tried to think about something else but the images would fly at me, taunting me like a horde of angry demons.

I called the library the next morning and told the branch manager that I had the flu. Lots of fluids and plenty of rest, he suggested. I couldn't face the strangers who passed in and out of the book-lined fortress I fantasized as my own. The people who came in to read or escape the weather never bothered me. And the erudite souls who truly love books, reserve several at once and return them on time, are so few.

It's the others who occasionally rouse the monster in me. They break spines, fold corners and confuse John Ashbery with John Berryman. I despise them and, by extension, the job. Sometimes, when the library is completely empty and it's just me and all those words, I feel a contentment that I've never found anywhere else. The silence is a symphony of white noise, and when I close my eyes I can hear the voices arising from the pages, discussing love and death, arguing theories, trading juicy gossip.

My real work is altogether different. I try to capture shapes, colors and textures with oil and canvas. Then I must persuade some suburban harridan to buy the work by convincing her that after I die, which could be any time considering the squalor of my existence, she shall have made a smart investment. Business is a pursuit that has never interested me, nor have I been successful in mastering its protocol.

I suppose I could have found work that pays better than the library. But I probably wouldn't have found the time to paint. Wayne had said he wanted lots of money. In fact, he informed me, he was one of the few who would know what to do with a fortune should he ever be in possession of one.

* * *

The money and hashish he had accumulated for his leave were beginning to disappear; he'd spent two hundred dollars on a three-piece suit. Burnt sienna. I came home from work one day and found him sitting on the bed, his suit disheveled and sweat-soaked. He clutched the classified ad section of the *Times,* with several positions circled in pencil. Leaning back, he tossed the paper aside and clasped his hands behind his head.

"Well, I registered with a employment agency and they made me up a resume ... Resume?" I nodded. "And I'm supposed to call tomorrow."

"How does it feel, job hunting in the big city?"

"It's fun! Lots of good-lookin' guys everywhere. I got lost, though. Finally just got in a taxi and gave the guy your — I mean our — address."

* * *

Ever since Wayne left, I have kept myself so busy that time is something that is no longer part of my conscious thought. I cannot gauge or measure it and have lost the ability to control it. I seem to exist apart from — above or below, I'm not certain which — the rush of time. Haven't escaped it. I can feel myself aging. Slowly. But still, somehow, I am removed.

On the third day of Wayne's search for employment, I returned home and found him cursing the heat and concrete sidewalks.

"What's the matter?"

"I called my sister to wire me some money 'cause it looks like I might not find a job as fast as I thought. Anyway, she told me that Mom is in the hospital."

"Is it serious?"

"Brain tumor."

"Oh, my God!" I hugged him and comforted him as best I could.

"I'm gonna catch the 9:47 bus."

"Is there anything I can do? Do you feel like eating something?" He nodded. I glanced at the clock.

"Just enough time to get some groceries. After we eat, I'll help you pack and we'll go to the station together. All right?"

When I returned from the supermarket, however, he was gone. He'd packed his belongings and left the keys in the mailbox. I could not find a note with a telephone number where he could be reached.

The next day, I received a call from the employment agency. Wayne had been accepted for the position of clerk at a "chic private hotel." I said I'd have him call as soon as I heard from him.

I went about my work absentmindedly for several weeks, wondering what was going on. Eventually I received my phone bill, which registered a long distance call to somewhere in Massachusetts, "between Boston and the Cape," as Wayne had once said. I walked around for a few days with the bill in my pocket, anxious to call, afraid of what I'd find out.

Late at night, a few days later, I dialed. His sister answered. He wasn't there, nor did she know where he was stationed. I introduced myself, and she said that Wayne had spoken of me. "As long as I have you on the phone," I said, dying of curiosity but fearful that I was intruding, "I'd just like to find out how your mother is doing."

"What do you mean? She's fine, as far as I know."

"I see. That's a relief."

"Did Wayne tell you she was sick or something?"

"In a word, yes."

"Oh, honey, that's just Wayne's way. He's been making up stuff like that ever since he was a kid."

A few days later, I received a hastily scribbled note from Wayne in which he apologized for having lied about his mother's health. He went on to explain that he was afraid he'd never find a job and would not allow himself to be supported by another.

I didn't really speak to anyone for weeks. When friends would call, I'd say that I was busy and would get back to them when I was able.

I'm desperate to let him know that he was accepted for a job, but he's always drunk when he calls, and he never lets me know where he is so that I can write to him. Although he stays in touch, communication is impossible.

All I have now is work, time, and memories, which function

together like an automated Mobius strip. And I still have the records he gave me. There's one song in particular that constantly runs through my mind. It's about a bold sailor who leaves his lover to go to sea, each one keeping half of a broken coin. Years later, when they meet, they do not recognize each other at first, but the parts of the coin match perfectly, and they realize that they have been reunited. Sometimes I have a dream that is like a surreal film of that song with Wayne and myself as the main characters, mandolins and concertinas snaking across the soundtrack. Only when we meet again, we recognize each other instantly. The two halves of the coin, however, do not fit.

Scott Humphries

Tinky

Like fully fifty percent of the world, she waited for him to come to her. She sat around the house for days, then it was weeks, now it was two months. She didn't go out. She came right home from work. She waited for him to call. "He must be busy," she thought; or "He's trying to make it without me. But he'll call. He'll start missing me as badly as I miss him. Then he'll call."

But he didn't. And she wasn't some kind of nut. No, this is not a story about somebody being or becoming a nut. She realized, after exactly ten weeks, the Christmas holidays, and a little of New Year's, that she couldn't sit around any more waiting for him to call. So she called an 800 number she saw on television and they sent her an answering machine. She hooked it up to her telephone and now she didn't have to sit home waiting. The answering machine would wait for her. She recorded the pleasant little message suggested in the instruction book by reading it aloud with the switch set on *Outgoing Message Record,* and then she added her own two cents. She said, "And if this is Barry, my number at work is 234-0032."

With the home front covered, she went out looking for him. She shopped on Sunday nights at the Diamond Heights Safeway — the same Safeway he shopped at on Sunday nights. And she always looked her best and smiled at everyone in the store and actually got to know a few of the employees so she could ask, "Do you know

Barry? Have you seen a short, stocky guy named Barry? Always buys two or three six-packs of diet root beer?"

But she never saw him there, and the clerks were vague, as if they were protecting someone's medical records. So she started going to the bars again. She went to the ones she thought he would go to on the nights when she knew he didn't play bridge or shop or work at home on his bills. But he wasn't in the bars, either.

"Well, why," you could say, "if she wanted to see him so badly, didn't she just call him?" Well, she could never do that since it had been her that had left him and besides, her mother hated him, her sister hated him, and all of her friends hated him. Despite the best things said about love, about being in love, and all . . . well, it just wasn't true. It wasn't just something between yourself and him. You couldn't keep loving someone that your family and all your friends hated and not end up looking and feeling the fool. You couldn't and you can't.

She did call him. She called him when she knew he wasn't home so she could hear his voice on *his* answering machine. She would listen to the message two or three times, using a button on her phone that would redial the number. Then she would sit and think about the good times they'd had, skiing in Squaw Valley or camping out of an old pickup truck in the desert. And then she would be all sad and have to fill the old claw-footed bathtub so she could sit in there and drink wine by candlelight and read Emily Dickinson's little swipes at fated love. Then she would write a little poem of her own and cry for a while.

Then one night it hit her. It was January 15 and she had stayed to watch the second feature at the big old movie palace on Castro, and it was too late to be walking home. But she was wearing blue jeans and a windbreaker with a hood, so a mugger would probably think she was a man and leave her alone. Besides, if it was too cold to wait for the bus, you sure as hell could count on it being too cold for the muggers to be out.

Walking past Courtney's Produce, she looked up and thought, "Oh, they left their pumpkins out." Then she realized it was long past Halloween and Thanksgiving, and no one would want these pumpkins. They were in no danger of being stolen and could sit there on those shelves until they rotted. Their fate made sense to her. Barry didn't want her because she was too old; and, if no one else wanted her, what good was she to him? If no one else wanted her, he wouldn't have the pleasure of their envy.

So she felt mad at herself. And she said out loud, "I hate him." From then on, she said it. She said "I hate him" whenever she thought of him, and after about two weeks of repeating it like some spiteful little *mantra* she felt better.

She went shopping and bought some new clothes. She stopped feeling so sad and empty when she ate in a restaurant alone. She managed to fake happiness and — she had to conclude — fake happiness had much more security to it than Real Happiness. You never knew when Real Happiness was going to be snatched away, but no one could ever steal happiness you were faking. You'd just fake some more. The supply was endless.

It was faking happiness that got her to thinking about Tinky. She'd been going to a new bar every Thursday night in an effort to Forget Him And Meet Someone New. This Thursday she was at the Caspian Sea, an old place out on Geary Street that had free caviar served from the top of a Russian samovar and waitresses with white beehive hairdos. She sat down and got out her cigarettes and lighter and the little folding ashtray she always carried. She faked away, smoking two cigarettes in the process, and fell to thinking about when, in all her thirty-two years, she had been really happy. And then, suddenly, she thought of Tinky.

She had met him when she first moved away from home. They both had rooms in an old rundown mansion out in a Chicago suburb. It was run by a drunken landlady who made iced tea all year round, only she made it with vodka instead of water. The gay bar across the street was so much warmer than their drafty rooms that they'd taken to spending their evenings there. For the price of one or two drinks, you could watch television or sit by a roaring fake fireplace or go into the back room and dance in the disco dream world the two old queens who owned the place had cooked up.

She'd spent most of her time back there. She danced alone until about ten o'clock when the regular clientele began to arrive, and then she danced with them. They were sweet and affectionate, and they never tried to put the moves on her, so it was like being in the living room at home partying with her brothers. No sex moves, just, "Oh, you can dance like that! Oh, you're good! Let's have a drink before the next one."

Besides, it had been better for her to stay in the back room. In the front, she would have had to watch Tinky pulling his scam. Tinky was as young as she was, a black man with green eyes. "Mommy's baby, Daddy's maybe," her friend Thelma had said upon meeting him. He was as handsome as a catalogue model and looked to be one until you heard him talk. Then he sounded like Prissy from *Gone With The Wind* or some vague movie queen he called Tallulah. Anyway, he had a scam he called "my little game." He walked around the room and watched for men drinking and leaving their money out on the bar. He'd carry a copy of *My Boy* magazine with him and watch for the traveling salesmen or strangers at the bar.

Spotting a newcomer, he'd walk up and start looking at the magazine next to them. He'd show them a few pictures and flash those green eyes. It worked every time. They'd look at the magazine and the handsome young black stud instead of watching their money. And they'd never accuse him. They always blamed the bartender. Said he'd shortchanged them. Tinky would be in back dancing with her by then. Ten, maybe twenty dollars richer.

So they'd had good times together and gone through lovers like elephants let loose in a peanut factory and decided by the end of that first cold winter to leave Chicago for good. To pack everything the two of them owned into her old Pinto and drive to California. On the road, he'd gone on about being gay and how it had it all over being straight and she'd asked, *How can you do that to your own kind?* He'd answered her very seriously: "Child, I am black. And everyone knows black folks take most of their money from other black folks. And it's no different with gays. Like steals from like 'cause it's the mindset the thief knows best."

He was full of convoluted logic like that, and it endeared him to her. Any explanation was better than no explanation at all. He explained to her why gay men were never happy: "You see, no matter what they say, their daddy — if they had one — never loved them like their mama did. So they spend all their lifes trying to get a daddy or another man to love them, but none of them's never been loved by the first man, so they got no idea what it's like. And besides, they're never satisfied when it does happen 'cause, in any case, it ain't like the love mama give 'em."

Tinky, Tinky. He was so weird. Arriving in San Francisco, they'd lived together four short weeks when Tinky announced he was moving in with Bike, a fellow he met the second night they were there. They continued to know each other for a while, but then she had started moving with a different crowd and they drifted apart. They had kept in touch only occasionally, passing a new address along, vowing to go dancing. But San Francisco was so crazy there never seemed to be anyone to do anything with or there was no time. One extreme or the other. Never any safe, sane, comfortable middle ground.

So she was sitting there in the Caspian Sea, finishing her fourth cigarette, and she decided to call him. After wrestling with the phone book, she finally found him listed under his brother's name, Theodore. Theodore Sparks. She called the number and was told by an answering machine that kept calling her "Girl" and "Child" and referring to Tinky as "she" that, "She out, Hon. So please, be a sweet child and tell all to her wicked ass at the beep." It was him. She heard that voice come screaming up at her out of the past and, for the moment, she felt as happy as she'd remembered.

She left a message asking him to give her a call. Then she went back and talked to some computer guy who expected her to consider him a genius. He bought her two drinks, and then she took a taxi home.

She forgot to turn her answering machine off so, the next morning, after two rings and the clicking the machine made as it answered, he was screeching into her bedroom. "Girl, come up outta that bed now. I know you're there. Come on over and pick up on your darlin' Tinky. We got the news, girl. Pick it up!"

She struggled over and picked up the phone. "Tinky!" she cried delightedly, "I didn't think you'd call back so soon."

"Uh-huh, honey." He made a little gasping sound. "We done been up all night, child. All night. And now you be up, too."

She cradled the phone to her shoulder and began to pull on tights and jeans. She couldn't believe how happy it made her just to hear him. He rattled on about no money, no job, and "Child!" no parking in his neighborhood. Finally, she interrupted him: "Tinky, I've got to see you. What are you doing? Have you eaten breakfast? Let's go to the Patio and have eggs Benedict and *caffe lattes.*"

There was an odd little pause. "Oops, he's got someone with him," she thought. But he surprised her. He sounded different; his mood had changed. "Babe, come on over here. I got plantain pancakes mixin' as we speak. I'm at 836 Delores, number three. Okay?"

"Sure thing, child!" she said, mocking him. "Should I bring somethin'?"

"Only roses and hydrogen peroxide," he shot back. Then he gave a high-pitched squeal that turned into a giggle just before he hung up.

* * *

Trudging up the three flights to his apartment with a little bouquet of sweetheart roses and, yes, some hydrogen peroxide, she was breathless and excited. Back to old friends and old times! She rounded a corner and she saw him; or rather it seemed, as she thought back on it later, she saw what was left of him. The once-muscular black frame was thin and gaunt, and the face from which those green eyes had shown like mischievous party lanterns was now drawn. He smiled at her. She smiled back. Neither of them said anything. He gave her a little hug and took the roses. Walking into his apartment, she managed to ask, "Where's the bathroom?"

"There, child," he said softly, pointing to a doorway. She headed for it, but he caught her before she got there and they fell together, crying. "Oh, Tinky," she said, choking on her sobs, "you've got AIDS, don't you?"

"I do, baby, I do," he said into her shoulder. "Now I got you to help me, too."

And so she forgot all about Barry, and happiness, and meeting someone to love. Her soul mate became, instead of a new handsome stranger, her old handsome Tinky. She fried every food she could remember from her farmhouse childhood, and eventually his weight and his color came back. He got infections from time to time and seemed to be taking drugs constantly, but they shared the valium he got, and they listened to music and talked for hours; and, thank heaven, the good times came back.

He had all of his same philosophies and AIDS wasn't any more immune to them than anything else had ever been. "I know," he told her, "I know why I got this. It's 'cause o' how much I liked sex. I liked it too much. Moderation in all things, child, including moderation." He winked at her. "I be like old Simon and the Zealots. He love this man Jesus too much. Made Jesus nervous. Told ol' Simon to back off. Well, somethin' had to come along and tell me to stop lovin' livin' too much. You get all caught up in livin' and you forget 'bout dyin' or people 'ats doin' it. Dyin' got just as much place in this world as livin'. I be backin' off, child. Whoop!" he yelled, and flailed his long arms in a disco sashay.

So she was around him and all his lust for life. And when she wasn't around him, when she wasn't rubbing oil onto the skin that hung from his bones, when she wasn't putting cold wash cloths on his forehead and pulling them off minutes later feeling as if they'd just come damp out of a dryer, then she was thinking of him and wondering why this AIDS, this ominous stranger, had cast its shadow into the bright light of a life so full of red peppers.

It was always there now, this threat of disease. It was like an evil old grandfather always in the room with you, and he stared at you, his eyes following you everywhere. You could cook and shower and eat and talk for hours on the telephone, but always the old man would be sitting there staring at you, saying things like, "I got him, and I'll get you, Missy. I'll get you all."

She got used to Tinky looking so sallow and began to confide in him again. She told him about Barry and about the interminable waiting she had endured. He listened, looking at her intently. Then he leaned forward and said, "Let me tell you about Wayne, child."

He went to a shelf in the kitchen and got a little wooden box she had given him. It was from Mexico and had a sunset painted on it in the familiar red and green reserved for tourist trash. He opened it and pulled out three pieces of paper. They were the fortunes from fortune cookies. She reached for them, but he placed a slender brown hand over hers. "Wait," he said softly. "I have to tell you."

He handed her one of the slips. It said, "This fortune entitles you to one introduction to a good-looking man." Tinky swayed his head like a cobra following a snake charmer, then leaned right into her face. "I did, hon. I met me the man o' mans. Twenty-four. Two years younger'n I was. Handsome . . . Child! Child!" he exclaimed, raising his eyebrows theatrically. "This man had a face. So straight and square, looked like you could fold it. A pretty little box of a face, open, without a lid. On every fold they was a line of fine hair. You know? Like his eyebrows, they went straight across." Tinky furrowed his brow and slashed a furious imaginary line across his eyebrows with his finger.

"And straight across the top of his fine, fine lips." Tinky drew another line. "Then his chin — his chin made another line, with a fine little dimple. Made it look like the end of a wienie." He let out a squeal. "And set in the middle of all this so serious was two of the laughines' blue eyes you ever saw. They made that boy look surprised when he wasn't and mad when he was sad. You wanted to know wuz he mad, or what? I didn't look in his eyes. 'Cept when we was screwin'. Then, my friend, they glazed." He looked at her triumphantly and threw his arms out. "Glazed!" he shouted as if he had just shouted "Saved!"

Tinky stopped. He took the first piece of paper out of her hand and handed her the second one. It read: "You will always have good luck in your personal affairs."

"I did, honey." He picked at the crumbs on the table a moment. His voice was sadder now, wistful. "I had good luck, then. This boy with the strong face was also an artist. I met me an artist. A concert pianist. Twenty-four years old, and a musical genius."

"A concert pianist!" she exclaimed, trying to brighten him. "Wow! Did you go to his concerts? I mean, black tie and all?"

"No. I never saw them," Tinky answered with the same slow sadness. Then, smiling, "He played for me personally. I laid on the couch, and he played these big huge pieces by Brahms. For hours! Child, second time he did it, I chanced a look at that face. He was talking. I seen him talking to his hands. Making all these expressions. Like he was listenin' with his mouth and talkin' with his eyes. The eyes was not at that time seein'. They was lookin' inside. I had to look away! I never could watch his hands while he did it. Too. . ." Tinky paused, and a shiver ran around him. ". . . spooky," he said as his eyes met hers.

"Anyway," he continued, getting up to make them tea, "I got this fortune twenty-four hours after I met him. And I thought, 'Good luck!' Dear God in Heaven, I'm gonna be needin' some of that good luck with what I got to tell him . . . I don't tell, you know, not right away, about this AIDS thing. I don't tell for two reasons."

He turned to the sink, drew the water, then walked carefully to the stove. "I don't tell 'cause safe sex is safe sex, and I don't think they need to know till we be gettin' ready to maybe not be so safe." He set the kettle on the stove and lit the burner. Then he turned to her. "And I don't tell 'em till I think they can understand. You know, I ain't gonna give this to nobody." He pointed to himself. "But ain't nobody gonna be givin' themselves to me, either, if they think I'm just gonna up and die on 'em . . . Pour all that love down the trash." He gave a rueful little laugh.

"But this one was different. I had to tell him and tell him soon. When we did it for the first time, we was layin' in bed and — well, you know — the sex was real innocent, nothin' we shouldn't be doin'. We were just holdin' each other. Just real affectionate like, and he had that pretty head on my chest. Like . . . like he was listenin' to my heart, and I stroked his hair. *That's* what was dangerous!"

"Then he went and played me some of them songs." Tinky's voice began to break. "I knew I's gonna have to tell him then, hon. It wasn't my fault I got this thing. But it was gonna be all my fault about not tellin' him." Tinky set the cups on the table and burst into tears. She got up and bent to put her arm around his shoulders.

"Ah, Tinky," she said. "Honey, I'm sorry." She rubbed her hand up and down his bony spine. He lifted his head. The tears were leaving bright, shiny paths on his beautiful ebony skin.

"So I took my last piece of 'good luck,' child, and I went to this beautiful creatin' artist. I set down on his front steps with him, and I handed him this one." He showed her the third fortune, then continued. "And I said, 'Here. I got to jump off the ladder.'"

She took the scrap of paper. It said, "Find release from your cares. Have a good time."

Tinky watched her read it. Then, wiping his eyes with the wrappers from the tea bags, he said, "I told him — 'Look, you need me. In the two years I got left in my life, I can change yours. Not that you need it changed, Wayne, but ... I can give you all that momentum, that magic you been talkin' about.' He didn't say nothin' at first, just looked at me with them blue eyes, then asks what I'm talkin' about. So I told him. 'Straight and fair,' I says, 'I got the AIDS.' Well, honey, to say you coulda knocked him over with a feather wouldn't be it. No, he just folded that face right up. Closed it. His eyebrows set right down on his mustache. And he says to me, 'Well, I don't need to be caring about AIDS. I'm sorry. Why invite it into my life?' "

Tinky started crying again. The kettle was whistling. She poured their tea in silence. He held up the tea bag wrappers and laughed. "Look, my hankies," he said. Then he went on.

"I said, 'Wayne, it's in your life. It's the fact you ain't got it personal that makes it such a threat. You got to learn to live with things like this. To feel 'em as much as the one's got it themselves. Then it won't scare you so bad. Anyways, losin' somebody to somethin' else 'sides the next man who comes along ... well, it can make a love for you to remember. Pure, like is hard to get, unless you live thirty, forty years with 'em. Till death do us part.' " Tinky looked heavenward with fake piousness. "I said, 'Wayne, my time'll come sooner than yours. You're older than me already 'cause of this.' "

They both laughed at his dramatics. She took a sip of her tea and burned her tongue. He blew on the rim of his cup. "Well," he said, "then I played my last card. I said, 'Mozart, Tchaikovsky — they all had to live with the threat of disease. What you think made Tchaikovsky write that thing *Pathetique?* He was sad with death, with death bein' part of life.' " He looked at her and waited.

"So what did he do?" she asked.

"He handed me back my fortune and walked into the house."

They sipped their tea in silence. Outside, a bus ground its way up a steep hill. When it reached the top and stopped roaring so loudly, they could hear the clock ticking in the next room.

* * *

In early March, when his birthday came, she wanted to do something special. She decided to take him out to a restaurant, a fine French restaurant. She called every one that was listed in the book and asked the same three questions: "Are you wheelchair accessible?" (They always misunderstood. Then they'd say that they guessed they were.) "How much are your entrees?" and "Do you take Master Charge?" Finally, she settled on a place called Petite Auberge over in West Portal. Tinky wouldn't like the neighborhood, but then he'd never guess.

When she went to pick him up, he thought they were going to the Castro. She nearly cried when she let herself in and saw him sitting, already propped in his wheelchair, in a black pinstripe suit. He smiled weakly and raised a wine glass filled with cranberry juice. "My dahling," he teased her, "y'all look mahvelous, just mahvelous."

It was when they rolled through the door into the tiny restaurant that her surprise started to seem like it was not such a good idea. The door was wide enough, but it took such an effort to get in. No one helped, though an exiting couple did hold the door open. She heaved and shoved, and Tinky smiled gracefully, giving soft directions and encouragement until she got him inside, whereupon they nearly rammed a huge floral display. It stood between the waiting area and the dining room and was impossible to negotiate. The *maitre d'*, a tight little smile fixed on his face, didn't greet her as "Miss" or as anything at all. He just said, "This way, please," and walked off.

She moved the flowers and started toward the end of the room, which looked to be a million miles away. Other diners were looking at them, and Tinky was now coughing badly. She couldn't just shove him along at ninety miles an hour, so she stopped midway and asked if he was all right. She could feel the room staring. The people trying not to stare were the worst.

As she bent over him, she knew her big black velvet butt was perched on the edge of someone's table, but she didn't care. Then she heard the word. AIDS. Whoever said it could have been talking about a friend or their cousin or someone else, but she knew they weren't, and all she cared about was that Tinky hadn't seemed to hear. He motioned her to go on. She was glad to be behind him so he wouldn't see her eyes fill with tears.

* * *

He died in April. She took six hundred dollars from the money her grandmother had left her and paid the Neptune Society to give her his ashes. Then she went to Golden Gate Park with a knapsack and a ghetto blaster. She laid out a little picnic in the Rhododendron Dell and then dug his grave with a kitchen spoon. She buried the can of ashes in the little hole and then put a second grade photo of Tinky in a gold frame on top. He had his lips pursed and looked like a bird. She put his name tag from his waiter's job right below the picture. Then she ate his favorite, fried chicken, and played a Tina Turner album twice, like he'd asked.

Months later, she was lying on her bed and staring up at the ceiling, listening to a year's worth of answering machine messages. Suddenly, he was in the room, saying, "Girl, come up outta that bed now. I know you're there. Come on over and pick up on your darlin' Tinky. We got the news, girl. Pick it up!"

She jumped up, frightened, and turned the machine off. She looked around the room. "Are you there?" she said shakily. "Are you here?" She waited for some answer.

Richard Hall

A Faustian Bargain

It was that moment, the worst, when he wondered why he was here. The worst possible kind of thought five minutes before the concert was due to begin, five minutes before he had to stride on stage, tails flying, looking as if he knew everything there was to know about Scarlatti and Schumann and Beethoven.

He could hear the audience from where he stood. Rustling, coughing, shifting, stamping snow from their feet. Getting ready for the tones that would stir them up, amaze them, transport them. The only trouble was that he, David Lichtenstein, third guest performer in the Young Artists Series, was in no condition to stir or amaze or even hold their attention. He was dead.

Well, that was a slight exaggeration. He held up his fingers, then wiggled them. He'd just had a good warm-up on the piano upstairs. His fingers seemed to have a life of their own. He wiggled them again. They would go on poking, spinning, sliding, no matter what else was happening. Unfortunately, that wasn't enough to make music. You needed other things — heart and mind and history — and they could not be counted on tonight.

The house manager was at the lightboard reading a paperback. Virginia Woolf. What would you expect at a concert hall in Bloomington? David envied her. To sit at a panel and push a few buttons and read *Orlando* seemed like a wonderful life. Maybe he himself had been meant for a life like that — mild and unexciting. No need to practice, no tyranny of scales and arpeggios, no fear of losing dexterity or forgetting. But he'd taken a wrong turning somewhere, gotten lost on the obstacle course to fame, and now it was too late. If he turned back, tried to retrace his steps, he would lose his place. He wouldn't know who he was. He was suffering, he thought grimly as the house manager looked his way, from a paucity of options. He was this or nothing. He nodded and the house manager put down *Orlando.* She looked wonderfully alert and competent.

David watched her fingers punching the buttons, heard the audience grow quiet. He felt as he had at summer camp when he was at the end of the high-diving platform and there was no place to go but up and out. Now he had no time to worry about being dead. There was only the leap, the falling, and remembering to keep his toes pointed.

The audience applauded with the exact amount of enthusiasm he had come to expect. Part politeness, part hope, part skepticism. We might like you, but you'll have to convince us. In the meantime, we know our manners. Certainly not the way they would have greeted Horowitz or Richter, but then he was David Lichtenstein, one of the Young Artists, and half the people in the hall had hopes of being Young Artists themselves in a few years.

And then he forgot all that. The keyboard, its white fangs bared, was directly in front of him. It was time to begin.

* * *

David called his wife when he got back to his room; not the usual hotel room but a suite the university reserved for visiting performers. This was the third time he'd used it. Unfortunately, there was still no television, his favorite method of unwinding after a concert.

"How did it go?" Frieda sounded sleepy. She'd probably been dozing by the phone in New York.

"Not bad."

"Did you do all the encores?"

"Yeah." As a matter of fact, he'd done only two, and that had been milking the applause a bit. But they had gotten the best hand of the evening. "How're the kids?"

As Frieda gave him a rundown on teeth, food, and amazing remarks, he felt the tension begin to ease. He kept her going with extra questions. As she went on, no doubt sensing his desire not to talk about the concert, David pictured her. She would be in the woolen bathrobe he hated, the one she wore only when he was away. Her blue eyes, without her glasses, would be bulging slightly, and her small, capable hands would shift the receiver from ear to ear. After a while she paused, waiting for another cue from him. But he didn't want to tell her about his problems, about the dead feeling that had come to him before each concert on this tour. It was too complicated. Besides, it would upset her.

"I'll be home next week."

"Next week," she murmured. She really sounded half asleep.

"Kiss the kids for me."

"I will."

"You too."

After hanging up, he poured himself a slug of Scotch from the leather decanter in his suitcase, then took out a paperback, a detective story. But it was impossible to read. The words didn't connect. His mind was still on the concert. The Schumann had been especially disappointing. That used to be a sure-fire number for him. But tonight the lights and darks so dear to the German soul had eluded him. He hadn't been able to release the rapture. The Fantasy had been as cold and unconnected as the words in this silly mystery. A sudden chill went through him. Where had it all gone?

He forced himself to read a little. Words always worked at times like this; it was just a matter of getting started. And then, as his eyes skidded down the page, the image, the unavoidable image, presented itself. Tonight it was the young man with cornsilk hair and sleepy gaze who had sat in the front row, stretching his long legs not ten feet from where David sat pounding and trilling and sweating. He had noticed the young man when he took his opening bow, spotted the lankiness, the casual grace, the arrogance. Then he had blocked out the sight. Simply willed it out of existence to make room for the music. The two could not coexist in his mind.

He wiped his forehead; a cold dew lay on it. There had been other images recently, too many of them, in fact. This tour, all six weeks of it, had been full of such things. Then a new thought struck him. Robert Schumann had been in touch with his fantasies — had written them down, harmonized them, dramatized them. Was it possible that the young man in the front row, like those before him, had been David's C-major Fantasy and that in banning it he had also banned Schumann's? It was a miserable thought and he quelled it. Music was music, and this other was . . . well, something else. If he didn't keep them separate he might end up blocked and paralyzed like his friend Jim Levitsky, who now sold sheet music at Patelson's because he believed his fingers were made out of glass.

He returned to the mystery story. A perfectly sterile but intricate plot was waiting for him. But he knew the symptoms by now. Nothing would work. Not the mystery or another slug of Scotch or the thought of his children. Sleep would only come if he allowed the forbidden image into his mind. It was getting to be a habit. A nasty and depressing habit with predictable results.

Ten minutes later, after cleaning up, he was fast asleep.

* * *

Frieda had brought the girls to the airport, a special treat. Perhaps, David thought, catching sight of them, she had heard something in his voice in the last few weeks. After five years of marriage, Frieda was in tune with all his moods — not the least of her burdens.

When Frieda saw him, she scooped up Bunny and waved her arm for her. David felt a surge of delight. The kids looked like Christmas ornaments in their snowsuits, and Frieda looked like an older sister. It was a wonder they had popped out of that miniature frame.

He kissed Frieda, noting with mingled guilt and pleasure how completely she yielded to him — her firm little body pressed spinelessly into his — then took Bunny.

"Did you miss Daddy?" He squeezed her bulbous behind, which she didn't like. She beat at his lapels with her fists. David lowered her to the floor and hugged Sandra.

Sandra looked away. She was suddenly embarrassed. Sometimes children had the shyness of wild animals. "Did you miss Daddy?"

"No."

"Why, Sandy, you never stopped asking when Daddy would be back."

"No I didn't."

David laughed, then stood up. Both children clung to him. They made a splendid homecoming frieze. Several elderly ladies were looking and smiling. He had the sudden sense that they were at the very center of the universe, which radiated outward from them in spokes of light.

"We're going to have a marvelous dinner," Frieda said as they headed for the luggage area.

"Chocolate pudding!" Sandy said, suddenly unembarrassed.

"Chocolate pudding?" David echoed.

"Yes." She was looking at him reproachfully for some reason. "I helped."

"She sure did," Frieda laughed, her sarcasm audible only to David. Again the sense that they were the very rock and core of life on the planet came to him. In the next instant, all his troubles of the last few weeks dissolved. They were minor, imaginary, products of performing stress. Only this moment, these children, the time they would have together, seemed real.

They took a taxi to the city. The girls took turns sitting on his lap. They couldn't get enough of Daddy, now that he was really here.

* * *

David stayed away from the piano for a week. He always did that after a long tour. He spent as much time as possible with the children, taking them to Riverside Park, to the Museum of Natural History, playing the games they liked, helping Sandy with a huge puzzle her grandmother had given her. During this week he slept extremely well, without tension or insomnia. Sometimes he wondered if Frieda, next to him, kept the old demons at bay. Her calmness, her penchant for order, permitted no untidy images in the house. Of course, he had occasional lapses when he was on the street. His glance seemed to have a will of its own, pulling powerfully and automatically toward undesirable sights. At such times he had to fight the urge to hurry home, lock the door and embrace Frieda. But in spite of this, it was a happy week.

Nor did he fail in his conjugal duties. Actually, Frieda wouldn't let him. When she was in the mood, she made him strip, arranged the lighting, put on her favorite tape, and assisted him with her slim, strong hands until they both got what they wanted. She was never self-conscious afterward, perhaps owing to the frankness about sex in her own family. Orgasm was on her menu of delights, like chocolate pudding, and there was no reason to diet. False shame was not in her. She insisted that both children take showers with Daddy. She said she wanted them to feel comfortable around the male body, right from the beginning.

It was Frieda or no one, he often thought, but she had not been his own choice. It had been arranged, more or less, by his grandmother. Nana had met Frieda at a Succoth party — she was the niece of one of her friends — and had invited her home to hear David play. He was always being produced, a genie out of a bottle, and expected to perform miracles at the keyboard. But he didn't mind. He'd play for anybody in those days. So he'd trotted out some of his showpieces for this slim, agreeable girl of eighteen, who seemed to be instantly at home in Nana's big apartment on Riverside Drive. After that, Frieda kept turning up — at Nana's, at his own house in the suburbs, making friends with everybody in the family, even joining them for the high holidays and helping out with the food.

He'd gotten used to her little by little, inviting her to functions at Juilliard, to concerts, to parties, to Jones Beach. When he played his graduation exam — he was then twenty-two — he'd known Frieda Zimmerman for two years. In that time he had rarely been alone with her. He certainly hadn't thought about marriage, despite the hints and sighs and suggestions dropped by almost everybody. It had taken a last shove, a final bit of manipulation by Nana, to bring that to pass.

* * *

At the end of his vacation week, David went to the piano at nine in the morning. He had decided to learn the Diabelli Variations. It had occurred to him, during his week of rest, that he might be getting too old for the big Romantic repertory. He was thirty, after all. Maybe he'd been having trouble with Schumann because all that yearning and burning, that Sturm und Drang, no longer suited his temperament. Maybe this was a sign of growth, maturity. The structural solemnities of late Beethoven might suit him better. He might even turn into a Beethoven specialist.

Even while he told himself these things, however, he had the unpleasant feeling that he was really kidding himself. You never outgrew the great composers. Still, he convinced himself that he ought to give it a try. There was the plateau theory to back him up. He had discussed that with Frieda just last night — artists reach a certain level, then have to wait around, go through a crisis, before they can ascend to the next plateau. This had appealed strongly to Frieda's sense of order, as well as confirming what she knew about her father's business. Jack Zimmerman, who was a dress manufacturer, had seasonal slowdowns. If David was stalled, it was like being caught between the spring and winter lines.

David spent all morning on the first three variations, then took a break around noon. He was alone in the house. The mail had arrived, slotted through the door. He picked up the envelopes and went into the kitchen. Frieda had left some lentil soup on the stove. As he heated it up, he looked at the letters. The usual, except for one from an upstate college. The Office of the President. He opened it first.

The letter, on creamy stationery with a seal embossed at the top, contained an inquiry. Would he be interested in applying for the post of musician-in-residence at Benson College? He had been recommended by several musicians and professors, and the president felt confident that his application would be viewed favorably, etc., etc.

David read the letter several times during lunch. It contained references to his growing reputation, his successful tours, his youth and his potential as an inspiration for students. It was all very flattering. But even as he basked in the praise, a note of caution sounded in his ear. Two years off the circuit would set him back. He was on the cusp now — not quite out of the Young Artists category and not quite into the next, whatever that was. A couple of years away might keep him from an essential progression. Agents, critics, recording companies, the public — they'd forget him. Even worse, he might end up as a music professor. He knew several of them: mild, embittered types condemned to play in school auditoriums forever.

He left the letter propped up on the table for Frieda. As he washed his dish, he wondered about her reaction. A few years in the country would be marvelous for the kids. A yard, a garden, a bicycle for Sandy, new friends for Frieda ... wasn't all that just as important as his career, his eternal career?

Feeling mildly depressed, he went back to the piano. It seemed that an important decision had to be made, but he couldn't find all the elements that would have to go into it. Even Frieda's bright practicality, which so often brought him back from his own confusion, wouldn't uncover what he needed. The roots went back and back, down and down.

Down, he thought, starting Diabelli's innocuous little waltz on which Beethoven had reared a scaffolding that grazed heaven, to his late-night fantasies in hotel rooms across America. Yes, they were part of the decision, too. And then he was able to put the problem out of his mind as he dug into the Beethoven. It was only later, when his family was seated around the dinner table, that he looked at their glowing faces and wondered again how he would ever be able to locate all the truths needed to make the right decision.

* * *

A few weeks later he was ready to play the Diabelli for Frieda and for Maria Boleslav, his teacher. She wasn't his teacher any more, of course, but a colleague, a friend. Still, he liked to try out new repertory on her. She would come for dinner Tuesday night; afterward he would play.

During this period, he and Frieda discussed the Benson offer several times. He could tell from the sparkle in her eyes, the animation of her manner, that she wanted to go. He even overheard her, once or twice, telling the kids about the birds and animals they could meet in the country. But it wasn't her nature to prod or manipulate him. She would, he knew, accept whatever decision he made — a decision based on the requirements of his career. She was in the habit of putting that first. Her mother, married to an entrepreneur, had been the same way. But every time he opened his mouth with the intention of announcing his decision — yes or no, country or city, teaching or touring — he stopped. The words wouldn't come. The knowledge that would produce the words was still unavailable.

On the afternoon of Maria's visit, he played the Diabelli straight through twice. It wasn't up to performance level, but there were some nice things in it. He knew more or less what Maria would say — eight years as her pupil had taught him that — but he looked forward to hearing it. They would have a discussion. Discussions with Maria were fun now. It was hard to believe he had once been terrified of her opinion.

Maria arrived with stuffed animals for both the children. She had, some years ago, appointed herself honorary grandmother and insisted on putting them to bed to the sound of Polish lullabies when she came to visit. Tonight this seemed to take longer than usual. David and Frieda waited in the living room, Frieda with her crocheting in her lap, amused, and David diddling at the keyboard, fretful. Now that the time was actually here, he was having serious doubts. Maria had a hopelessly reverential attitude toward Beethoven. She even placed him above Mozart, which was absurd. Once, when he was a teenager and mangling the Appassionata, she had advised him to avoid any impure thought or action while preparing the piece. And he had done it — approached the sonata like a novice in a nunnery. What nonsense! Beethoven's music was about sex as much as anything else. And tonight she'd probably start handing out the same kind of gobbledegook. Irritation spurted through him. Maybe this wasn't going to be as much fun as he'd thought.

Maria came out of Sandy's bedroom at last, looking guilty. She had her purse with her, which meant that she had been slipping the children chocolate drops, against orders, but neither of them said anything. She lowered herself swiftly to the couch; although she was past seventy, she was decisive in her movements. In her opinions, too, David thought, watching her. You never had to wait long to find out what Maria thought. Her square glasses, rimless, sparkled in the lamplight like windows at sunset.

"The piece is just beautiful, Maria. He's been working so hard." Frieda was making obligatory sounds, which increased David's irritation. There were so many rituals in his life, so many things that had to be said. None of them had anything to do with his music, which depended on impulse, spontaneity. And on other things that now, in his living room, seemed hopelessly remote.

"Ah, good, good." Maria pursed her lips, and a humming sound emerged — the Slavic *schwa*. She nodded rapidly. "The Diabelli..." She moved her slender hands through the air. David tensed. Something reverential was coming. It was hard to believe, in Maria's presence, that Beethoven had ever picked his nose or gone to the bathroom. "...the Diabelli is one of the mountain peaks, like *King Lear.*" She stopped there, thank goodness. "You are taking the repeats, of course." He hadn't intended to but he found himself nodding. Why was Maria always so sure? Why didn't she have any doubts? Maybe it had something to do with being Catholic and Polish.

And then, as Frieda poured Maria some coffee from the service in front of them, his irritation disappeared, and he wondered if he should discuss his dilemma with Maria. Not the offer of the job upstate — they'd already gone over that at dinner, and Maria had been vehemently opposed — but his confusions about it. Perhaps even the images that had plagued him during his recent tours. It wouldn't be the first time, after all.

He looked at the two women. Maria was examining the crocheting, a sweater for Sandy, and making suggestions. She was an expert at handicrafts, too.

It had been one of his bad days, when he was nineteen. Maria had asked him to stay for tea after his lesson. She did that once in a while, when she sensed personal problems, heard trouble in his playing. He had never liked to confide in her — she wasn't the motherly type, and most of her private attentions went to her husband, a dim man with several fingers missing (frostbite in a Soviet labor camp), now dead — but this time he had taken the plunge. He told her about some escapade involving a subway john where he had been spotted by police and sent home with a warning. She had listened quietly, nodding rapidly from time to time as if she wanted to get it over with as quickly as possible, and when he finished, she had hissed out her reaction like steam from a radiator. "David, you must fight against this. You must not hurt your great talent because of some little-boy desires, some few minutes of excitement. You will regret it all your life."

He had started to argue, to bring in Tchaikovsky and Moussorgsky and Saint-Saens and Gershwin, but she had cut him off. There was nothing more to be said. He had to be strong and that was all.

And, miraculously, her words, harsh as they were, had helped. Sent him back to the piano with new determination, at least for a while. Was it possible that now, more than ten years later, she would infuse him with strength once again?

Maria consulted the watch on her lapel, which had an upside-down dial. She never left the house without it. "All right, it is late. We begin now, please." The old command — how many thousands of times had he heard it? He smiled. Some things never changed. And Maria would help him with his trouble, pass on some of her sureness, her simplicity. He reached out and touched the plaster cast of Paderewski's hands on the little table to his left. It had been a wedding gift from Maria, one of her precious possessions. She said it would be a talisman for him, a source of strength. She had been right, as usual. Before she left tonight, he would ask if he could come to see her in the old apartment on 110th Street.

They were ready. He faced the keyboard, gathering his forces. For an instant, he was baffled by the knowledge that there were too many ways to play this music. Then his eyes closed in the powerful perception that there was only one way to play it, and that was his, David Lichtenstein's, way on this particular evening on West 74th Street in New York City; and that it was up to him to convince his hearers that this was the right, the inevitable way.

He dropped his hands and began. By the time he was into the sixth variation, the first real stinker, he realized that the important things were eluding him. The twentieth variation, the *andante*, did not move behind the stillness, and the fugue lacked surprise. He tried harder, going for sharper rhythms, more rubato, dynamic reversals, but the center of the music didn't hold. Beethoven's intellectual passion, his honesty, his recklessness, everything that should have been natural, was forced. He couldn't find the secret entrance to the music. It was as if his special talent, his private line to the piano, had broken. When he lifted the pedal for the last time, staring dully at the keyboard, he felt naked and ashamed. The deadness had come back. Right back to his own living room, his own Steinway.

"I thought it was beautiful, dear." Frieda, tuned into the tension, was being helpful.

He took out his handkerchief and wiped his forehead. He was sweating like a pig. He didn't turn to look at Maria. He could almost hear her mind snapping.

"Why don't you have some coffee, dear?"

"Oh God!" He turned his face away. Now everything was worse. He was acting like a child.

"David." Maria's voice cut like a razor blade. "You must not be too hard on yourself. You have made a good beginning."

He looked at the two women side by side on the couch. Boxes, he thought, they live in little boxes, and they have no idea what it's like outside. The next moment a terrible thought took possession of him. Was it possible that they were secretly pleased? Pleased because his failure at the keyboard gave them power over him? If he had played well, there would be nothing for them to do. But he hadn't played well, and now it was up to them to correct, advise, comfort. His performance had made him their captive.

He stood up. They stared at him. What was he doing? He hadn't acted like this in years. He walked out of the room, wondering if they would forgive him. Beethoven, who should have made sense of the world, had confused everything.

In the kitchen he poured himself some Scotch. He could hear muted voices — not hard to imagine what they were saying. "He's always irritable with a new piece." "I've known many musicians, dear, such difficult men." He doubled the amount of liquor in the glass, added tap water and drank off half. As he did so, he heard laughter, low, discreet. They were amused! His rotten playing, his tantrum, struck them as funny. But of course. People were always delighted to find they had power over others. The next moment, in his rage, he saw Nana. Nana on her deathbed, at the very instant she had said the things that led to this madness in his kitchen, the Diabelli in ruins around him, the two women he loved most discreetly celebrating his failure. She had had power over him, the most of all as it turned out.

She'd been lying in her bed, the mahogany four-poster that had been her marriage bed, looking thin and jaundiced. She was dying of liver failure. Still, she had managed to give him a fierce hug when he approached. Her David, her precious grandson. When he pulled away, almost losing his balance, she had hung onto his hand, searching his face as if looking for the least scrap of information he might selfishly wish to withhold. *Tell me,* she had cried silently, *tell me everything you think, feel, know, imagine. Keep nothing back.* Even now, standing next to his daughter's highchair with a bear in a gingham apron stencilled on the back, he could feel the violence of his grandmother's gaze.

After he'd gotten loose from her grip, he had begun to humor her, tell her she was looking better, but she would have none of it. "Don't be a fool," she said quite furiously, lying back. She had become even more tyrannical in her last illness. Perhaps the sickroom had its consolation too — total control over everyone who entered.

"I'm leaving you something in my will, David," she had said a few minutes later. "I want you to use it for your music."

Tears had welled up in his eyes. Tears of gratitude, love, guilt, responsibility. A regular mishmash of conflict and confusion. But he had cried too soon. Nana was watching him, her yellow tiger eyes ringed as usual with too much mascara. She was making her calculations.

"You'll get the money when you marry, David." And then, as he said nothing, too surprised and puzzled to sort out his speech, she had added, "I want you to marry. It will be good for you."

He stared back at her, his tears drying, his throat constricted.

Had she guessed something, looked into his private passions without permission? Was this her last bit of meddling in a lifetime of meddling? There was a lot of money, he knew. From her father, born in Germany, who had wound up the only doctor in a small Ohio town. From Grandpa, who had made a fortune supplying buttons to the military. For a moment, he thought she was going to mention Frieda — after all, she'd been the one who met Frieda, invited her home to hear him play — but she didn't. She didn't need to. With that yellow stare of hers, with that bottomless probing of his shadows, she had seen it all. Seen, and acted accordingly. It had been the final, overwhelming expression of her love as well as an act of fierce posthumous control.

He could hear footsteps coming toward the kitchen. Frieda would be here in a minute, ending both his tantrum and his reverie. He polished off the Scotch. There was one last thought, mixed up with all the rest. He'd sensed it, glimpsed it, several times in recent months, but hadn't gotten it free. Now he would, quickly, before Frieda walked in.

Money plus marriage. That was the bargain he had struck with Nana, and it had given him an edge at the start of his career. He'd been able to finance his early tours, send recordings to critics, hire a publicity agent, avoid the contest trap, even buy this co-op. By the time he'd been out of Juilliard for three years he was ahead of the pack and had stayed there, at least until recently.

"David, what's the matter?" Frieda was almost bloodless with exasperation. Her small face was clenched like a fist. A shudder went through him. Frieda was part of the bargain, part of Nana's legacy. Was it possible that he had never really examined the cost? That in fact its two halves — money and marriage — had simply cancelled each other out? That his career was failing precisely because of his marriage? Another shudder went through him. Who was he? And who was this small woman glaring at him in the blue fluorescent light of a kitchen whose appliances looked like the accoutrements of a morgue?

He shook his head, coming back. "Nothing's the matter, Frieda."

"Maria is very upset."

"I know she is."

"You were the one who invited her."

"I know. I know." He twisted away. "Gimme one more minute and I'll go talk to her."

Frieda exhaled sharply. "I hope you say the right thing when you get there."

She wheeled out, heading for the children's rooms. He had transgressed. Frieda would tolerate a fair amount of temperament on her own account but none toward friends or guests. He fought back the sense of dislocation and returned to the living room.

Maria sat on the couch, a ramrod. Her glasses glittered coldly. What could he say to thaw her out? An absurd sentence took shape in his mind. *Listen, Maria, at night I have these thoughts, these pictures, in my head, and I know you think they're a sign of weakness, that I can get rid of them whenever I want, but it doesn't work that way...*

He took a deep breath. It was time for honesty, or at least an imitation of it. "Something's been wrong lately." He sat on the couch.

"I can tell."

"I don't know what's causing it." He drummed his fingers on his thigh. "I've been playing badly all winter."

"I heard that."

Of course. She had connections everywhere — Bloomington, Pittsburgh, Chicago, Denver. The jungle telegraph had throbbed with the news: *David Lichtenstein has lost it.* He scanned her face, trying to read it. Impossible, as usual. She didn't betray her emotions easily. He used to think the nuns had caused this iciness, but now he wondered if disappointment might be the reason. She had given up her own concert career to tend to her husband, that dim man in grey clothing who was missing two fingers.

"Perhaps you'd like to come up tomorrow. We will have tea."

The old summons — confessional tea amid the busts and portraits and posters. But now he didn't want to. He could see too clearly what the result would be. Another injunction, a greater exhortation, to restrain himself, be strong.

She heard, or sensed, his reluctance. "I would like to play the Lhevinne recording of the Diabelli. I think you would get something out of it."

She had sugar-coated the pill, but still he didn't want to. He could see Frieda's shadow just outside the living room, wavering against the wall. She was eavesdropping. A sudden impulse to get up, walk out, run away, came over him.

"Yes, why don't you go, David?" Frieda hurtled in, a small, intense presence. "You haven't been up to Maria's in ages." He had the impression that a trap was closing, one of those pincers movements in tank warfare. "I'm taking Sandy to the doctor anyway and I'll take Bunny too."

Yes, a closing trap, and the crazy thing was that he had set it up himself; given the women in his life, going back to Nana, the power to run things, make his decisions.

"Good." Maria was still examining him with steely eyes. "Three o'clock, how is that?"

"No."

Whose voice was that? Could it have been his? It certainly didn't sound like his. Too deep, too hoarse. As if somebody else had popped out of his larynx.

"David!" Frieda was deeply angry. Fans of color ascended each cheek and her lips disappeared. He had only seen her like this once before, when a babysitter had been careless in her duties toward the children, endangering them.

"I'm sorry," he began, then stopped. Why was he apologizing? He didn't want to go, that's all. They wouldn't understand. He had a sudden vision of Maria at home tonight. What would she do? Weep? Laugh? Sit down and unwind her hair and think about Paderewski? He didn't really know any more about her than she knew about him. And what, for that matter, did he know about Frieda, this small, positive woman whose life was tied to his own? A fierce jab of inauthenticity went through him. Was it possible that his relationship with these women was unraveling because it had been a masquerade from the very beginning?

He stood up. He had just seen what he had to do. It was too bad it came to him only now, when it would cause the maximum amount of pain and upheaval, but there was no help for it. He'd waited too long. To postpone it further would be obscene. He suddenly recalled the young man in the front row at Bloomington, the one with the long legs and sleepy blue eyes. The young man had been in the receiving line after the concert. He'd actually shaken David's hand and looked at him curiously, invitation in his glance, ready to respond to the slightest hint. But David had averted his eyes, passed on quickly to the next well-wisher, then forgotten the whole thing. Forgotten it until tonight, when it had returned with dreadful vividness as Maria and Frieda stared at him. But of course its return now was a signal, a confirmation.

Aware that nothing would ever be exactly the same, he went to the hall closet and got his coat. The apartment was silent around him. It was silent when he opened the front door and when he closed it. He thought of faces frozen in a photograph as he waited for the elevator, then he refused to imagine anything else.

* * *

He had passed the bar often in his strolls around the neighborhood, noted the men going in and out, glimpsed the interior. It had always seemed quite out of reach, as if it were on the moon or Mars instead of the corner of Amsterdam and 76th. Now, walking in, he marveled at the simplicity of the act. He was like a homing pigeon that had lost its way for years.

He asked for a beer. The bartender was wearing a metal gauntlet; he opened the can by hooking the tab with a little ring on the pinkie. The he rapped the bar twice and said, "Enjoy."

David moved to a corner and looked around. His excitement and anger had given way to lightheadedness. He really felt quite dizzy. He leaned back, closing his eyes, but reopened them quickly. Frieda and Maria were waiting just under his eyelids.

The men around him seemed to be having a good time. He had never participated in this world, even while he was still a student. He'd been too busy, too scared, too involved with music, family, career. He hadn't learned its ways, its code and signals. He would have to do that now. A slight confusion seized him. If he learned how to operate in this world, would he forget the other? Would he lose his knack of talking to other parents, playing with Sandy and Bunny? He shook his head. There was no need to think about all that yet.

A young couple entered the bar, two handsome men, both dressed in loose white jeans, white blouses and sneakers. A gem sparkled in one ear of each. As David watched them greet friends, hug and kiss, his dizziness returned, but this time with a thrill of recognition. This was what he had in mind. He had a vision of intense conversations, shared wardrobes, and seasons by the sea. Beyond that, he glimpsed the happiness that would open up the music of his youth again, the fantasies and variations and sonatas, just as the great composers — passionate men all — had meant them.

"This your first time here?" A man his own age had appeared alongside him. He had dark blond hair, a square face with a thin nose, cloudy blue eyes. David nodded. "I thought so. Haven't seen you around. You live downtown?"

David studied his beer. Now that the moment had arrived he didn't know what to say. "No," he managed at last. "I live right around the corner."

This seemed to please the stranger. "So do I." He put out his hand. "Merrill."

"David Lichtenstein."

The man blinked rapidly, appearing to flinch. Then his blue eyes lightened a bit and he said, "My last name is Sparks. Merrill Sparks." This was followed by a smile and an appraising stare. David had the impression he had broken a rule of some kind, but he didn't know which one. "Can I get you another beer, David Lichtenstein?" The man was teasing him, but David laughed and said yes. Everything seemed very dangerous and very easy at the same time.

Watching Merrill return with the beers, David felt that things had been decided too quickly. That they hadn't had a chance to talk, to get acquainted. Then he wondered if this wasn't one of the rituals here too — the slightest gesture, the least acquiescence, was charged with meaning. Again his confusion returned. Yes, he would have to learn a whole new language.

"Here ya go." Merrill's hand was large and square and covered with curling caramel hairs. David couldn't help comparing it to Frieda's tiny, dextrous paw. His life would be very different if hands like these were sharing and shaping it. He lifted the beer to his lips. "I work right around here too." Merrill spoke cheerfully, quickly. He was a partner in a video store on Broadway. Business was good. They were thinking of opening a second store farther up-town. His open, easy manner, David thought, came from speaking to strangers all day. Maybe he was at his best in situations like this.

Merrill changed the subject to health. His chief fear was disease. He peered at David as he said this, as if trying to see into his bloodstream. David murmured that he had the same fear himself.

"Of course, safe sex is just as much fun as any other kind," Merrill said.

"That's the only kind to have," David replied, wondering where all this glibness came from. "You can't be too careful."

His answer seemed to reassure Merrill. "What d'ya say we get out of here, David?" He obviously expected no resistance because he put down his beer, then went to the door and stopped. Again David marveled at the speed and efficiency with which he had com-promised himself, though he didn't really care. Merrill Sparks was more or less what he had in mind when he walked out of his apart-ment tonight, crossing a space wider than that which separated the moon from earth. He put down his beer and followed Merrill outside.

Merrill lived on 80th Street between Broadway and West End. As they walked, Merrill chatting easily, David thought he might have passed his new friend on the street many times. He might even have been one of those young men whose glance he had always avoided, whose appearance made him hold his children's hands more tightly or sent him scurrying back to Frieda. Well, that was behind him now, thank God.

As they crossed Broadway, David suddenly had a clear picture of Frieda. She would be in bed by now with her pink curler, the only one she used, hanging over her forehead. He glanced sideways at Merrill. With his height and good shoulders and square hands and easy manner, he was about as far from Frieda as could be. Then an exciting notion struck him. He was now on a new life, parallel to the old one. Why couldn't he maintain the two tracks forever? Frieda and the children on one line, Merrill and his music on another? The two would never have to intersect — just go on and on, as far as the horizon. It would be easy in New York, where you could live for years and never even speak to your neighbors.

By the time they got to Merrill's apartment house, one of those slightly decayed, doormanless structures from the 1920s, David was filled with euphoria. Hadn't he solved his problem? Tonight and with a minimum of fuss? Solved it with a logic and daring that were completely beyond Maria's limited experience? Why had he ever thought of turning to her for advice?

Merrill's apartment consisted of two large rooms, separated by sliding doors of small glass panels, plus a kitchen. David could tell it had been carved out of a larger apartment. He remembered these spacious flats from his childhood, their rooms often bounded by tuck-in glass doors like these. Nana, in fact, had resided at 210 Riverside, a huge place of many rooms overlooking the Hudson, not far from here.

But the resemblance stopped there. Where Nana's apartment, like his own, was full of heavy, middle-European furniture, this one was hardly furnished at all. By the light of the one lamp Merrill had turned on, David could see two futons, a low bookcase, a wall devoted to audio and video equipment, and dozens of wicker baskets. In fact, there were baskets everywhere — hanging, sitting, dangling. They were all empty.

"What did you do, inherit a basket factory?"

Merrill laughed. "Don't worry, they'll be gone this time next year. I like to keep changing things around."

David sat on a futon covered in a bold geometric pattern while Merrill got some beers. Again he marveled at the suddenness of change. He might have fallen through a hole in the sky. From the nineteenth century right into the last of the twentieth.

Merrill sat next to him on the futon. They had to lean their backs against a radiator, which was quite uncomfortable. After they had opened their beers, Merrill turned toward David, whose heart began to beat rapidly.

Merrill's lips were rubbery, probing, aggressive. His tongue darted quickly into David's mouth. The sensation was not pleasant. David broke away. Kissing Frieda was very different.

"You're not supposed to kiss anyway," Merrill said.

"You're not?"

Merrill eyed him skeptically. "You didn't know that?"

"Oh yeah, I guess I forgot."

Merrill examined him for a while, then got up. "Let's go in the other room."

David followed him, then stood around indecisively as Merrill unrolled a large red pad. It reminded David of a gym mat. When it was flat, Merrill began to undress. Apparently they weren't going to use any sheets. "What're you waiting for?" Merrill asked. His voice was brisk, authoritative. David had the feeling that everything was scheduled from here on with no detours or hesitations permitted. Again he thought of Frieda. Once she got them started, she never tried to control things. She left that up to him.

Merrill was nude. He was terribly handsome — wings of caramel hair flying upward on his chest, his stomach flat, his thighs powerful, his sex lengthening into a massive club. David didn't take his eyes off Merrill as he undressed, hoping Merrill would find him equally attractive even though his stomach was flabby (a bit of a rubber tire around it) and his posture poor. Still, he had a naturally good physique, shoulders and hips in good proportion, nice legs, smooth ass. He had nothing to be ashamed of, really. Besides, Merrill had already reached out to grab him. "Nice," he said, yanking David down so that it hurt.

"Be careful!" he yelped. But Merrill was on top of him, grinding him into the mat, squashing him. David managed to wriggle free so that they lay side by side. Merrill's body now felt wonderful, its hills and valleys fitting perfectly into his own. He stretched his legs against Merrill's, pointing his feet in ecstasy. He wanted to make contact with every square inch of skin, every nerve end and tissue. He began to kiss Merrill lightly, just grazing. It was tremendously exciting.

"That's a no-no," Merrill said between breaths.

"A no-no," David mocked. He felt that a door had finally opened — a door behind which waited thousands of sensations as exquisite as the ones he was now experiencing — and he would be able to pass through that door any time he wanted, for the rest of his life.

In the next few minutes, he was gently prevented from doing

half the things he wanted to. Merrill would whisper or shake his head and raise David to another position. As they battled their way toward orgasm, David had the feeling he was making love only to the surface of Merrill's body, to its contours instead of to its entrances and exits, but that was okay. His climax, the result of minimal friction, was satisfactory; and, judging from Merrill's noises, his was too.

A towel appeared and Merrill mopped up. Then he lay down beside David. It was cold without a cover, but David didn't complain. It was so good to feel Merrill next to him, as if they had undergone some trial and could rest now because they had come out equally successful. Best of all, he didn't feel alone. He often did after sex with Frieda. The bridge between them seemed to vanish. But this time he had shared everything with his partner, not only the beginning and end but the instrumentalities along the way. It was an entirely new sensation and would, he thought, last as long as they lay here.

But Merrill, after no more than five minutes, sat up. "It's getting late," he said. He looked down at David. "Do you want to sleep? I'll get some covers."

David struggled up. He couldn't spend the night. That was out of the question. He pictured his apartment with its sleeping forms. They seemed to exist on the other side of a vast divide.

Merrill was waiting for an answer.

"I . . . I can't stay."

"No?" He looked amused.

"No."

"Somebody waiting for you in bed at home?"

Several lies passed through David's mind but he dismissed them. If his plan was going to take effect, if he was going to run his life on two tracks simultaneously, he'd have to start with the truth. "I'm married," he said.

Merrill didn't reply at first, just stared at him in the dimness. "That explains it," he said at last.

"Explains what?"

"There were some things you should've known. You didn't."

David thought back. He had been stupid, given himself away.

But did it really matter? Did anything matter except his desire to see Merrill again, to repeat tonight's experience? "We've . . . kind of come to a dead end. My wife and I." That wasn't strictly true, but it would do for now. Later, maybe next time, he could talk to Merrill about his music, about the Schumann Fantasy and the Diabelli Variations and all the rest of it.

"Yeah? A dead end?" Merrill's voice had gotten neutral. It was as if somebody had opened a little trapdoor under the syllables and all the affect had fallen through.

"I'm not getting everything I need." Stated that way it sounded quite selfish. Childish almost.

He sensed rather than heard Merrill snicker. "You and everybody else." He turned slightly away. "I don't think I can help you, David."

"I'd just . . . just like to see you again." He tried to keep the urgency out of his voice.

"When? When you get tired of fucking your wife?"

"No!" He reached out and touched Merrill's back, which now felt cold and slab-like. "I'd like to see you all the time." He paused. That wasn't what he had in mind. "Regularly," he amended, which didn't sound as good.

"You got kids?"

"Yes."

"Then it's all bullshit, David." Merrill lurched upward and disappeared into the gloom. A light went on in the bathroom. The toilet flushed.

David started to shiver. It was really freezing in this room. He got up and started putting his clothes on. He felt quite disoriented, though that was probably due to the cold and the lateness of the hour and his general exhaustion. He tried to marshal his thoughts, to find the words that would explain his needs to Merrill. It struck him that if he couldn't find the words, couldn't convince him now, his own future would consist of brief engagements like this — hundreds of Merrills standing in line behind the magic door, each a little more aloof, a little less interested, a little more impatient.

Merrill reappeared, wrapped in a robe. David thought of a model in a Macy's ad. Merrill had the same rugged, tender look. A slight terror darted through him. Would he ever meet anyone like this again?

"There's no reason we can't go on seeing each other." His voice was calm and firm, no trace of terror.

Merrill didn't reply. He was waiting for David to finish dressing and leave.

"I could arrange it any time you want. Almost any time," he added, thinking of his tours. "My wife wouldn't object."

Merrill's eyes flickered. "You mean she knows about this sort of thing?"

David twisted away. "No. Not exactly." As Merrill became stony-faced again, he said, "Not yet, anyway."

Merrill took a few steps. "You ready?"

David felt himself flush. Merrill was practically shoving him out the door. It was really quite rude considering what had gone on here just a few minutes ago. "Yes, I'm ready," he replied with equal coldness.

But in the hallway, waiting for the elevator, Merrill standing tall and empty-eyed at his door, his iciness gave way. "Give me another chance, Merrill." And then, without premeditation, he cited his address. "I'm in the phone book. My wife's name is Frieda. You might even get to like her."

A slight smile appeared on Merrill's handsome face. "No way," he said, and then the elevator arrived and David stepped into it.

He leaned his head against the inlaid paneling and closed his eyes. Merrill had turned nasty out of jealousy, selfishness, fear. Why wasn't there room for more than one partner in a life? Why was everyone so exclusive about love and sex? Why did they parcel them out so stingily? It was the curse of the human race. Or — a new thought came to him — maybe it was a feature of men living lives like Merrill's. Maybe they suffered from extra insecurity, possessiveness. They hadn't been tempered by marriage, by children, hadn't really learned to share.

But as he stepped out into the street, deserted at this hour, that thought collapsed. Merrill was right. He realized at once that a life couldn't be split in half, couldn't run on two tracks, not even in New York, a city of countless nooks and crannies. The price of Merrill's companionship, he saw now, was divorce. But that was impossible. He'd never considered divorce — not when he walked out on Frieda and Maria tonight, not when he stepped into the bar, not when he walked home with Merrill, both of them choking with lust. He would never leave his children, never deprive himself of their growing up, even at the price of a career that had gone cold and dead. The children, he thought, stopping in the street, meant more to him than his music. The children and Frieda and, yes, the apartment with its awful middle-European furniture and maybe even Maria's frozen reverence for Beethoven. It was too late to abandon any of that. They had become part of him. They were what he was.

A brief pain darted through him. He wondered if he had been unequal to his destiny, the destiny he had glimpsed from various keyboards and platforms as a teenager, as a young man, when he thought all the world's music lay within the curl of his ten fingers. And then the pain passed, and he was left with only a faint bitterness and the taste of Merrill's cologne on his tongue.

The next instant he had a clear vision of Nana. She had materialized at the corner of Broadway and 75th and was staring at him with her yellowish tiger eyes, now alight with triumph. His flesh chilled and he hated her. "You won," he said to the vision, "you won." Then she moved, and he saw that she was trying to reach him in a gesture of love and apology, but it was too late. He shook his head and marched on.

Frieda woke up when he got into bed. She turned on the light and reached for her glasses, but he refused to answer her questions. "Go to sleep," he said. "I'll tell you in the morning." She studied him, then threw herself down, her back to him, keeping as far away as possible. He tried not to touch her, even by accident, during the night.

* * *

The house was really very nice — yellow brick, federal, with Doric columns on either side of the front door. This afternoon, a time of bright sunshine in upstate New York, Sandy and Bunny wanted to bring their box turtle inside.

"You can't," David said. "It doesn't like the house, it likes the outdoors." To divert the children, he invited them inside to play chopsticks. As he sat Bunny on his lap and positioned Sandy alongside, it occurred to him that although he had sold his soul to his grandmother, he had gotten two souls in return — two brand new ones, in fact.

"We have to play softly. Mommy's taking a nap," he whispered.

"Softly," Sandy shrieked, banging her fists on the keys.

"Softwy," cried Bunny, imitating her sister as usual.

Yes, two brand new souls; and if that was so, couldn't it be argued that he had gotten the better of the bargain after all? Perhaps, he thought, removing the children from the piano. It all depended on your point of view or, as the students at Benson were fond of saying, where you were coming from. Besides, his recital last week had gone quite well. He had even managed to get through the Schumann. Of course, the people around here hadn't heard him in the old days. But those days were fading even for him, except at certain times, when he was alone in the woods or face to face with a particularly dazzling undergraduate. At such moments, he would hear a distant harmony, faint echoes of the old forbidden fantasies. But the next instant these tempting sounds were gone, thank heavens, and he was himself again.

William A. Reyes

A View of the Freeway

Nothing interfered with Rafael Saavedra's unperturbed sleep, not even his infant son's kitten-like outbursts at the crack of dawn. It was his wife's obligation to rise like a sleepwalker and tend to the baby's troubles with her precariously sung lullabies. *Duerme, duerme, dormilón,* Ana Maria would croon halfheartedly. Through the course of the night, Rafael would continue to sleep soundly while she cradled away the effects of infant nightmares provoked by — she hastened to guess — sudden lightning at the window mistaken for some evil foreboding. She imagined the child's unformed mind instinctively knew danger and would blare out fears automatically, in a fashion too impulsive and natural for adults to emulate. But then she realized that instinct could only interfere with the discipline needed for a long day of work ahead. One day, she thought, she'd also expect a miracle out of life, a miracle...

When he opened his eyes that morning, Rafael found not the child in its mother's arms nor even the mother, his wife, in the spartan matrimonial bed. Ana Maria was sleeping on the couch, soundly and alone, without her husband and apparently at peace, which didn't seem right to him. Then he went to check on the baby, who showed no awareness of his father's hovering shadow and let out no cries but only a gargly snore.

Rafael moved away, careful not to bump into the cradle, and headed for the window. A hum of emptiness arose from the freeway outside in the dark of night. Only a few cars sped by, at nearly twice the legal limit. The average Angeleno's dream consisted, it seemed, of a wish to immerse himself in the freeway like the Hindu who swims the Ganges.

He jerked his neck around a bit and flailed his arms in the air to bring some circulation into his head. Then it dawned on him, as if a spark of oxygen had awakened him at last to reality, that starting today he would no longer be sharing this miniature dwelling on the edge of East Los Angeles with wife and child.

"I'm not necessarily abandoning them," he reassured himself. He had sat Ana Maria down a few days before and attempted something men from his village near Guadalajara would never have done: to justify his actions to his wife. It was, on the face of it, an unmanly act; but one vital in this case to Rafael's peace of mind. There were, however, too many reasons that had to go unspoken — "for the sake of decency," as he put it, and he stumbled his way through the explanation until he no longer sounded coherent. "I'm just a dummy, you know me," he said, as if reminding her of the fact. "What kind of explanation did you expect, *mujer*, from a son of a peasant like me?"

All the while, Ana Maria had gradually shifted her position on the couch, getting further away from him. Her smile of incredulity lingered, refusing to vanish, as if meant more for her benefit than his. She had decided she would sleep on the couch from then on. "Until his madness passes," she said, thinking of outbreaks of typhoid back in the village, where such things did come and go. Yet a few days had gone by and his decision still stood.

When Rafael awakened that morning, he felt that Ana Maria had grown too attached to that old spring-busted couch, which they'd picked up at a garage sale for a suitably low $5.50. He would have volunteered to sleep on it himself had she not been so determined to bear the brunt of the bad news. How like her to choose a hard surface to sleep on so she could wake up groaning and lamenting her lot in life. To his surprise, however, she hadn't overdone the sound effects of self-pity. She had resorted instead to pouting and suspicious glances. Even her back stretched reticently each morning, without the cracking sounds of guilt.

He pulled a cigarette up to his mouth, stopping the fluttering of restless hands. There were fierce red streaks of sunlight on the horizon as he breathed in his first whiff of smoke. The freeway still looked abandoned, empty, like the thinning flow of a river in the middle of a dry, sizzling summer.

* * *

"You're our best friends..."

He could hear the voices of Ana Maria's parents as they stepped over the heel-marked tiles in his parents' back yard in Taracapa not too long previously. His mother escorted the Basualtos inside and sat them down to light tea and crackers, while they talked of their children's future like ranchers trading a few head of cattle.

"You're our best friends," said Don Orlando, Ana Maria's father, a stocky black-mustachioed man in his forties who wore the same dark suit to both weddings and funerals. "Just look at her," he said, pointing at the girl who, firmly convinced she wouldn't have reason to smile ever again, practiced a surly smirk. "She's sixteen now, *comadre.*" He addressed himself chummily to Señora Saavedra. "Sixteen, the same age as the boy, and they've known each other for too long not to get together now. You can't just send him off to the United States, *comadrita santa,* not by himself. He's a young man in search of adventure, true, but he must come home every night to a clean room and a hot meal, and she's a very hard worker."

Doña Edna, Ana Maria's mother, was eager to back up her husband's claim. "She learned to milk cows at five." Her face was suddenly shadowed with discomfort, as if she wished she hadn't said that at all. "Not that milking will come in handy in Los Angeles, from what I've heard." She glanced through the window to catch a reassuring glimpse of the rustic tavern that had divorced the Basualtos from the land, if not from the farmers who congregated there to get drunk on every convenient occasion. "She's a fast learner," Doña Edna threw in. "Not afraid of machines, for instance."

In truth, Ana Maria's first encounter with an electric blender had nearly resulted in the dismemberment of a nun. But those friendly Sisters of Hope, with their worldly ways and links to the outside world through their foreign magazines and newspapers, had familiarized everyone in Taracapa, including Ana Maria, with civilization. She imagined an entire universe fully lit at night by sparkling neon signs; and colorful hairdos to match them, a foreshadowing, actually, of Melrose Avenue in Los Angeles, as she eventually discovered.

"Between the two of them," said Don Orlando to Señor Saavedra, who'd come in to join the party, "they'll send back more dollars." The conversation had hit the right key, and it took off merrily from there.

Meanwhile, Ana Maria's eyes had strayed and met Rafael's across the room. For the first time, she found him staring at her as a man stares at a woman, given the proper stimulus. She smiled in a flattered way, breaking the code of misanthropy that had overcome her recently. Her eyes immediately shifted in embarrassment, but when they travelled back for a second look, Rafael's had gone wandering off to take in his own reflection on the tile floor. It was as if his initial look had been a fluke, only a bare attempt to take her into consideration as a woman.

Their eyes hadn't met again until a quick reception arranged for them not long after that fateful afternoon. By then, his look had grown weary and arrogant. His condescending attitude, his eventual bossiness, confirmed her suspicion that he was eager to enact the role of the man of the house. Out of resentment for her and her parents, he seemed perfectly willing to play it to the hilt. It would never have occurred to her at that point, knowing how well he was enjoying it, that he would ever willingly surrender, even seek to escape, his privileges as Boss.

Nothing elaborate was done for them on their wedding day, no town feasts, no disorderly drunken festivities. Instead, there was something along the lines of a "Yankee Wedding," which was what people called the type of rushed ceremony Americans went through on brief stops in Tijuana.

* * *

Ana Maria was suddenly up and running as Rafael turned to face her. She dashed to the bathroom and locked herself in. She let the water run longer than it usually took to wash her face, as there was no time for a full-fledged shower. Then she stepped out, her evasive eyes searching for the uniform she wore at Las Delicias, the twenty-four-hour Mexican diner where she worked the morning shift. She put on the brown and yellow striped vest and was fastening her name tag on it when it suddenly occurred to her that she could no longer avoid him with the oblivious attitude she'd recently taken. Time was running out. His packed cases surrounded her in an ambushing manner.

She caught his nervous, ninnyish smile and had to look away as she said her first words to him in a week. "I guess now I know," she said. "You must have met some blonde gringo broad. Is that it? Is that why you're leaving?"

He had already told her — he was only moving in with a friend in Westwood. He'd be sharing a room with another Mexican, just two blocks away from La Fonte, the restaurant where he worked as a busboy. "It's not a gringo broad at all," he said quite truthfully, not wanting to volunteer more than that.

She conjured up a valiant, martyrical smile that surprised him a bit, but he remembered that the more philosophically minded ladies of their village believed it was best to smile at the crucial moment of desertion, because a man would be more likely to return to a smiling woman than to one who puts up a fight. For her part, Ana Maria figured that grinning like an idiot was an inferior ploy, but it consoled her nonetheless. It served as an earthy version of the "coping strategies" she'd learned from reading the Spanish edition of *Cosmopolitan*.

She approached Rafael as he leaned by the window, feeling the pull of his body, his smooth naked chest, the way it parted itself in a male cleavage with grace and form. She couldn't help wondering why he always admired that freeway. No one else could have stood the roaring flow of bumper-to-bumper traffic that had already started to form as the sun sparkled through the window. She figured she might as well not reproach him for his bad habits at a moment like this. She'd do as well to join him in a cigarette, but he didn't offer one.

She went on the offensive, quietly, subtly, with those coping strategies fully at work: "One day you might want to explain it to your son, at least." That was hitting a bit low, and she tried to soften the impact. "I mean, I'm aware that you're responsible, that you'll keep up support for him, but the boy — when he grows up, I mean — might want a better explanation."

Which was to say she sought an explanation that very moment. He shook his head, as if indeed eager to lay out the details. But he ended up volunteering something karmic-sounding about following his "currents of life" — no doubt the result of working around the people of West Los Angeles who, she'd heard, measured the value of meals according to their organic vibrations. These people did seem amusing to Ana Maria, but she never thought her Rafa would adopt their lingo. Currents of life? She indeed had reason now to suspect a gringo broad, who'd no doubt use him for his well-formed masculinity, then send him right back to East L.A. after getting a good taste of Latin spice.

"Just don't write the folks back home about it yet," he said almost pleadingly. "They wouldn't understand."

"Oh, they'd understand, all right," she said, breaking out of the humble mold for a second. "They just won't approve, that's all." But she wasn't much of a fighter, not with the scent of nervousness his skin was exuding, and this need she felt to bury her face in his chest. She leaned forward and seized his arm, then gave him one tight embrace. He wouldn't be there when she returned from work and she figured she deserved to get a final feel of him, even if only of the lightest, least demanding sort. He gave her a little kiss on the cheek, stroked her hair as one might that of a relative departing on a long trip, then withdrew.

* * *

At about the same time in Westwood, a man in his mid-twenties stood nervously by the reception desk at the Bon Vite restaurant. He was looking at his watch when the hostess startled him with a sharp and radiant set of teeth passing for a smile. "Will it be just one, sir?" she asked, clutching a menu offering an assortment of Earth's natural bounties.

"I'm waiting for a friend," he explained, "but it looks like he'll be a little late. Would it be all right if I sat down and waited?"

"Oh, no problem, sir," she said agreeably. "What's your name, in case he asks for you?"

"Pedroza, Michael Pedroza," he answered, giving the last name a flat Spanish pronunciation with affected pride.

"Pee-droazz-ah," she enunciated. "Did you by any chance go to Hollywood High School?"

"No, I grew up in the Valley."

"Oh, a Valley boy!" she said, amused, making him doubly nervous as she led him to a corner booth far from the natural light that was southern California's only saving grace. "I was good friends with a Pedroza family in Hollywood. I bet there weren't too many Pedrozas in the Valley, were there?"

By then he was staring at one of the busboys, a dark Latin in his early twenties, perhaps. He reminded Michael of someone he knew quite well and admired deeply. As the hostess continued her monologue about Hollywood life (she was probably an unemployed actress, he figured), Michael looked around, hoping to find distraction in the fake adobe decor. To his surprise, what he saw was the scowl on the face of young Rock M. Toshiwara, who stood behind the hostess, having come in without warning like a mugger.

"Why, you started without me!" he nagged, in an accusatory tone.

"It was my idea to sit him down," the hostess said protectively. "But I'll get you another menu, sir. No prob."

Michael had actually planned on doing brunch that morning, but Rock, a law student at UC-Berkeley, in town now for a visit, had imposed a last-minute change of plans. "Not brunch," he'd blared through the phone curtly, "but breakfast! I have to go to visit this older gentleman I'm dating. He's twenty-six and drives a Ferrari, owns a mansion in the Hollywood Hills."

Rock himself was twenty-two years of age and already in his last year of law school. He expected to pass the bar exam by the time he was twenty-three, to have a condo by twenty-five, a house on the beach by twenty-seven, and a lasting relationship with a man by the time he turned thirty; but only after compiling a long list of disposable lovers that would include a few well-known actors, heirs, maybe European royalty — whatever he could get his hands on that could be boasted of afterwards. Rock had always been in a rush, completing his high school education at sixteen, rushing through college by adding summer courses, then going directly to law school to avoid "being one of the masses." But he was a registered Democrat, believing that only "vulgar people" voted for the likes of Ronald Reagan.

All along, he had also dabbled in a series of lovers in his own income range, of whom Michael (though he hated to admit it) had been one. There wasn't much Rock could have boasted of in Michael — a fifth-year senior at UCLA, unemployable because he was in full command of the English language and enjoyed reading obscure books. But, like many people in the humanities, Michael believed his lack of marketable skills was a sign of moral superiority, and that was the kind of arrogance that appealed to Rock. Now, though, they were only good friends, by mutual consent inspired by mutual embarrassment.

"So what on earth is up?" Rock asked, biting into the whole wheat bun he'd just drenched in butter. "You look like a nervous wreck."

"Do I?" asked Michael, surprised, since he thought of himself as being quite composed.

"Well, it shows through," said Rock with a wink. "I know you too well. What's up?"

"I suppose you might as well hear it straight out . . . It's happened," he stated gravely, hoping he was being perfectly understood.

"What? Got accepted to a top law school like mine?"

"No, never mind law school. I'm taking a year off after this quarter."

"Why? What for?" Rock demanded, shocked to hear that someone could possibly delay on the road to easy riches, which was what the law meant to him.

"I'm in love," Michael admitted, ill at ease. Such words had never crossed his lips, and Rock acted as if they had never reached his ears. He lowered the sunglasses he nowadays wore indoors, giving him a stark mafioso look. (Until recently, Rock's name had been Roshura Toshiwara. But he'd suddenly decided he no longer wanted to be known as that and had filed a court petition to have his name changed to that of his favorite star, the late Rock Hudson.)

"You?" Rock took a sip of water. "I thought you said that such things didn't happen to you. I thought you were jaded, self-defeating — the classic queen syndrome, you know."

Michael pointed toward a window that offered a view of another restaurant across the street. "See that?"

"What? La Fonte?" asked Rock, giving the name a perfect inflection. "I've dined there on many occasions."

"Then you might know one of the busboys there."

"I used to know several," Rock admitted, "but then I went to Berkeley and I lost contact. But why?" he added with great suspicion, "why on earth?"

"Well, his name is Rafael. He works there."

Rock signaled the approaching waitress that he wasn't ready to order yet, not at all. "You mean, maybe, that he's the manager of La Fonte, or maybe the owner? That's it, the owner, right?"

"No, one of the busboys."

"But why?"

"He has no money, his English is poor but I'm teaching him, he has a brain but hasn't used it to half its potential . . . and yes, he is a Mexican, but so are all my ancestors. Is that really so shocking, Rock?"

Rock crushed an ice cube with his teeth, then placed his sunglasses in neat fashion back atop his nose. "Just tell me one thing," he said, pressing Michael's hand as if to express condolence. "Is he *illegal?* Say it isn't so, or I'll walk out right now."

Michael resented that. After all, Rock's parents had spent part of their childhood in detention camps in the Joaquin Valley. "Illegal" was only an invective applied to minorities currently not in vogue. Japanese-Americans were once quite "illegal," with the Supreme Court's blessing; and Michael wasn't vituperative enough to say he wished that Rock Toshiwara personally still were. "Yes," he answered patiently, "Rafael is an undocumented worker. But what difference does that make? I'll eventually specialize in immigration law anyway."

Rock lifted his napkin as if the revelation had brought tears to his eyes and maybe even moisture to his nose. "I wouldn't want to be one of your parents," he said, crumpling the napkin in his hands. "All right, so what are you going to do about it?"

"Plenty. He's moving in with me this afternoon," he said, watching Rock's face grow paler and more dismayed with every word he uttered. "I even bought a queen-size bed."

"I bet you did."

"He's also married..."

"Pardon?" Rock now motioned for waitering help.

"He's got a six-month-old baby, in fact."

"The next thing you'll tell me is that they're all moving in with you."

"No, he decided to leave them," Michael said with a pang of guilt.

Rock homed in on it like a beast jumping on a trickle of blood from a wound. "Why, you've broken up a home!"

"Perhaps it's a home that needed to be broken up," said Michael, figuring he might as well play the *femme fatale* to the hilt. "They were kids when they got married. It was an arranged marriage, like something straight out of the Bible."

"Ready to order, sir?" A bubbly waitress hovered over them. "Protein maybe?"

"Eggs and sausages," said Michael hastily. He saw the disgust on her face and then started to time Rock's expression until the latter finally let out, predictably, "Cancel his order before I barf. Bring him a whole wheat croissant with a plate of tofu. I'll have a protein drink and the fruit plate."

While they waited for the food, Michael explained. The affair had started as a matter of accommodation, one might say. Rafa had been staring into the West Hollywood bar where they'd met, inspecting the place like a child at a candy store window, afraid to walk in for lack of cash. Michael walked out instead, curious to know what the young man was hoping to find inside. It started to rain, and Michael resisted the urge to run inside again. So there they stood, barely protected from the rain by an overhang of the building, until a first kiss suddenly produced itself like a miracle.

Michael's perfect Spanish impressed Rafael, who still thought of him as a gringo. Then, in the heat of titillation and anticipation, Michael's tongue had slipped, mispronouncing a simple word like *sábado*, Saturday (the day they agreed to meet again), as *zapato*, shoe, which sounded too awkward to hold any sexy connotations.

"How sweet," said Rock, putting on an acrid semi-smile. He suddenly brought out a silver brooch given to him by the 26-year-old he'd been dating. "He made it himself," Rock said, pointing to tiny sparkling chips of diamond. "It commemorates two thousand years of gay oppression since the fall of the Roman Empire. He's one of those social historians, I think — a professional gay. Impressive, no?"

"A person with brains, no less," said Michael, amazed. He wondered how Rock had managed to find and keep one.

"But it's not a relationship," Rock asserted, to set him straight. "It's a momentary courtship already on the road to extinction. Meanwhile, I have another suitor." He brought out a picture of a tall blond thing from Nebraska, a bodybuilder and gas station manager. Not the type of person Rock would marry but somebody he was glad to know on a very temporary basis.

"If you combine his body with somebody else's brains — mine, for instance — you've got perfection. But then there's his family. I met them, drove them to Seaworld. Nebraskans are landlocked, you know. They didn't seem very friendly. I don't know why. I mean, we didn't make it *too* obvious."

Michael's attention was slipping a bit as he called for the bill. "Yes," he commented, "maybe they were backwater people who've never met an Asian-American." Rock's face grew pale and Michael was taken aback. He wasn't quite sure what he'd said.

"Are you trying to say that Asian-Americans are somehow . . . aliens? Funny-looking people?"

Michael didn't want to honor the question with an apology. "Rock, would you please. . . ?"

"You're saying that we're so exotic that a Midwesterner would think of us as a tourist attraction!"

"Believe me, I've come across all kinds of hicks." Michael was trying to undo the damage; although it was to the people of

Nebraska that he might after all have owed an apology. "I've met Mexicans, for instance," — like Rafa he wanted to add, but didn't — "who come from such isolated villages that they've never even seen black people, much less Japanese or Koreans..."

Rock banged his fist on the table. "...who are like picturesque birds that people come to look at. You owe the entire Asian-American community an apology!"

Michael's face dropped. He could see people at nearby tables looking alert for scandal. "You can't possibly be serious," he said, but Rock was up by then. He threw a ten dollar bill on the table and went running out, tears welling up in his eyes and a fiery flush blemishing his face.

Michael untangled a clump of bills and reticently placed them on the table, leaving just enough for a fifteen percent tip. Then he walked out, avoiding the hostess's eye as she blared out airily, "Come again, Mr. Perez!"

Rock's habit of storming out of places at the least expected moment conveniently liberated the rest of Michael's morning, allowing him to run some errands. He was actually pleased, in a way, since there were times when one couldn't get rid of Rock.

As soon as he stepped into his apartment, shutting and locking the door to exclude humanity, he remembered that Rafael was due to move in that morning. "I guess it's the start of a new life," he said grudgingly and headed toward the kitchen to tackle a week's worth of dishes. "I must be neat," he thought.

Once he set out some roach motels, which he tried not to think of as a symbol of his entrapment of Rafa, he circled back to the living room to straighten out his library. He regretted the coffee stains all over Dante's *Divine Comedy*, but he nonetheless closed the book on them, probably for a long time to come. (He figured the *Inferno* was the only part that was a real masterpiece.) The book went into a dim corner next to Thackeray, with the best access to the dust. *Pride and Prejudice* went the way of *120 Days of Sodom,* and *David Copperfield* did quite well with *Moll Flanders.* There was no time to sift true from false, so St. Augustine's *Confessions* were lodged in uneasy company with the likes of Norman Mailer and John Irving.

He pulled up the blinds to let in what he called "the sunlight of reality." Then, when he went to the bedroom to make the bed, he found to his shock that Rafael had already brought his belongings in. Cardboard boxes lay all around the unmade bed with its over-washed, dimly greying sheets. He wondered if Rafael had noticed the mess. Still, he believed that no one could fail to regard his apart-ment — with its silky cobwebs, dying plants and peeling paint — as anything other than "an intellectual garden overgrown with weeds of brilliance." That was a line from Michael's journal.

He dragged himself back to the living room, furrowing the car-pet with his heels, sidestepping a Garbo poster that was peeling off the wall like a crust of paint. Plopping himself on the brick-like couch, he scanned the few pieces of mail, hoping to find an accept-ance letter from the *Atlantic Monthly*. He'd sent them an autobio-graphical piece, "Why I Cultivate My Ego," inspired by Nietzsche's *Ecce Homo*. What he found instead was a letter from his mother. She'd actually written, rather than just calling across town, as she needed to use exactly the right words to air her many grievances.

He skipped the introduction, a formal recounting of everyone's doing reasonably well and trudging along with their normal lives, and reached a passage couched in a more moralistic vein. "Your father has worked all his life to keep us away from the *barrios* of East L.A. and to help you pay for your apartment in Westwood. We've looked the other way about a lot of things, but now you tell us you're putting off going to law school so you can spend an entire year reading the Great Books. (And is the Bible going to be one of them?)"

No, it wasn't included, but that was only to make up for the fact that it had once been the only book officially allowed in his room.

"We consented to let you attend college rather than go into the Air Force like your brother, and now you want to use our money to read books. I hope you'll come to your senses. . ." A few tearstains, probably fabricated with saliva, blurred the next few words. ". . . anyway, I hope your new roommate works out all right."

He went back to the bedroom, not even bothering to stash the letter in the File of Infamy he kept for parental messages and edito-rial rejections. He moaned, mourning his fate, then decided to look through Rafa's belongings on the pretext of helping to straighten them out.

"You're the most intelligent person I've ever met," Rafa had once told him; and Michael believed it, as he doubted poor Rafa ran across many educated people. He didn't know if a combination of pity and desire could move a person into one's life; though Rafa had managed to endear himself further one evening by saying, "I'd like to wake up every morning and hear you say something beautiful." All that because Michael had read him a portion of *Leaves of Grass* in Spanish translation. Yet vacuous people were often quite adorable. There was so much one could teach them and no danger of their attempting to teach back. Looking through Rafa's things would be a sort of test for the boy, to see whether he continued to fulfill Michael's need for innocence in him, a need for fresh loving beauty divorced completely from intellect.

He opened one box, uncovering sets of work clothes, the black pants and white shirts busboys usually wore. Another box held a few homemade sweaters, hinting at a touch of taste in the women — Rafa's mother and sisters, perhaps — who'd knitted them. He knew he ran no danger of finding a book of any kind, so he was startled by a pamphlet stashed deep under some shorts. Was it a *Watchtower* publication, he wondered, fearing? But it only turned out to be a "How to Obtain Your Residence Papers" leaflet.

A few Julio Iglesias cassettes had to be forgiven under the circumstances (of poverty and its effects on taste). But then, under documents such as Rafa's birth certificate and his passport, was a picture of the tiny baby Rafael Junior, with the exotic flattened features that recalled the Aztec element in his blood. He resembled his father in his darkness, and perhaps in the deviational, non-European nature of his beauty. Worse yet for Michael's nerves was a picture of Rafa as a teenaged bridegroom, dressed up in a somber three-piece suit. Rafa gazed blithely at the camera as he stood with Ana Maria's limp hand resting on his arm; the both of them smiling as if to please the others, especially the parents, who surrounded them and squeezed them together.

A tear ran from Michael's eye, and he threw himself down on the bed. He felt a deep exhaustion at the prospect of a struggle that couldn't be waged with the intellect. He didn't care to face it and so he surrendered, dissolving like a child into easy sleep.

He was awakened by sounds in the room. He looked up, startled at first, and caught sight of Rafa as he ran a white towel over his dark smooth skin after a shower. Several hours had passed and the afternoon had settled in.

Rafael noticed the eagerness in Michael's eyes as soon as they opened and he was surprised by it. He regarded Michael as older and wiser. Yet this sign of weakness on the "older man's" part encouraged him to go on the offensive, to rush at him brandishing his towel like a flag of liberation. "Wake up, you *dormilón!*" Rafa shouted, shaking the water off his drenched hair like a wet dog until Michael reached up to grab it, pulling Rafa down to press their lips together tightly.

* * *

Baby Rafael clung to Ana Maria's lips with five twirling fingers, while his other hand beat his rattle against her head. She struggled along the street, squinting for the right address while dodging the child's blows. She was further distracted by groups of fraternity boys hooting at her out their windows. The focus of their attention seemed to be her new hairdo, a curled and moussed spectacle of a mess that was the last word in style. She ignored the boys as they began speculating on whether the university chancellor or the student body president was more likely to be the baby's father. She simply declined to translate their words in her mind. (Only in Spanish could she be stung by an insult.)

She began to wonder whether the West Side was actually an improvement compared to the East. The media were, after all, in the hands of the people of the West, and it was only natural that they should invariably portray their side of the city as the place to be. Meanwhile, the fraternity boys, the country's future leaders, were waving pirate flags and belching loudly. Well, at least they were responding to her new look. She had wanted to provoke some reaction and was glad to have nearly provoked a fraternity riot. Even so, she thought it wise to pick up her pace.

A few moments later, she stood outside a brick building with a dying jacaranda tree in its front yard. She double-checked the address and took a deep breath, which lifted the baby awkwardly along with her chest. Then, slowly, she began climbing a steep flight of stairs, careful not to miss a step. She reached a furry mat with a welcome sign inscribed on it; but she began to waver, as she'd been told many times not to trust everything she read. Her hand was shaking, the child wriggling about, and she couldn't quite bring herself to knock on the smooth green door with a gargoyle for a knocker.

She tapped lightly with the tips of her fingers and knew that she wasn't being heard. Then the baby let out an incredible hyena-ish cry that shattered her ears and must have gone through the door as well. The boy started beating at her again with his rattle, creating a commotion that seemed to be inspired by the behavior of the fraternity brothers outside. Through the hush inside, she heard the murmur of low voices and steps going back and forth across the room in confusion.

Somebody looked through the peephole in the door, so she put on a nervous smile. The baby's fingers were now entangled in her moussed hairs, ready to rob the scalp of them. Her Rafa opened the door in the midst of this struggle, standing there with his shirt unbuttoned and the sock on his left foot covering the bottom of his pants.

"I know you only moved out today," she said with a smile, "but I thought I might pay a visit. I hope I'm not intruding."

Rafa looked shocked at what he saw: an Ana Maria he hadn't ever witnessed before, if witnessing was the right word for catching a glimpse of this hairdo whose worm-like strands reminded him of a palm tree on Sunset Boulevard. A blue eye shadow covered her lids, reminiscent of that used in rituals indigenous to their home state. She wore a loud green skirt that revealed her trunk-like knees and was too tight at the seams, suggesting that she'd been taking generous advantage of the employee discount at Las Delicias.

Nervously, Rafael took the child from her and told her to come in. His own hair was wet and messy and looked very much as if fingers — maybe tongues — had been running through it like forks.

Ana Maria inspected the room. Just as she had suspected, the decor looked unmistakably feminine. Clearly a gringo broad, she thought, as she heard the toilet flush with a smooth pull of the handle that only a soft hand could have given it. She saw posters of Greta Garbo and Barbara Stanwyck and imagined Rafa's new woman in that vein, a struggling young actress perhaps. And she felt a pang at seeing so many bookshelves not all neatly stacked, proving that they weren't there just for show. An intelligent gringo broad, no less! She imagined her as a tall, glamorous lady who read without glasses and spoke wittily in various languages; a ravishing, luscious being, the likes of whom Rafa clearly didn't deserve ... Then the bathroom door opened and she saw, to her surprise, a young Latin man in a bathrobe with his arms crossed as if to keep them from shaking.

Rafa stood quietly, his eyes focused on Ana Maria's pink hideous nails. He still held his son, needing to hide behind the little body, and shook him as if he were playing a set of maracas.

"I'm Michael." Rafa's friend finally introduced himself. Ana Maria noticed that he spoke in nearly perfect Anglicized Spanish. This Michael couldn't be another busboy, she figured, but she couldn't understand what else would have led him to choose Rafa as his roommate.

"I'm sorry," she said, feeling a need to explain her presence to him; not to Rafa, but to this gentler-seeming Michael. She found him pleasant already. "I went to my hairdresser, as you can see, and I thought I might stop by and say hello."

"Never mind that her hairdresser's in the other part of town," Rafa stuck in, with a clear need to ridicule.

Ana Maria wasn't in the mood yet to launch her own complaints, to lay blame, to confront. She was there officially on business. And this nice Michael was bringing her a chair and a bottle of sherry. Such royal treatment! She never would have expected it of any of Rafa's friends. There was something about this Michael that delighted her completely, this politeness she'd never seen in Latin men before.

"I took the afternoon off," she announced. "I thought I needed a new look."

"Looking for a job at the circus?" asked Rafael, laughing it up. Michael reached out to subdue him with a tap of the hand, which Ana Maria found suspicious. Rafa looked away and fell silent, as if he actually obeyed Michael's touch. Very suspicious.

"And I had a little talk with the girl there," she went on, nervously observing the two young men, not knowing precisely why she kept talking or what she was saying. "I mean the girl at the salon. Her specialty is acrylic nails like mine, see?" She fluttered them in the air, to Rafa's horror and Michael's awkward tolerance. "So I asked her how she'd gotten into that business, and she told me about this cosmetics school in the area, and, well, she gave me the address, and I went to make a visit. They even have classes in Spanish and it's full of *nice* ladies, nobody too pretentious, just ladies doing their best. I decided I could enroll as soon as I can get a bit *more* support from my, er, husband — and I'll pay it back if I have to, as soon as I start doing makeup for the stars . . ."

"You doing makeup for the stars?" Rafa snorted. "They want to look like real actors, not clowns!" Then he went off on a vituperative speech about Ana Maria barging into this household uninvited when he'd specifically instructed her to call ahead before coming.

Michael was shocked and daintily inserted his hand in the chest of his robe. He'd only rarely witnessed a Latin husband at work on his wife's discipline like this, and he admired Ana Maria's equanimity under the circumstances. Rafa even shrieked that no wife of his should walk fraternity row looking like a tramp. Michael himself thought the poor girl had not been done justice by her makeup artist and stylist; she did look garish, even a bit tart-like. But he was too polite to mention that.

Rafa suddenly thrust the child at her and instructed her to go make a call from the phone booth on the corner, to ask if it was all right to come by. Such treatment, Michael thought, was something Rafa had better not try with his new spouse. Here was a side of his Rafa he hadn't seen before, a machismo that hadn't been directed at him, since Rafael tended to admire him and revere his intellectual powers. It looked ridiculous, this twenty-year-old Latin dad playing a role for which he obviously wasn't suited.

Ana Maria didn't seem at all shocked. She was smiling defiantly. She put the baby into Michael's hands and got up to face this Rafael Saavedra.

"Look, I didn't come here to spy on you," she said, though to herself she admitted to being awfully curious about his new life. "I only came here to tell you that I'm not going to sit around crying because you left..."

"Why not? What kind of woman are you?"

"...and that I'll be needing an extra fifty dollars a month."

"Fifty dollars!"

"It'll help me save up so that in September I can start attending classes."

"Fifty dollars? I live off tips, you know, the tips waiters share with me when they're generous enough to give me anything at all."

"Sorry, but you owe me that and more. And besides, if you're getting what you want, then I'm going to become an artist!"

"I've seen your third grade sketches — stick to fast food!"

"Nothing you say will hurt me at this point, Rafael Saavedra." The remark stabbed at her heart, as had those about her hair. But she would stick to her demands. "Fifty dollars."

Michael felt compelled to intervene at that point as he detected an urgent moisture beginning to seep out of the baby's diaper. "We can handle it," he said, wondering how his parents would feel about some of their money going into a slush fund for his male lover's wife. "Fifty dollars is manageable..."

"Stay out of this, you intellectual!" Rafael screamed. Michael was shocked. He'd never been called an intellectual in so many words, and not with such a negative connotation. Ana Maria sat back and sipped her sherry with a look of satisfaction.

"See?" she said. "This is what I've had to live with for the past four years." Her tone of voice suggested that she also meant, *Now it's your turn.*

Michael felt he ought to go and cool down Rafa, who was beating his fists on the wall; give him a lecture on ethics, maybe, or wisdom from some great mind. At that moment, however, the front door flew open. They all turned, even the baby, and saw on the threshold the outraged, thunderous-looking figure of Rock M. Toshiwara. For once, Michael actually felt relieved to see him, regarding him as a sort of dramatic outlet, a bell ringing to signal a break.

* * *

"I've been betrayed!" cried Rock Toshiwara with a tragic ring to his voice as he sauntered into the house and headed for the bedroom. "I need some privacy," he added, clearly intimating that he wanted someone to follow him and beg for details of his sorrows. Michael handed Baby Rafael back to Ana Maria, warning her about the wet diaper. Then he excused himself and rushed inside. The husband and wife picked up where they'd left off, with a couple of shots of sherry already making for slight but noticeable differences in temperament. Ana Maria was talking along the lines of, "I could have been great," and Rafael answered with surly scorn.

Michael was relieved to find that Rock hadn't locked the bedroom door, showing that he had indeed wanted to be followed. "Rock," he said, still uncomfortable with his friend's Hollywood name, "what is the meaning of this?"

By then, Rock had dried his tears and was sitting on the bed trying to seem engrossed in a copy of *Hollywood Husbands*. "It's the sequel to *Hollywood Wives*," he explained.

"You do this just to irritate me, don't you?" asked Michael.

"I told you I don't read books that were written before I was born."

"Forget the damn book, I mean you!" Michael realized that if Rock moved an inch from the corner of the bed where he was sitting, he'd uncover the moist remains of lovemaking on the sheets. "Come sit over here," he pleaded, offering a comfortable swivel chair in front of his desk.

Rock was suspicious of the false ring of politeness in Michael's voice and he went instead to look out the window. "I just don't want to talk about it!" he said, shutting his book violently and throwing it on the bed, where it landed right on the stain. Books of that sort were probably meant to be stained, thought Michael, more worried about his reputation than the book's pristine state. "I can't talk about it, I just can't," Rock continued to wail.

"Look, you'll get around to it sooner or later, whether I beg you to or not. So please don't waste my time."

"If you put it that way," said Rock, and he was off. He'd gone to visit his friend in the mountains, hoping for a week of amorous intimacy. But when he got there, he found that he wasn't the only one invited. The place "reeked" of old men, thirty-year-olds mostly, who to Rock appeared nearly senile. They were drinking and playing cards like old hags and talking about some Brigitte Bardot. "A French *chanteuse* or something," Rock figured. "They paid very little attention to me. Mostly I was encouraged to run around the pool in my Speedos and swim for their benefit, like a showgirl or something."

"And did you?"

"Of course I did, but that wasn't why I went. And when I confronted Teddy, he said, 'I figured it would be good for you to meet my friends.'"

"What's wrong with that?"

"He meant I should meet his friends so there would be somebody for him to pass me along to once he's done with me."

"So — did you meet anybody else you liked?"

"A couple. But that isn't the point, Michael Pedroza! Even *I* get tired of using people."

Michael's eyes widened in genuine surprise. "You do?" Rock actually sounded sincere.

"Of course I do! What do you take me for? ... So I made a dramatic exit — said I was not a stripper, a kept boy, a teenage runaway. They may be my alter egos, but I am none of those things. See?"

"See what?"

"I didn't come here just to remind you that you owe me an apology."

"Which I don't."

"But I won't demand it. If you don't mind, though," he said nonchalantly, "I'd like to park in your living room for a couple of days before I go back to Berkeley."

Michael was too astounded for words.

"You're a doll."

Michael bit his lip, then proceeded in an agreeable tone. "Of course you can stay." Then he added a warning: "As long as you cool it!"

"You're so thoughtful." Rock smiled with a hint of flirtatiousness. "I thought you were so handsome once ... I mean ... Oh, you know what I mean. In the rush to fulfill oneself in one quick night, one ends up flattering half the world. But of course you're more special than that. What I mean is, I hope I didn't just use you, and that you got something out of it."

"Yes, I got humiliation out of it, but it's in the past. You were seventeen, and if I'd known you were so young . . ."

"You broke the law!"

". . . I would have sent you home to your parents. Sometimes I still think about that, sending you home."

"Oh, you're such a comedian." By then, Rock was peeking out into the living room. He was astounded by the sight of Ana Maria's medusa-like hair. "What on earth happened to her? Where did she get that god-awful do? And what is she doing here, anyway? Giving you a few pointers on how to handle the macho man?"

"If you're going to make fun of us . . ."

"Oh, no, no, no," said Rock, rushing to reassure him. "That's just the way I talk. You know me, a complete snob. I thought you were a snob, too, once."

"So did I," Michael said, looking as if he'd begun to regret leaving his past behind to mate with an illegal alien. "I don't know what will become of me now."

"You have enough pride, I know you do. It will just be channeled in different directions. Just find yourself a good law school. Meanwhile, dear Rafael will satisfy physical needs, and that will give him a purpose in this world."

"But it's not just physical."

"I know, you'll teach him to read and write, the Pygmalion syndrome." Michael's eyebrows slid upward in surprise at this reference. "Yes, I have read some G.B. Shaw, though I would never admit it to my friends. They wouldn't understand."

"And I thought reading books was a challenge," sighed Michael, thinking of other challenges to come, the struggle to civilize the beautiful but primitive.

"Stick to bestsellers," said Rock. "But now we must celebrate your new life. Believe me, I need something to cheer me up as well." He flashed daddy's plastic in the air. "I must treat you all to dinner, even the poor widow."

Michael thought about it and decided that Rock did deserve to pay, literally, for so many past misdeeds. Even if it was with credit.

"All right, Mr. Rock," he said, "take us to dinner."

In no time, Rock was in the living room, offering a limp hand with a proud upward pull of the shoulders as he introduced himself. "Rock," he said, one raised eyebrow suggesting solemnity, even royalty, "Rock M. Toshiwara."

* * *

Ana Maria sat quietly, assessing the value of the furnishings, the dishes and silverware, the waitresses' uniforms, as Rock and Michael engaged in an esoteric discussion about law schools. Meanwhile, she and Rafa smiled like pretty people. "They're both going to be attorneys," she told him, nudging his elbow, "and I'm going to be a makeup artist. What are you going to be, Rafa, when you grow up?"

Rafael held the child in his arms and turned his back to her. "Can't you just sit there and behave? They're all looking at you, asking where did that peasant come from."

"Why, from Mexico," she said confidently.

"We can't take you anywhere!"

"Settle down, you two," Rock interjected, then went back to talking to Michael.

"Yes, Mr. Rock," said Ana Maria, offering toasts with her third glass of cabernet sauvignon. She had her eye on the busboy assigned to the table. Every time he came to refill her water glass, she'd gulp it down to prompt his quick return. Rafael complained that the busboy was incompetent, too insistent on returning, that he felt harassed by him. "He's not harassing you," Ana Maria said, grateful for some attention from a man. "He's harassing me."

"He should stick to his job."

She moved on to other topics, her mind unsettled by the cabernet. "So, isn't this nice — to be treated to dinner by a Chinese gentleman?"

Rock's eyes grew fierce at that supposition. "I'm not Chinese!" he exclaimed. "I'm Japanese. Please get that right." He seemed ready to make a scene but was restrained by Michael.

"*Mil perdones, señor,*" said Ana Maria, surprised that Rock understood Spanish. In their village, all Asian people had been referred to as *chinos* and she didn't understand why Rock would take offense at that.

"See?" said Rafael, as if his worst fears about her had now been justified. "You're embarrassing Rock, *mujer!*" Then he turned and gave Michael a mean stare. "It was your idea, wasn't it? To have her here. To humiliate me."

"Yes it was," Michael barked back, not in the mood to let Rafael have his way. He thought Ana Maria was perfectly charming, as endearing as Rafael could be when he wasn't trying to create a dichotomy between man and woman as master and slave.

"Everybody relax," said Ana Maria, trying to reduce the tension in the air. Just then, the busboy returned to refill her glass. She took the opportunity to introduce herself, surprising the young man, who looked flattered. He was from Oaxaca and was glad to meet a *compatriota*. He was also so handsome that Rock and Michael fell silent and stared at him. To her surprise and relief, he was clearly interested only in her. At least she felt she'd gotten something out of the evening.

The exchange was brief. He had to go clear an empty table and lay clean silverware. Then he went into the kitchen. She felt a sudden drunken fear that she'd never see him again. That would mean the loss of two busboys in a single day.

"I have to go find him," she announced, getting up in a rush.

"Ana Maria, don't make a fool of yourself!" Rafael commanded, but to no avail. Rock and Michael laughed, encouraging her to "go for it."

In no time, she was in the kitchen, surrounded by the sounds of washing, cleaning, cooking. The dishwashers and busboys and the corpulent chef all stopped what they were doing and stared at her with great curiosity.

"It's Miss Mexico," somebody whispered, probably figuring that her passionate hairdo meant she was a "Miss" something or other. The boy from Oaxaca introduced her to an assorted lot of Mexicans, Salvadorans, Guatemalans, and even a Chilean from the southernmost tip of the continent. In seconds, she had collected phone numbers and addresses and been invited to a few parties to be given in honor of "Miss Mexico."

The manager walked in, looking not at all impressed by Ana Maria's turbulent hair. The kitchen workers immediately scattered and resumed their duties. She apologized and walked out, clutching the pieces of paper with new names and numbers. She smiled at the idea of having brought the kitchen workers a respite from work and a promise of future pleasures.

* * *

Ana Maria floundered into the apartment with a headache coming on and landed on the couch that had been her bed for the past week. Michael stepped in, the soberest of the four, and put the baby in his cradle. Rock and Rafael had remained in the car. Ana Maria grabbed the windowsill to lift herself up and catch a glimpse of the car out in the street. Rafael's shadowy figure could be seen in the back seat, legs crossed impatiently and resentfully, as if he'd been the one to be abandoned by wife and child.

"Such a big baby," she said, her hand cradling her head as she leaned casually, merrily on the sill. She turned to Michael, who was rocking the cradle. "Perhaps Rafa just hasn't learned about coping strategies." She felt quite sophisticated to have heard of such things. "He hasn't become accustomed to his new life. He doesn't yet know how to explain it to himself, much less to his wife, and never to his family back home. He may be a daddy but he's not quite a grown-up."

Michael looked surprised. She seemed livelier than he'd expected her to be, almost completely at ease with her own new life, as if he'd lifted a burden from her shoulders. "And you understand, then," he asked with some discomfort, "about him and me?"

"Of course I understand," she said. "The moment I stepped into your apartment, I knew there was a woman in the house, of sorts. I've read about these things." She reached out to give him a congratulatory hug. "He's your problem now, dear," she said, but didn't mean to imply she felt sorry for him at all. "You're the strongest, like a true woman. You can handle anything. You're educated — blessed with wisdom."

Michael hadn't seen so much faith in the power of education

since the bookies had installed a California lottery for the benefit, so they claimed, of the state's schools. "I'll do my best," he said.

"He'll need the best," she stated. "Meanwhile, I'll learn about nails and split ends and colors and tints. I love tints. And men's hair — I really want to get into men's hair."

Michael left her in her bed, repeating this fantasy of dazzling colors, a dazzling future. Ana Maria heard the door close and rushed to take one final look at the car as it departed for the West Side, that other half of the city that was so detached from the rest but still managed to dominate the whole. No partition was needed to keep the residents apart, only the power of pretension and hard cash. Perhaps she and Michael, having so much in common, could break this barrier through their bizarre comradeship.

She heard the motor start up, then watched as the car drove up the street. She sought a way to capture the sight, to distinguish this Toyota Corolla from all the rest, like a departing plane that carries a close relative. But the car reached the freeway entrance and blended with the lights, the hum, the colors of the city's lifeline, carrying away with it part of her life, her dear Rafa, a prize she'd never earned but had been appropriated for her by others. The car disappeared from sight but she had something richer, livelier — the picturesque view of the freeway, whose scintillating lights flashed promises of love and beauty ahead as she slept and, of course, dreamt.

SHADOWS
OF
LOVE

T.R. Witomski
for Alex

Within You/Without You
Aria, Duet, Cabaletta and Recitative

Aria

I am in mourning for Alex. No, my dears, he has not died. What would have killed him? Alex (and I) won't die from an overdose. (We calculate dosages very exactly; we're Ph.D.'s in recreational — and mandatory — drugs. And, anyway, dying from drugs is now much too retro, too 70s.) And — dare I write this? — we probably won't die of the plague, either. Because, if we are ruled by principles more developed, more inspired, more heartless than throws of the dice (God may be a son of a bitch, my brothers, but He *is* there; He must be there), it would be more fitting, more dramatic, more inhuman for Alex and me to live, scarred, scared veterans of the sex wars, horribly guilty survivors full of self-loathing. For we are still here while the lights are going out all over, spared to serve as witnesses to the cataclysm unless the Savior comes (let us pray).

My sense of plot being what it is, I cannot allow Alex to die from "it." While I suppose I have wanted to kill him, I can never martyr him, never write a praiseful obituary for him, never let him be idolized by others who might read of him, never contribute to making him a saint before the tribunal. I must always act as the Devil's Advocate. I will not let Alex die of the insidious plague because I refuse to continue to deify him.

But Alex, though alive, is gone, gone from me, gone somewhere; I suspect somewhere "out there," somewhere over the fuckin' rainbow, somewhere where he can get a blasé job not on a yuppie-esque career track, somewhere where he can find a nice young man who will love him and try to protect him from his demons, a kind-hearted guy, someone very much unlike me. Perhaps Alex has gone to Milwaukee or one of the Portlands and if he reads this will laugh and think, "Christ, he is still at it? Will he never stop?"

Probably not.

When Alex first left me (I can hear him: he is saying, "No, I didn't leave *you;* I left everything — Wally's parties, The Spike, the goddamned opera, Drexel Burnham Lambert, Claire, you, the whole fuckin' shooting match"), I painted madly. Years ago, before any of this, before Alex, before "it," I had wanted to be an artist, had even sold a bunch of paintings, gotten a few gallery shows, been favorably mentioned in the correct journals; but somewhere, somewhere in the midst of all the men and all the money and all the booze and all the epic dawns at the Mineshaft, that desire, that yearning to create images and not merely to be a part of the images, fled from me. But when Alex first left me, the urge to exercise what was left of my abilities — naturally? ironically? masochistically? — returned.

It helped that there was not all that much else to do.

My paintings this time around were, as you have probably surmised, all of Alex. Alex crucified. Alex drawn and quartered. Alex hanged, beheaded, castrated, sodomized with a white-hot poker, torn apart by wild dogs, executed by electricity, by lethal injection, by poison gas. Alex, the dinner of cannibals, the patient of concentration camp doctors, the sacrifice to bloodthirsty gods. Alex tortured, starved, the flesh ripped from his body, his eyes gouged out, his teeth extracted, bamboo sticks shoved under his fingernails, his bones broken, his corpse left for the vultures and hyenas. All of these delightful images rendered, I hasten to add, in a wildly abstract, "intensely personal" and "creatively vibrant" style, in rigid lines of black and swirls of red and splats of white, hundreds and hundreds of different shades of black and red and white, quite mad.

At first I showed the paintings to no one. Like a Victorian

miser, I hoarded them. ("Mine! All mine!" he howled diabolically.) But Rene had heard, or maybe simply intuited, that I was painting again. He *had,* he said, to see the paintings. Not wanting to risk one of his psychotic outbursts (when Vincent refused Rene an interview for *Artforum,* Rene retaliated by stabbing Vincent's fourteen-year-old lover), I let him see them. Impressed as only a crazy art queen can be, Rene arranged for a show. And I made a great deal of money. And I again stopped painting, thus getting myself noticed by the *Times* for refusing a Whitney show and then getting praised to the skies by Annette in *October* for the refusal.

Duet

It is time for the ritual. Naked, except for sweatsocks and engineer boots, I position myself in the sling. As Alex, hooded, watches, I pull my cock to hardness. "Yes," Alex says, "yes."

As I jerk my cock, I think of . . . well, this will sound odd, but . . . as I jerk my cock, I think, I try to think (I fail but I try to think) of nothing. I try to clear my mind of all images, to — ha! — purify my thoughts, to paint the impossible. To capture the idea of a blank canvas, that screen on which there is nothing but possibility, the void that contains everything, the emptiness that holds all being.

I am never successful. The concrete intrudes. I see: a hand pushing into an asshole, the marks left by a riding crop on a milky white inner thigh, a tongue lovingly licking foreskin, a silver ring through a nipple, a kneeling man begging, "Please, please, Sir, let me swallow your load, please, I don't care about *that,* I need your cum, please, please, Sir, please give it to me," a face contorted in searing agony as an electric cattle prod touches balls, a silent chorus mesmerized by the spectacle of a branding, Callas as the dying Violetta, a straight razor scraping over a crotch, black cock, Arab cock, Hispanic cock, Japanese cock, leather against leather, leather against flesh, flesh against flesh, flesh alive, pulsating, enraptured.

Alex watches silently. The images surge incoherently. I grunt. The cum spews out of my cock. The sling rocks, its chains clanging. The canvas is perfectly blank now, pristine, open, welcoming, waiting, needing. I whimper. I am satisfied.

The penetration is sudden, complete, excruciating. Alex

shoves his cock into me. He withdraws. He re-enters. He pulls out. He rams in. "Yes," I hiss, "yes."

His strokes — brutal, masterful, all-knowing — recreate me, destroy the nothingness, saturate the canvas with brilliant colors: bright oranges, deep blues, insane greens. I am: tied to a St. Andrew's cross and scourged with rose branches; pierced with fine sterilized surgical grade needles; raped by Cossacks; roped like a calf in the rodeo; gagged with a tremendous black lead dildo; blinded by the light reflected in his mirrored sunglasses; imprisoned among thieves and murderers; slaughtered in the Colosseum as thousands cheer; burned in an auto-da-fe while the crowd praises Jesus; annihilated by the will of Sir Stephen; humiliated by Beauty; tormented by O; violated by the Divine Marquis himself . . . fucked, fucked, fucked by my forever lover Alex. Fucked then, now, eternally. Fucked fully, overwhelmingly, remorselessly. Fucked until he becomes a part of me and I a part of him, his cum signaling my rebirth, his being being my being.

"We must move on," Alex said. "Both of us."

"What is this 'we' shit? This 'us' crap? You're the one who's leaving. For me Die Tote Stadt.*"*

Toward the end, I had no patience with Alex. For in some silly, untouchable part of his mind, he still held sacred the ideal of a country house with that fuckin' white picket fence, lovers drinking good brandy by the blazing fireplace, tender kisses, Christmas, a piece of crewel-work framed and hanging on the kitchen wall asking the Lord to Bless This Home.

I just wanted him to promise me that if I got "it," he would put a bullet through my head.

Alex left three days after I bought the gun.

Cabaletta

"You don't have to wear a rubber." The voice of the trick is heard. "I want to do it the way we used to. I mean, if I'm gonna get it, I'm gonna get it. Nothing I can do about it, ya know? Might as well have fun now."

How do you answer that? After you say that you *will* use the rubber, of course. I like the SM-ish approach: "You don't deserve to have my cum inside you, you worthless fag." I have now learned to manage to say that without laughing, without breaking the scene.

Could Alex have learned how to say to me, "You don't deserve to have my cum inside you, you worthless fag" without laughing, without breaking the scene? Could I have listened to him say that and still have been able to hiss, "Yes, yes"? Could he? Could I? Could we?

I can hear him. I can hear Alex asking, "Why do you torment yourself and why do you torment *me* with unanswerable questions? Don't you know the lyric that goes, 'If you believe in forever, then life is just a one-night stand'?"

Ha! Is that all there is? Is that all there is? Am I to be left with trite song lyrics? Can I spend the rest of my life in mourning for Alex? Or will I again start to paint so that I can once more see white, a blank canvas, so many possibilities?

Alex, Alex...

Recitative

The final painting took eighteen months to do. (And it *will* be my last painting. After I completed it, I submerged my right hand in scalding water and, using a scalpel purloined from a bar friend who specialized in mad doctor scenes, severed the nerves in the fingers I used to hold my brushes.) I'll not describe it; it has been too much described already. I would like nothing more than to firebomb the house of the critic who compared it to *Guernica*.

"Why not," Kenneth asked, after reading that wrongheaded review, "to *The Last Supper?*"

"Because *The Last Supper* isn't a painting."

"Then what the fuck is it?"

"A fresco."

"Well, that's *like* a painting."

"You know, my mother thinks my stuff is *like* painting, too."

"Do tell."

"You know that old line, 'There are two kinds of people: those who only like a painting when they can see what it's a painting of, and those who only like a painting when they can't'?"

"I do now."

"Do you think that was the difference between Alex and me?"

"It's Sunday, so The Spike shouldn't be too crowded."

"I'm almost ready. Shit, after all these years, you'd think I would have learned how to get these damn things on without all this effort."

"What we go through to be butch."

"Why'd you change the subject?"

"Aren't you tired of talking about Alex?"

"No. Don't you see? Haven't you gotten it yet? Alex was — is — *it*. There's nothing after him."

"But what about the young man you're seeing?"

"Jack's very hot. *Very* hot. And I'm getting good at safe — well, safer — sex. So good it feels natural. I guess we really do learn by doing. Or not doing."

"But he's not Alex."

"There are no second acts in gay life."

"I like to fuck you after you've just come," Alex says. "I like that most of all."

"Yes . . . yes." The ritual is complete.

"Was Alex really *that* good in bed? You've never told me too much about that. The really lurid details."

"Not especially. Jack's got a much bigger cock. *Much* bigger. Christ, he's practically a tripod . . . Do you feel — I don't know — funny, knowing you'll probably never take cum up your ass again?"

"I never really liked cum up my ass anyway."

"I did. *Did.* That's all over now. It seems. . ."

"Funny?"

"Yes. Odd. To know that, with Jack . . . with Jack it will never be . . . complete. Is that the word? I want to say to him, 'You don't have to wear a rubber. I want to do it like we used to. I mean, if I'm gonna get it, I'm gonna get it. Nothing I can do about it, ya know? Might as well have fun now.' I want to hear myself saying, 'Please, please, Sir, let me swallow your load, please I don't care about *that*, I need your cum, please, please, Sir, please give it to me.' But I don't. I won't. I can't."

* * *

On fall Saturday afternoons now, is Alex perhaps going to college football games, loving the innocent homoerotic brutality the muscular young studs demonstrate so avidly, so sacredly, so that the fans may be thrilled, satiated, saved from the petty torments of quietly desperate lives that feature only one musician keeping the beat? On Sundays now, is Alex perhaps going to church services — Episcopalian, I would think — getting hard from the perfect ritual, dull, stoic, sublime, hearing in a voice from the choir a memory of a perfect Marschallin? Does Alex perhaps now have a good, solid, uneventful middle management job in a small, pleasant company (one that would never be investigated by the SEC) where he tenderly, patiently, guiltily listens to his co-workers chatting of their bright new romances, their small concerns, their quaint notions of a fine future? Does Alex perhaps now come home to a good, balanced meal, *Moonlighting* and *L.A. Law,* and the companionship of a charming wide-eyed suburban man, aging just a bit, who listens with a courteous, passionate, bemused mortification as Alex, like a demented version of that Arabian bitch (you know the one — don't make me look up the spelling of that name), tells his vile tales of the city; wanting, needing, having to tell them, to revel in the sordidness, the bright horror, the dark loves, lest he be killed in the morning for the crime of not remembering the lost time?

Most of the great places are closed now, and there are hardly any lights except the shadowy, moving glow of a lost taxi in the meat-packing district of Manhattan. (What a great irony that used to be!) And as the moon rises higher, the inessential buildings begin to melt away until gradually I become aware of the old island that flowered here once for Dutch sailors' eyes — the fresh green breast of the New World. Its vanished trees, the trees that made way for the great places, had once pandered in whispers to the wildest of all human desires. For a transitory enchanted moment, man must have held his breath in the presence of this continent, compelled to an aesthetic contemplation he neither understood nor desired, face to face for the last time in history with something commensurate to his capacity for wonder.

As I brood on the old, unknown world, I think of Alex's wonder when he first picked out the light at the entrance to the

Mineshaft. For him, it was the green light at the end of Daisy's dock. (Note for someone's thesis: my eyes are green, though frequently bloodshot.) Alex had come a long way to this great place, and his dream must have seemed so close that he could hardly fail to grasp it. He did not know that it was already behind him, somewhere back in the vast obscurity behind the city where the dark fields of the republic rolled on under the night.

Alex believed in the light, the orgiastic future that year by year recedes before us. It eluded us then, but that's no matter — tomorrow we will run faster, stretch our arms out farther . . . And then, one fine morning. . .

So we beat on, taxis against the night, borne backward ceaselessly.

Alex, Alex. . .

We played a dangerous game, full of more than its share of trite lyrics, meaningless encores, and I'm still here, going through the motions, resolving to stop mourning for Alex; but not yet, not just yet.

After enough cognac these nights, I think: white — a blank canvas. It will never be filled now. There is no longer anyone available to carry the rose.

Alex. . .

Fade to black.

Alan Neff

American Dreams

That's insomnia and 48th," said Spiro Mattress.
"That's imminent and 48th," said Ben Klaid.
"That's omniscience and 48th," said Kid Newton.
Well, the disco was there, anyway, on the corner.
The disco was there, but it was too early to go in. They went in anyway. And ordered drinks.
"A tonic," said Spiro Mattress.
"Ummm . . . the same for me," said Ben.
"A beer," said Kid.
"Would you like your tonic with a twist of lime?" the waiter politely asked Spiro.
"Yes, please."
"And yes," said Ben.
"A Coors for you?"
"No, I found out they don't pasteurize. An Oly."
"The music should start soon," said Spiro, after the waiter left.
"Oh? That's nice," said Ben.
Kid said nothing: his eyes were roving.
They sipped their drinks sparingly, waiting for the disco to fill up. Soon a great many people were arriving, and the music and light show started. The waiter came by to get their order for more drinks. He said there were an awful lot of people in the disco for a Sunday night. He didn't explain why.

Spiro, nervously biting his lower lip, wondered why there were so many people tonight. Not that Spiro didn't like people; in fact, last night he'd had amusing thoughts of the disco and dancing. It was just that he hadn't been to a disco for a long time. He was old, pushing thirty, and he felt conspicuous here among the young disco set. Ben, who was shy and compact and several years younger than Spiro, didn't look conspicuous. Spiro wished he was as young as Ben. Kid was as old as Spiro but looked so young and carefree. He didn't look conspicuous either (though he was certainly of determined expression).

The three had met at Seattle Mental Health. Spiro had been seeing a counselor about depression; Ben was flipped out totally; and Kid never did say what his problem was. None of them had a car or a regular job. They all lived together (Marilyn Monroe sings melodiously, "Me and Jackie O. and Liz together, We all live together") and the state sent them monthly welfare checks. They lived on Capitol Hill, several blocks from the Group Health Hospital and not far from the Seattle Mental Health Building. This was a big night for them, especially for Spiro. Usually, he slept a lot.

Spiro wondered for the umpteenth time why he slept so much. Here he was at a disco and he just wanted to go home and sleep. He felt guilty about sleeping a lot. It seemed to him he didn't do anything with his life; he just went to counseling and slept and slept. Some days were better than others. Some days he did some grocery shopping and cleaned the bathtub or washed a few dishes. And he did write short stories.

He thought about friends he used to have. Now that he slept so much, his friends were Ben and Kid. They were the only ones that understood. Well, maybe sometimes his counselor understood. Maybe.

* * *

The blinking lights of the disco were giving Ben a headache. Or maybe the lights were just making the same old headache throb more. His medication soothed his head, but he had forgotten to take it, and his headache was very bad. It had sounded like fun to go to the disco when Spiro first mentioned it. He had wanted Spiro to get out and about, but Ben knew now the disco was a mistake. Spiro and he should have just taken a walk or gone to a show and not joined Kid, who was always going to the disco.

The lights were frightening. Ben hoped he wouldn't start seeing images in the lights. Those images of his mom and dad who were dead. There was no one alive now. Just the memories. They were very much alive.

A very fine lady asked Kid to dance. And he danced and danced and would not sit down. Ben and Spiro decided they would go home. They finally motioned to Kid that they were leaving. Kid came up to them and told them goodbye, saying he didn't want to leave yet. He said he was going home with someone after dancing some more, and would be back at their place the next day.

"How will you get home?" asked Ben. The question seemed absurd, since home was not far, and they had walked to the disco in the first place. But Ben had actually asked the question to try and get a clue as to where exactly Kid would be spending the night. In Ben's opinion, Kid was entirely too frivolous about sex.

"What are you talking about, Baby Ben? I think I know how to get home. Don't worry about me. If you guys stick around, I can get you a ride home." And Kid swirled around, back to the dance floor.

Ben motioned to Spiro. "Come on, I think I have the will power to put my left foot in front of my right foot."

When they got home, Ben rushed upstairs to take his medication. If Spiro didn't go to sleep right away, they could talk until the medication took effect, and then Ben would be sure the faces wouldn't come. He watched as Spiro entered the apartment and immediately began fixing a peanut butter sandwich.

"What did you think of that disco?" asked Ben. "Fix me one, too."

"Quite a riot! But not for me. Awfully congested, didn't you think? I felt like going home to bed the instant I got there. But did you notice the strange hairdos...?"

As Spiro babbled childishly on, Ben felt his headache and his oppression oozing away. Spiro was the only one whom the demons respected.

II

Spiro awoke the next day after noon. He listened: no one was home. He tried to get up, and the inside of his head swirled around, and he was stupefied and felt unrested. How long would he go on feeling like this?

He couldn't blame any medication; he had stopped taking Elevil months ago. Maybe he would always be like this, or maybe there would be some way out, sometime. He lay resting a few minutes more. Someone opened the front door of the apartment and asked, "Hello, anyone?"

It was Kid. Spiro pulled himself up from his bed and went to the kitchen. Kid had pulled out some raisin bran from a bag of groceries, poured milk, and was eating. Kid ate a lot and never seemed to get fat. Spiro thought his own stomach was not as slim as it once was. He poured himself some cereal.

"Don't leave the milk out on the counter, Spiro."

"I won't."

After cereal, Spiro forced himself to do the few dishes. He kept looking out the kitchen window; they lived on the second floor. The day was kind of nice — a nice fall day. Spiro knew Ben was out somewhere, enjoying the weather. Ben was usually an early riser. Spiro thought it would be nice to find a way to sleep forever. But that wouldn't be fair to Ben. Ben really liked him. Someday things would be better. Someday he'd stay at the disco all night and not be sleepy at all.

In the meantime, he was working on a short story, and he periodically pecked away at his typewriter. He had recently sent a story to the *New Yorker* magazine but it had been rejected, and he was now working on another. If it weren't for his writing, he probably *would* go crazy. He was a fast typist. Spiro always forgot to tell people he was a writer and could type fast. When anyone asked him what he did, he said, "Nothing."

Today, Spiro went walking down around Lake Union.

* * *

Ben came back to the apartment in the early evening while Kid was making dinner and Spiro was still out walking.

"Set the table," said Kid.

Ben did that, and asked, "Where on earth is Spiro?"

"He left earlier, said he was going for a walk. Where have you been?"

"I earned some money today — I was raking leaves for someone."

"For that old fag," said Kid.

Ben's face turned red. "Please don't call him that, Kid. I earned over twenty dollars and got to work outside. What do you care? Don't call him a fag. Everyone teases him..."

"I'm sorry."

"So, did you get some money last night?"

"Yeah. You hungry?"

"You bet. I wonder where Spiro is. Is dinner almost ready?"

Spiro arrived just in time for dinner. Ben's face lit up and he grinned when Spiro came into the apartment. Ben thought Spiro was looking very attractive today. His cheeks were flushed, his very blue eyes were ... well, they were very blue, and his hair was blown about his face in an exotic way.

"I'm hungry," said Spiro. "I've just walked for several hours, it seems like, and it's something I didn't think I had enough energy to do."

Ben looked proudly at him. Spiro saw Ben's face and was comforted. In a way, just like Ben, he didn't have any parents either. Or at least he might as well not have any parents. His parents lived in the Midwest and couldn't care less about him. And yet, Spiro wondered again why he had ever left Lawrence, Kansas, and his family and friends. One day, he had just packed up a few things and left, and ended up in Seattle. (He had read in the *New Yorker,* "Seattle is a God-forsaken place.") His depression did not leave him when he came west; it became worse. Spiro felt as if he had no understanding at all of the way his brain worked.

Throughout dinner, Spiro was very tense. He was thinking about his favorite obsessive topic, his parents. He would not forgive his parents. Years ago, he had had a very rough time in the army; he was discharged after an emotional breakdown. He had lasted almost six months in the army. Six noxious months without enough sleep! Wasn't there enough sleep to go around in the army? Spiro hadn't gotten his share. His parents' reaction to his army disaster had been discomforting — they had considered Spiro an embarrassment.

Spiro was getting lots of sleep now, and at least he didn't drink. His parents were drunks. And at least he had graduated from college. (Spiro wondered, at times, how he had ever had the vitality to get through four years of college; but, of course, he was younger then and had lived at home.) And now he was writing short stories that were never published and living on welfare. Spiro just wanted to sleep forever, and practically fell asleep on his kitchen chair.

* * *

After dinner, Ben watched Kid cleaning up the dishes. Kid actually seemed elated doing household chores. There was no accounting for tastes. Ben would rather go to the movies as often as possible. Suddenly, he jumped up and gave Kid twenty dollars.

"I want you to have this, for our food," said Ben.

"That's very nice of you," replied Kid, deftly depositing the haul in a pocket of his slinky jeans.

Ben wouldn't be using *that* money for the show. But it was only fair to take on some responsibility, he knew, and then maybe Kid wouldn't have to screw around so much. Because Ben didn't think Kid was totally happy with his "dates." Ben wondered if Spiro was concerned about Kid's sexual behavior. Sex was a topic hardly ever openly discussed. Ben didn't think Spiro participated in sex. (Ben certainly didn't, unless you counted masturbation.)

Ben looked passionately at Spiro's hair — it was so shiny, so wonderfully blond, just like the hair Ben always wanted, instead of his own curly, dingy brown hair. He wanted to reach out and feel Spiro's hair and tug on it. And he wanted to touch Spiro's teeth, too. Spiro's teeth were very white and very straight, and he had a small mouth. Spiro's mouth was quivering slightly, and Ben noticed he was biting skin off his lip, and his fingernails were bitten way down.

* * *

While Kid washed the dinner dishes, he watched Spiro and Ben watch him. There could be a nuclear holocaust, thought Kid, and they would sit there being mildly, vaguely entertained. Luckily, he had gotten money last night. Those two certainly didn't have any money for food. They would probably starve if it wasn't for him. They didn't realize how the household was constantly on the brink of financial disaster. But it was really nice, thought Kid, Ben giving him twenty dollars. Ben could be so thoughtful sometimes, and there just happened to be an electric bill that needed attending to.

Kid studied Spiro, who looked as if he was biting his nails down to the quick. Spiro was a zombie, the most intelligent, attractive zombie Kid had ever known. And Ben was a really swell person. He felt an intense attraction to both of them. He was already too emotionally attached to them, he knew. But, then, why should he fear emotional attachment? It wasn't as if he had anything going other than one-night stands.

At about eleven o'clock, Kid walked down to the disco, leaving Ben and Spiro playing cards. (He didn't think they'd ever go back to the disco.) He was a little early for the dancing — the crowd was just now arriving, even though the music started at nine — but he wanted to think a little.

He watched the people filing in. A few of the women waved timidly to him. He barely smiled. Thank God I'm still slender, he thought. But I can't have too many more years of a life like this. Imagine, only a few years ago I wasn't lazy and had a job at the phone company. It wasn't easy for me to get on welfare — not like Spiro and Ben, who managed it just like one, two, three.

Kid was mumbling to himself, and people at other tables were coyly scrutinizing him. He could have cared less: he had a reputation for being slightly loony. No one really seemed to mind. Fact was, the word was out that Kid had a very large scrotum. Fact was, Kid was quite a guy.

But I'm lazy, thought Kid. That's all there is to it. I'd rather be on welfare and have this life of one-night stands (Another euphemism? Why do people insist on euphemisms, isms, isms, isms?) and take care of those two brats than accept the responsibility of being a productive person. But I do see a counselor once a week. That's productive. I am seeing a counselor. As long as I'm seeing a counselor, no one can deny that I need welfare. But I certainly don't have any problems like Spiro and Ben. Being sexually promiscuous isn't being mentally ill. Lots of people are promiscuous. I need a rich lover. My condescending counselor says I have an inferiority complex. That's ridiculous — why, I practically take care of Spiro and Ben. And, Kid thought, what in fact is wrong with taking care of them? I really like it. And who would take care of them if I didn't? They are the only stabilizing influence in my life. We are a family.

But Kid couldn't decide if he needed to accept a life of his own. A slow tune came over the speakers and a tall redhead asked Kid to dance. At the end of a few songs he sat down again, still thinking. He left, alone, a few minutes later and went home. Spiro and Ben were listening to the radio. Lucky we don't have a TV, thought Kid, or they would be watching it all the time.

"So you're up, Spiro," said Kid. "That walking is doing you good. Keep it up, babe."

"How's the outside?" asked Ben.

"Fine." Kid, restless but tired, went to bed. He lay there, kicking around sheets and ideas, thinking; thinking he wanted a permanent lover. Someday...

The radio remained on. He could hear his boys warbling about nothing. He relaxed.

* * *

Ben could remember exactly when he had started hallucinating: it was right after the automobile accident. He'd had at least a few hallucinations during the years right after the wreck. That was when he was twelve. He had been left uninjured, at least physically, but his parents had died. Ben had been raised by different families, some relatives, some not. He tried very hard sometimes to remember when the hallucinations had become such a nuisance, but thinking about it always gave him a headache.

After being forced to live on his own, his problems had become almost unbearable until he met Spiro. Spiro, effortlessly, relieved many of Ben's anxieties. Kid was a tough punk but Ben had seen Spiro cry at night for hours, or laugh over silly jokes. Spiro's laugh was infectious. All in all, Spiro was the most fascinating person Ben knew. He could be very kind and, since living with him, Ben had actually, at times, almost forgotten about his headaches. Of course, he was still taking his medication, but life was fun. Spiro gave a sense of security to his life. Or maybe it was the combination of Kid and Spiro. Ben wondered . . . do I take Kid for granted? But then he noted, Kid acts as if Spiro and I are children. *His* children. What a laugh. Ben started laughing to himself.

"What's so funny?" asked Spiro. "Something on the radio?"

"I was thinking about Kid."

"Oh?"

"He thinks we're his kids, he's a Kidder, get it?"

"You better take your medication, Ben! You're acting weird!"

They laughed.

III

Spiro looked dully into the bathroom mirror and wiped the sleep out of his eyes. It was afternoon, and he had just awakened. I shouldn't have stayed up so late listening to the radio, he thought. I feel tired. Instantly, his brain started churning bad thoughts: he hated his parents, and no matter what his therapist said, he couldn't stop it. One by one, Spiro ran the slights by his parents through his mind, until he finally forced himself to put it all on the back burner to stew. He wondered why these thoughts about his parents kept erupting. He had hoped to leave them behind in Kansas. And he hoped to God he wouldn't start missing them. That would be the ultimate defeat — to start missing people who had helped destroy him. They had only bothered to write a couple of letters since he'd moved to Seattle, and they rarely called. Nothing on his birthdays. Spiro's eyes narrowed. Maybe his parents didn't like to write, but they could at least call.

He could hear Ben and Kid setting up a board game. "What are you guys playing?" yelled Spiro from the bathroom.

"Clue," said Kid. "Hurry up, we need you to play."

"I haven't eaten yet."

Spiro heard the phone ring. Suddenly, Kid came bursting into the bathroom. Spiro was brushing his hair. Kid looked upon him majestically for a few moments until Spiro finally said impatiently, "What is it? Is the phone for me? I can't imagine who. . ."

"Your mom is on the phone!" exclaimed Kid.

Spiro was stunned.

"Come on, hop to it, baby," said Kid. "Go on and answer it."

Spiro ran to the phone. Kid and Ben tried listening but all they heard was Spiro saying, "Uh, uh, uhm, uhm."

"Well?" Kid inquisitioned Spiro as soon as he was off the phone.

"My dad is going into some hospital for treatment of alcoholism, that's all. It doesn't concern me."

Ben and Kid looked disappointed. Spiro couldn't blame them — it was a pretty dull family he came from. Kid finished setting up Clue and they all played. Soon, though, Spiro said he was tired and, taking a peanut butter sandwich and a glass of chocolate milk with him, went to his bed.

He thought about the phone conversation: his mom hadn't even asked how his life was going. Furthermore, she didn't say if *she* had stopped drinking. She should have asked him home for a visit or something, but no, that had not happened. Spiro was beginning to realize, once and for all, what a rough world this was going to be. He wasn't ever going back to live with his parents; he was going to have to live on his own forever and ever.

Spiro bit his lip and it bled. He squished it into the pillow to make little blood designs, then turned back over to stare at the ceiling. His short stories were never published and he wondered if he should try to expand some of them into a novel. That would be hard. Living in the world alone was very hard business. Yet Spiro still had quite a bit of persistence left in his insides. And besides, he wasn't on his own. Kid and Ben were his friends. It occurred to him that maybe he should just try to forget about his parents. They didn't seem to have trouble forgetting about him.

* * *

Later in the afternoon, Ben walked into their shared bedroom, saw that Spiro was sleeping, and knelt down beside the bed to look

closely at him. There were laugh lines around Spiro's mouth and little lines next to his eyes but, all in all, he had wonderfully clear skin.
There was a distinct and shining aura about the face. Surely, Spiro
had the most perfect face.

Ben put his hand on Spiro's stomach, the flat stomach that was
breathing steadily up and down. Then he left the room to go and
have a glass of milk and he kept thinking about Spiro. Ben was
afraid he loved Spiro and felt guilty about loving another man.
What would Kid think?

* * *

After the aborted Clue game, Kid stayed in the living room
pretending to read, but he was actually amusing himself with smug
thoughts. He decided that Spiro and Ben had a symbiotic relationship based on mutual ignorance of the world. Recently, Kid had
come across the word "symbiotic" in the newspaper and immediately sought reference, but Webster's definition was vague. Even
now he wasn't completely sure he knew how to use "symbiotic" in a
sentence. But he liked the word. He had thrown it around in front
of Spiro and Ben until Spiro had said, "Will you shut up with that
word! I don't even think you're using it correctly." Kid felt renewed
chagrin recalling the incident. You had to be careful: Spiro knew a
lot more than anyone would suppose.

IV

In the morning, Ben and Spiro were sitting at the kitchen table lan-
guishing over peanut butter and banana sandwiches, their eyes
drifting naturally toward the window where, from their vantage
point, they could see a few branches swaying slightly in the breeze.
Kid came out of his bedroom.

"Are you two still mooning over each other? You've been sitting there for hours. What is your problem?"

"I've been reading this *Newsweek,*" said Spiro, "and it feels good
to be up earlier for a change." Ben merely burped.

"*Well,* what are you guys doing today?" asked Kid.

"Ah . . . going for a walk, maybe, huh Ben?"

For Kid, the day stretched out; no doubt about it, his life was boring. He was thinking seriously of finding a part-time job and getting off welfare and chucking his dates. He didn't feel like he was sick enough to be on welfare, and had tentatively decided to discuss his feelings with his counselor. Besides, and furthermore, he knew he didn't have dates. Technically, thought Kid, I'm probably a male prostitute. But he didn't like to think technically. He shuffled over and stood by Ben and Spiro, and all three stared out the window.

"What do you see?" Spiro asked Kid. "It's funny, we never looked out that window during the winter — we always had the curtains closed.

"Yes, and it will be winter soon, and we'll close them again to keep out the cold. They're thermal-lined. I'm a prostitute," said Kid.

"Yes, I know," said Ben. "And I'm in love."

"And I'm a writer," said Spiro.

But Kid just laughed, impetuously. Then hysterically. And then morbidly. Spiro and Ben smiled at him knowingly and petted his neck.

V

Picasso's daring inventiveness, his ability to use so-called useless materials of everyday life and transform them into works of enduring art, continued throughout the forties and fifties. A sculpture called "Head of a Bull" was the result of the artist's having found an old bicycle seat next to a rusted handlebar in a garage. His vision saw these ordinary castaway objects as a bull's head. His hands followed and he soldered the handlebar and bicycle seat together until they became the horned head. Picasso himself has said of this: "Everybody who looks at it says, 'Well, there's a bull,' until a bicyclist comes along and says, 'Well, there's a bicycle seat.'"

In 1950, he created what was to become the most famous goat in history — from a wicker basket, palm branches, metal tubes, terra cotta jars, nails, and other thrown-out objects. The following year, two toy cars bottom to bottom inspired a baboon's head; a strip of metal became a tail, the handles of pitchers were transformed into ears and shoulders. The rest was modeled in wood and clay, and the final result when cast in bronze is a work both humorous and touching called "Baboon and Young."

The list of his miraculous transformations is endless.

"What's this? What are you reading, baby?"

Spiro looked up from the dining room table. Kid was being a smartass. Baby, indeed. "I'm reading *Picasso: An Introduction.* I'm reading for background. The artist had a mania for farts."

"What did you say?" Kid let a faint expression of surprise come into his voice, although he wasn't surprised but amused. "In any case," he said, "what a strange man, Picasso, so square. I think I like Louise Nevelson better. She never fits in, but is so tasteful about it — all that black mascara and those dark clothes. The Architect of Shadow, you know. Takes wood she finds in the New York city streets, paints it black."

Spiro had no earthly idea who Louise Nevelson was and didn't care to get into an esoteric conversation with Kid. He was having an obsession, his own, and wanted to be let alone.

Kid looked askance at Spiro's expression. "Well," he said smartly, "she's only the most famous living sculptor."

This was certainly a new and different side of Kid, thought Spiro. Obviously, the man had run across Ms. Nevelson somewhere.

As if reading Spiro's thoughts, Kid had his last few thrusts on the subject: "I saw a play, a one-woman show, all about Louise; I asked you to go with me. If you'd gone you'd know all about it, like me ... You've sure got enough books around here — all from the library? What a wonderful library system we have ... We're having lunch soon. Clean up your mess after you're done. How come you don't use your bedroom?"

"Ben is sleeping."

"That's a switch; *you've* turned more lively. Trying to stay youthful, huh?"

Spiro merely looked nonchalantly at Kid, then went on reading and making notes. That's the trouble with him, thought Kid — you never know what he's thinking, or even *if* he's thinking. Spiro in his fantasy world.

VI

Hollywood's most famous writer, Spiro Mattress, announced today his com-

mitment to write the screenplay for the major motion picture Picasso the Square. *Mattress is the winner of three Academy Awards for his screenplays. At the same time, the Screen Writers Guild announced that it might take Mattress to court. Why? . . . Mattress' contract provides that he work from noon to four* P.M. *He is a notorious sleeper, who feels that office hours from noon to four are quite sufficient. The Screen Writers Guild president, Dave Hagen Dasdorf, stated that Mattress' contract was ludicrous.*

"We'll take you to court," said Hagen Dasdorf to Mattress at a press conference. "Fine," responded Mattress. "Just make sure the court date isn't in the morning. I usually don't get up until noon."

Mattress went on to say that his contract for Picasso the Square *is no different from other contracts he has had. "Marilyn Monroe didn't have to arrive at work before noon, so why should I?" he huffed. Hagen Dasdorf laughed in Mattress' face and stormed out of the press conference. Mattress then stated, "He's just mad because he's got insomnia and I don't."*

Hagen Dasdorf campaigned for, and won, the Screen Writers Guild presidency after writing sixteen bomb pictures in a row. His present position earns him $11,000 a year. Spiro Mattress will not reveal his earnings for the past year, but a reliable source estimates that they were way over a very popular seven-figure number.

"What are you writing, Spiro? Let me see." Ben came into the bedroom, back from grocery shopping with Kid.

"It's nothing."

"Please let me see." Ben didn't like Spiro to have secrets.

"No, no, it's just too silly. It's not a story I'm working on — I'm just playing around."

"Oh." Ben thought he would just look at it himself when Spiro was out for a walk. He liked Spiro's writing very much and couldn't wait for him to earn lots of money. "Have you gone for a walk today?"

"Yes, but I'll go for another if you want to. It gets dark so early now, it's depressing. What can we do? And it starts raining . . . It would be nice to go away," Spiro added dreamily.

"Yes it would, if we were together." Ben stared into Spiro's eyes. He was hypnotized by Spiro's breathing, and his slight smile, and his eyes that almost always looked down at the ground, eyes not quite hidden under heavy lashes. And his voice.

Ben thought Spiro's voice too often sounded apologetic. He wanted to ask him if he felt victimized by life but knew the question would only sound pedantic and hurt Spiro's feelings. I know *I* feel like a victim, thought Ben.

Spiro was now tilting his head down and biting his thumb. "What are you thinking about?" asked Ben.

"I was just thinking." What is this feeling, thought Spiro, that I've had so long for my parents? They can't give me the affection I need. Why did I ever think they could? Or did I know they couldn't, but clung to the idea they could just to avoid intimacy with other people? I wonder what Ben thinks of me. Does he like me as much as I like him? So much ego is involved in intimacy. "Do you like me a lot?" asked Spiro. And what if he says yes, thought Spiro, what if he says yes, won't that be scary?

"Do I like you?" Ben sounded astonished. "Do I like you?"

Spiro didn't know what to do. He wanted to rush to Ben and hug him and make him feel better but he was frozen. He wanted to touch Ben, but he couldn't do that. Spiro was Greta Garbo just now. And he had this complicated, woozy feeling, too, that he would like to do more than just touch Ben. He would like to touch Ben and kiss him, and unbutton his shirt, and...

Kid called for dinner.

VII
THE MYSTERY OF PICASSO

With regard to the "just so damn beautiful" $4 million Picasso painting purchased by the Kimbell Art Museum (NEWSMAKERS, Sept. 6), I beg to differ. Like a lot of Picasso's work, it isn't juvenile, but it certainly comes close. Just look at the man's idea of anatomy — if a real woman had legs like that, she'd be in a hospital for surgery (or an autopsy). Michelangelo would have laughed — or cried — at it. Picasso has long been an example of the emperor's clothes syndrome.

Paul J. Nahin
Durham, NH

Spiro was reading in bed — a letter to the editor in *Newsweek*. He had just come from the downtown public library, situated among the oppressive skyscrapers, and had brought home a stack of about a dozen magazines, including the *New Yorker, Newsweek, Modern Maturity* and *World Press Review.* The magazines were free: he had grabbed them from the "Put and Take" rack. Spiro never put anything in the rack but he was always taking gobs of magazines.

He read the letter in *Newsweek* intently. A man was criticizing Picasso's work. Spiro was under the impression that Picasso's paintings and sculptures were created to evoke a mood. Looked at piecemeal, any of the figures in the paintings might well appear to be some sort of disembodied mess. But the point, Spiro thought, was that there was something *emotionally* fulfilling in them. What about emotions was so fucking offensive? What image was this man criticizing, anyway? Would he, to satisfy his angry curiosity, have to go back to the library and check a previously published article to view for himself this so-called "juvenile" piece of Picasso's work?

Then, looking through a *New Yorker*, Spiro noticed a mention of a *Picasso Anthology: Documents, Criticism, Reminiscences.* A *Time* had an article about the sculptor Julio Gonzalez who, it reported, had worked in collaboration with Picasso. There was a photo of a 1902 portrait of Gonzalez by Picasso.

Spiro felt his anxiety and depression hurl themselves forward. Why had he done this — started noticing the criss-cross of patterns of information about Picasso in the magazines? Kid had been right. He should have checked out books on Louise Nevelson and not gotten involved with Picasso. Picasso was much too complicated. Spiro began biting his lip. It was three in the morning. Kid always accused him of sleeping too much but lately he wasn't sleeping much at all. He couldn't sleep, and now here was this Picasso thing. And to think he had just ordered a whole bunch more books on Picasso from the library. I'll just send them back, thought Spiro, I'll just send the damn things back.

Spiro got up and put on his black pants, a light blue sweatshirt and white tennis shoes and he left the apartment. He had recently begun taking secret walks late at night. This seemed to relax him, so he walked many miles every night. Everything looked so different at night; it was peaceful. There were no irritating crowds, and the lone person he might come across was cause for curiosity.

He walked along the downtown streets, amazed that they were deserted. He never ceased to marvel at the hugeness and ugliness of the newer buildings compared to the rich, detailed architecture of the older ones. On First Street there were quite a few porno shops, one of which, Sudden Heaven, stayed open all night. Sudden Heaven reigned unique: people *always* seemed to be strolling in and out of there.

Tonight, as he walked past, a prostitute tried to give him the hustle. Spiro smiled kindly at her but then looked away. A man in a Gremlin pulled up beside him and asked for the time. He noticed that the man was wearing a watch but politely told him the time anyway. The man, now most assuredly a seducer, asked Spiro if he had a cigarette. Spiro coldly said, "I don't smoke," and moved briskly away. He really wanted to continue his walk.

Spiro walked down Second, where legitimate movie theaters abounded, and checked to see what was playing at each and every one. The Imperial was a shoddy place, but on Thursday night you could get in for a buck. The Majestic played first-run pictures. Spiro liked that plush palace. Once the manager had let him and Ben in free.

Spiro always chose to return home via Burnside Avenue. Powell's Bookstore, advertised as the largest bookstore in the Pacific Northwest, always had a cardboard box of discarded books in front of their door. They were there for pedestrians to take, and Spiro always found one or two that were worth carrying home. Further down Burnside was the brewery. He kind of liked the smell of the hops.

His apartment building was on the corner of Twelfth and Howell. Twelfth was a *potpourri* of shops and Spiro found it to be, all in all, the most vital, fascinating street in the world. A main attraction for him were its half-dozen thrift stores. People complained about the high cost of living, but yesterday he had assembled his entire winter wardrobe at the thrift stores for only twenty-eight dollars. He had to be assertive with the cheeky salesclerks and haggle over certain pricey items. But what bargains!

* * *

It was one of the last nice fall days and Ben didn't want to miss any part of it. He awoke early and saw all the magazines and books surrounding Spiro's bed. It must be true, thought Ben — Spiro must have a new hobby. He dug into the pile to see what all the commotion was about ... Picasso! He left the room in disgust. He'd thought Spiro had much better taste than that.

After a shower and a quick breakfast, Ben decided to walk up and down the street and glance in at all the thrift shops. Spiro had found bargains, so he wanted to find some, too. As soon as he walked outside, he ran into some smart-alecky young men who were smoking cigarettes and talking about "queers." Ben stopped to stare at them. He felt self-conscious, yet he knew the young men — they weren't boys — couldn't know how he felt about Spiro.

One of the gang shot, "What are you looking at?" Another volleyed, "Are you a queer?" and slapped him hard, then ripped open his shirt. "Look," he said, "the little boy has some hair on his chest." Then they walked away. One of Ben's teeth had cut into his mouth.

Ben, shaky, went back upstairs. He came into the living room panting; blood was running down his chin. The torn shirt was a favorite. He cried and hung his head.

"Who did this to you?" Kid jumped up from the couch.

"I don't know," whined Ben.

"Who did it?" Kid demanded again through clenched teeth.

"Down there, outside. They called me a queer."

Kid ran outside and looked down the street. Four guys in tight Levis and army jackets were walking along jauntily, laughing and smoking. He galloped up behind them. "Hey, you fuckers," he yelled, "did you hit my friend?" They started running. Kid knew he could have caught one of them, but what was the use? Most of his rage was spent. "You go fuck yourselves," he screamed after. "You're just afraid you might be a little bit queer yourselves!"

Kid felt uncomfortable when he saw a few amazed bystanders staring at him. He stomped back to the apartment building. His eyes watered from the exertion and excitement, but he felt more composed by the time he got upstairs. Ben and Spiro looked at him expectantly when he came in.

"What are you doing up?" he asked Spiro.

"I heard all the noise."

These two, thought Kid. Oh, Jesus. "Come on, it isn't a big deal. It happens all the time. Quit looking like a couple of sick dogs. For heaven's sake, Spiro, go help Ben clean up." Spiro and Ben moved sullenly to the bathroom. "Just forget about it. After all, it makes you stronger . . . And those assholes will never bother you again, believe me."

Kid went to his bedroom and lay down, exhausted.

* * *

Ben couldn't believe this had happened to him. Nothing else bad in his life was supposed to happen because he already had such a hard time with all his mind trouble. Why had this happened? Did everyone now sense his affection and sexual attraction for Spiro?

Spiro pushed him toward the bathtub and took off his shirt. "You look okay," he told Ben. "This blood will come right off your face . . . In fact, why don't I wash you all over?"

Spiro felt him and Ben giggled involuntarily, shocked at feeling incredibly, sensually insane.

Guy-Mark Foster, III

Immortally Yours

A close friend is getting married in two days. Mondale (no rela-
tion whatsoever to Fritz) is heterosexual, but that detail has
never mattered to either of us; or, rather, to him. On my end, relo-
cating to another state is what has made it matter less. This was the
sole purpose of moving. It is quite okay that he does not acknowledge it in the way I do — acquiescence comes with the territory; it is
a fact I have come to accept, and not wrestle with.

This is how I am. My Manhattan friends call me "The
Cushion" because of the way I absorb the brunt of romantic entan-
glements with white men. They are amazed at how complimentary
I can be toward these "Caucasoids" who, in their eyes, do nothing
but use me up. Calmly, I ask them what is the advantage in resent-
ing these fellows. Whatever is heaped upon me is because somewhere along the line I've obviously invited it. Those past lovers
were only performing roles scribbled in my own karmic ink many
centuries ago. But a non-comedic belief in past lives is not a trait
shared among us, so the topic seldom comes up.

And anyway, Mondale was never one of those spiritual boy-
toys. He drew the line at that point and, in order to remain his
friend, I knew not to cross it, not to push his panic button. Yet, if I
regret anything in my current life, it is this position of being a tan-
gent in his world, forever stepping on his heels.

I am, by Mr. Webster's book definition and by my own say-so, a coward for letting things continue in this way. It was never necessary that I reply to his letters, to play advisor when society and women gave him the runaround blues. I should have struck a match to each of them without opening a single envelope. But I never learned to resist his handwriting and therefore read and promptly answered every one — including the invitation to this most inconsiderate of weddings. What can I say except that I am bound to perpetuate things as they are? Mondale and I will forever be confined to the reasons separating us. He will marry on Sunday this female he refers to in his bi-monthly letters as Sharon or Shari, or whatever it is he calls her, and I will continue searching for his replacement, someone who has his look of bewilderment on the face, a little boy's expression of being always lost.

* * *

He tells me his name is Tim — not Timmy or even Timothy, but Tim — and he has, next to Mondale, this century's most uninformed smile. We spoke while in line for 6:30 P.M. train tickets to Washington, though he is traveling only as far as Wilmington, Delaware. A girl behind us joined the conversation when he half-jokingly referred to himself as a pessimist, seeing as the clock read 6:20 and we still had not purchased tickets. She confirmed his guess that we could buy them on the train, if push came to shove, for only a few dollars extra. Intuitively, I knew Tim was her perfect match and so gave them my back for a while; but when he touched my sleeve and made a joke, a not particularly funny joke, I knew it was all right to face them again. My laughter on the flat punch line put her off, I could tell, as she took a quarter-step backward and somewhat distractedly re-counted her two twenty dollar bills.

It is 6:29 by the clock over the escalator, one minute until the conductor pushes the button for the train to leave the station. I am holding one of the doors open in case he makes it. I need to be certain we'll sit together; and since he is not really my friend yet, I could not with any degree of comfort wait while he paid for his ticket with that female behind him listening in. To relax, I tap my feet in a staccato to the internal rhythms I always hear in my ears. A second later, I breathe air into my palm and cup it to my nose for possible signs of halitosis. A young girl in an Afro-cut drags her child behind her while looking into my eyes. Where is the baby's father, I ask her. Why isn't his face clean? But she ignores my intrusion with a glance of her own that says, Hi! Wanna be my husband and pay my bills?

I turn away from her when I see Tim coming down the escalator with his duffel bag in tow. And when I see that he is alone and not with his "most perfect mate," I lean against the door and let the sweat bumps break out freely over my back. It is happening again, and I will do everything in my power to aid it. As he walks toward me, I take notice of how similar the hairstyle is to Mondale's: it is neither Ivy League nor metropolitan, but college-boy suburban. The fact that he has no lips is minor, since he has plenty of teeth to make up for this deficiency.

He is behind me as we dodge fellow passengers in the aisle. I am looking for a needle in a haystack trying to find two seats together; but, since he is a pessimist, I know there is hope for our future when, on his own, he spots an empty pair further to the left of us. He arranges his duffel bag and smaller knapsack on the overhead rack. When he is finished, I ask him to find room for my things and he does. These early moments between us seem promising if the pace remains unrushed and casual. I take the window seat and as soon as he's down he jumps up and asks if I want anything from the bar. Without hesitating, I answer "No thanks," but he brings me back a Molson Golden anyway — this first one being on him, he says.

It is perhaps too easy to pick out the resemblances between the two, especially since each passing thornbush outside my window is bringing me closer to Mondale. In addition to the hair and nearly pink-rose complexion, they grip beer bottles in the same way: with the neck wedged firmly in the vertex of the thumb and forefinger and the other three digits drumming against the bottle. The edges of his nails are ragged from chewing. Mondale, because he is a worrier, also bites his off instead of using clippers. He once told me, years ago when we worked on our college paper together, that brittle nerves made him chew at them. I can see him now, pacing in his apartment on Longfellow Street in Washington, second-guessing his every decision about marrying this woman.

Tim tells me he is an actor, and instantly the connection is made. Many of my Manhattan friends are in the wonderful world of show business: dancers, actors, singers — some are even unlucky enough to be all three. However, these friends, unlike Tim and Mondale who ravage their nails, suppress their disappointment and worry behind overlarge smiles, scented musk oils, and the Buddhistic healing powers that come from chanting for hours at a stretch "namyohorengekyo." I often, when in a room with them, find it soothing deciphering the crossword puzzle of their colorful gestures and words.

In time, Tim speaks to me of partying, and then specifically of his long-standing involvement with the other sex. He is twenty-two, he says, and hardly a weekend goes by that he does not get disgustingly drunk and lay one of them. Having no comment, I only nod my head. I cannot pretend, and this has always been a major blemish according to my Manhattan friends. But they can simply go to hell. I will not compromise myself and fake enthusiasm just so a man will like me. If a nod of the head won't do, then so be it. Besides, I am much too sober right now to act any other way. I grip the neck of my Molson's and take an extra long swig — maybe it will help to relax me. But he changes the direction of the conversation anyway, and speaks to me of how close the trains pass one another along the track, of how fast the speeds must be.

We finish our beers and he is up again. This time I give him four dollars, it being my round to buy, and turn to watch him go down the aisle behind me. This man is handsome in his own right, but my reasons for wanting him have little to do with the soul eddying beneath the brown hair and pale skin. He will remain infinitely unknowable to me, just as the other white faces who've reminded me of Mondale all have. Yet my city friends are quick to blame these ex-lovers. After all, we see too much of one another to unleash harsh character judgments, no matter how to the point. It would be too risky when we depend so pathetically on the camaraderie of our little informal group.

But, regardless of them, I know myself far too well to be surprised by any of my own choices. In fact, I might suggest, as a way of teasing Tim, that we exchange phone numbers when he returns. All things considered, my eyes are wide open in this thing, and they will stay that way until the second coming of our Lord and Saviour Jesus Christ, when, perhaps, we will all be rescued from the merry-go-round of our lives.

After a while I sense him and cock my head to the right. He is smiling that neon smile and extending a second Molson toward me. I watch him hitch the fabric of his tan trousers at the thigh and sit. For the first time in over an hour, I smell him. The scent is of grass and wind. Upon sitting, he tells me that, in addition to acting, he models and also does landscaping to round out his income. I take a drink from my bottle, laugh, and slap, quite by reflex, the top of his knee. This second beer is much too confident and gushes through my system like nobody's business. We talk more about the world in general and I tell him of the afternoon I gave a homeless man a five dollar bill, only to have him chase me a whole city block protesting about it being too large a sum.

Before long, he is back on the subject of females and tells me of the time he screwed one on his front porch while his father mowed the lawn not fifteen feet in front of them. She sat sideways on his lap, he says. It was a Sunday in July and both their families were at home, so there was no alternate place to go. They positioned themselves on a swinging bench and he stroked her hair while she pretended to be asleep. He came so hard, he tells me, that some cum bubbled out of the ear she had on his shoulder. I pull my jacket over my lap to conceal my erection. Tim doesn't have a jacket and his knapsack is overhead, so he uses his forearms as a shield. Because of the mature themes of our conversation, he can no longer respond to me as an innocent, as he could at the beginning of this scenic train ride. I tell him I have to take a leak and he gets up to let me cross. Out of habit, he stretches his legs in the aisle, momentarily forgetting his protruding condition, and smiles; while I, feeling expectedly triumphant, foam at the mouth and head for the bathroom.

I lean against the wall of the tiny compartment while my urine streams down into the silver platter. Some of it washes up and around the base and swirls to the floor. Without inhibition I take my dick and point it at the back wall and spray-pee his name on the blue paint. I have enough fluid left to spell it out three times. When finished, I look into the mirror over the tin sink and see how droopy my face has become. The beer has depleted the muscle tone in my head and torso, and now everything above my waist has dropped below my belt. I want to masturbate, but he will be getting off soon and I cannot waste any of our time together. I wash my hands, dry them, and pull back the metal latch.

Tim is waiting for me as I walk the short distance down the corridor. He has the aisle seat and can study me from head to tennis shoes. Like me, he has noted the time and is not smiling now, but considering the possibilities. And before I can even sit, the speakers come on and a girlish voice announces Wilmington as the next stop. This time Tim does not stand but stays put, with his eyes fixed on the food tray in front of him, and motions for me to scoot my fanny low across his lap to reach my own seat.

"You know, we oughta get together, dude," he says, "seeing how you like movies as much as me." (We never discussed anything of the sort.) "Man, I'll see anything, you know: foreign films, comedies, dramas, romance — you name it. You got any paper?"

I open up my shoulder bag and take from there the pad and pen I keep for these predestined meetings and hand them over. Though he's right-handed, I notice he slants the pen awkwardly; the same as Mondale, who writes with his left. I can easily see him growing up in Wilmington, with the train tracks so near to his parents' house. I could even paint a watercolor, if called upon, of him and his buddies trekking across blacktop avenues, and the girls eyeing them and becoming slaves because of these boys' looks.

I take the pad and pen from his hands and scribble down my own vital statistics. I then tear the sheet off and fold it so he cannot read it, and put it into his shirt pocket myself. No one can see us clearly and so he lays his palm over mine and mentally strokes my skin. Again, he does not smile, and out of mock consideration neither do I. I want, in fact, to laugh out loud when his left eye goes moist and a drop falls before he wipes it; and surely not because I am unsentimental or lack that type of feeling myself. But because I know far too much about *everything* these days to become weak in the joints at the sight of a man near tears.

I probably won't even cry at Mondale's wedding. So what if his marriage sends me reeling further out among the stars than even I expected? One day he'll come to his senses and realize he all the time belonged with me, and not Cheryl or whatever the mugambo her name is. And when he does, all he'll need do is whisper my name and, like a comet streaking through infinity, I'll *zing* right back into his arms. But...

...now, in order to catalogue this one's face and identity with at least some uniqueness, I have refrained from writing either my correct address or legitimate last name on that torn slip of notepad; and what I did write was not legible. I will, through him, have my own fun and stretch out a long-wished-for fantasy of being sought after but never found. I want desperately to pick up the *Village Voice* and see, week after week, year after year, the following message repeated on the back page:

> (5/23 Amtrak to Wash.) You: Jamal, a Native Son in blk jeans. Me: Tim, a Tom Cruise type. You liked my longer hair & we drank 2 Molsons. Exchanged #s but can't read your writing. Pls call actor enroute to Delaware. 874-6342.

Tim gets up before the train stops completely and unloads his duffel bag and knapsack from overhead. For the public at large we shake hands and say we'll get in touch for that movie or something. I can tell he doesn't want this to be the end by his furtive glances toward my seat while he waits for the brakes to catch; but, like Mondale, he is uninformed and does not realize that this isn't, not by a long shot, one of those predictable, see-ya-soon kind of good-byes. Oh, no. In fact, it ain't a goodbye at all. Because when the seeds I've planted in him ripen, he'll find himself, quite unexpectedly, on the lookout for ... well, if not me, then someone reincarnated to look like me, a snow queen dressed in my clothes maybe, with my look of false calm about the face and all that rigmarole.

Robert Boucheron

African Gray

Onstage, the ballet dancers execute patterns of great precision. They wear archaic costumes: stiff, bejeweled skirts that stick straight out from the women's hips, like inverted flower petals, and doublets for the men, cut very close and short. The lighting is brilliant. Though they move with perfect grace, the dancers are all arms and legs, with no body to speak of. The women have no bust; they are almost painfully thin. Everyone's flesh is pale, a faint pink, but that may be the tights they wear. Two black dancers by contrast seem exaggeratedly dark.

I look for Bunny in the first row of seats but I cannot see him from the rear of the balcony. This is a new ballet, so I wonder what he thinks of it. Probably he will like it, since it is "pure dance," with no overt symbolism. He approves of art that is not too obvious, and I suspect he likes the ballet precisely because it is non-literal. Bunny detests mime.

When the house lights come up at intermission, he looks around inquiringly. He is a slight man with a boyish shock of hair and a pleasant face. Like me, he wears glasses. We met at Yale more than ten years ago, where we both studied English. He wanted someone to go to the ballet with him, so we took the train down from New Haven on Sunday afternoons. After graduation, we both landed in New York, and Bunny continued our Sunday night subscription. He now lives with a man he calls Bear, who does not care for the ballet. So I am still his dance date.

I stand and reveal myself.

"Sorry I'm late. I got a last-minute phone call, and then I had to wait for the subway. The trains don't run very often on Sunday."

"I knew you would come. Either that or you were sick. You haven't missed a performance yet."

"You make me sound so dedicated. What is that word for a ballet fanatic?"

"Balletomane."

"As in 'mania,' I suppose. But it sounds sort of horsey."

"That could be. Those teenage girls who take ballet classes and fall in love with horses: the *My Friend Flicka* syndrome."

"I think that was a boy."

"Well, how about *National Velvet?*"

"Better. No ballet, but no one could call Liz Taylor a boy."

"Definitely not."

We stroll around the lobby at our level. At each ring of seats, a catwalk runs around four sides of the lobby. We sit in the top ring, where we always have. We could afford better seats now, but Bunny says we can see everything from where we are. Maybe we feel younger, sitting in the cheapest seats high above the stage, like students reading the score by flashlight. Or maybe it is some unacknowledged sense of tradition, of the sort that impelled the ancient Romans to perform sacred rites they no longer understood to gods they no longer believed in. Bunny has a genius for creating these habits and rituals, although he never discusses them as such. He never discusses anything. With Bunny, everything is understood. Or not, as the case may be.

This stroll has become a ritual: we make one circuit, then stand at the rail and chat until the first chime, at which Bunny goes to the men's room. Around the catwalk, lights are trained either on the walls or on the beaded curtain at the glassed arcade, so the other strollers appear as dramatic silhouettes, an animated frieze. We study the main floor, which completely fills with people. Mostly what we see are the tops of heads, shoulders, and shoes. It is hard to get a good look at a person from directly overhead. In past years, Bunny would point out the gay men and perhaps add a brief critique. Now he just looks, out of habit. The crowd is densest around the Gift Bar, which has expanded over the years. Women hold up t-shirts, flip through souvenir books, and read buttons. Bunny points out the toe shoes for sale, worn by star ballerinas. He is unusually lively.

"Bear and I went to a pet store today on Long Island."

"You had to go all the way to Long Island to find a pet store?"

"We were visiting his mother, and it was very close to the train station, practically in it."

"How convenient for the commuters. You know, instead of bringing your wife roses for your anniversary, you buy her a puppy or a guinea pig. So you went in?"

"Of course. Bear wanted to look at birds. You remember Andrew and Edward. Well, now he's talking about a big bird, something like a macaw."

"Andrew and Edward are the parakeets?"

"Conures. A conure is a type of parrot, but small."

"Oh, yes, they look like parrots, green and orange, with yellow circles around the eyes. Andrew perched on my shoulder at the Christmas party. He also bit my ear."

"Yes, he had a great time. He loves people, but he sometimes has trouble showing his affection. Edward is shy and tends to hide. He spent most of the party in the kitchen, on the chandelier."

"I thought they were more your birds. You do more to take care of them, don't you?"

"Bear helps. He sometimes cleans the cage. He buys toys for them. They tend to destroy their things."

"They haven't learned to play nicely, you mean."

"Andrew gets excited and tries to bully the other one, but Edward is bigger, so it ends in a tie."

"Do you always let them roam freely in the apartment?"

"I put them to bed in the cage, partly for their own protection. Also, they feel safer there. During the day, they're out. They don't fly around much: birds are very territorial. Bear built a complicated perch for them, sort of a bird environment, but they prefer the curtain rods and the tops of picture frames. The metal ones are slippery, so I discourage that."

"They don't mess on the curtains and floor?"

"No, they seem to have an instinct about that. They come naturally house-trained."

"Well, what about the commuter pet store?"

"Oh, yes! We've been looking at birds in the city. What Bear really wants is one of those South American parrots, about two feet long, that come in bright colors. One that can talk."

"Like something a pirate would have on a chain. Long John Silver."

"Right. You may have seen them at Bird Jungle. That's one place we go to look."

"They have sales. I see signs on the door. Those birds are expensive, hundreds of dollars."

"Thousands for the really big ones. But they live up to seventy-five years and retain their value, if they can talk. Bear was reading up on parrots and found there's one called an African Gray. It's smaller, doesn't cost as much, and is an excellent learner."

"Didn't you try to train Andrew?"

"We made a mistake. If you put two birds together, they will pay attention to each other and ignore you. He may have been too old at the time we got him, anyway. After a certain age, it's too late."

"You still haven't told me about the pet store."

"Well, they had an African Gray asleep in a corner. How anyone could sleep in the midst of all that barking and squawking and mewing is beyond me. Bear tried to get its attention, but it was determined not to wake up. Meanwhile, a *very* friendly white cockatoo crawled up my arm, saying, 'Hello, how are you? Hello, how are you?'" Bunny imitates the bird's voice, quick and mechanical.

"It might as well have said, 'Take me home.'"

"That was a *very* friendly bird. 'Hello, how are you?'"

"Did you buy it?"

"No, Bear wasn't really interested in a white cockatoo, although Mae West would have been, I'm sure. Besides, he wants one we can train. They're less expensive, for one thing."

"Too bad. Did *you* want to buy it?"

The chime saves him. He looks up from the crowd below, which begins to disperse.

"Time for me to do my business."

* * *

Normally we meet at the theater, but on our next ballet night, I go to Bunny's apartment early to look up a classical reference. He has an impressive library, most of which dates back to college and graduate school. He went through two years of a Ph.D. program in English before becoming a civil servant. Since then, he has avoided any "serious" reading, and in the past few years he has gotten away from reading altogether. He and Bear have "invested" in all the latest sound and video gear, so now Bunny rents movies and catches up on programs the machines have taped in his absence. Even so, he is the most literate man I know in New York. I throw an allusion into the conversation now and then, just for practice.

Bunny has the book ready on a table by the door. I find what I am looking for and begin to browse. I notice that Bunny's name is stamped inside the cover, last name first. It is a venerable Anglo-Saxon name, and that of a seventeenth-century dramatist. His ancestors were among the earliest English colonists, but Bunny never talks about his family, dead or alive.

"That must have been just before college. The stamp was my mother's idea. It was really for clothes, like sewing in labels before you go away to summer camp. I don't know what she thought Yale was going to be like."

"Pajama parties and panty raids."

"It wasn't coed yet."

"Ah, the old days." I shrug.

"Would you like to meet Philip?" It is a leading question.

"All right, who is Philip, or what?"

"The new bird. We bought an African Gray. He was on sale at Bird Jungle. Come this way to Bear's bedroom. We're keeping him isolated from the other birds at first. He doesn't know they're here."

The apartment is a rambling series of rooms, actually two railroad flats thrown together. I follow Bunny down a miniature hallway to one of the largest rooms, with a window on the street. Bear's bed is unmade. There is a male nude calendar on the wall, and in one corner a stationary bicycle and a bench press. As everywhere in the apartment, there are shelves and stacks of books. Most of them here relate to the theater.

"Hello, Philip. Hello, Philip. How are you? Hello, Philip."

"Where did you get the name? Is it from Philip Sparrow?"

"No." Bunny does not get it, or he is not interested.

I sing the first strain of an Elizabethan song, a relic of our college days, when such things were our occupation:

> Of all the birds that I do know,
> Philip my sparrow hath no peer,
> For sit she high or sit she low,
> Be she far off or be she near . . .

"She?"

"I don't understand that myself. I think all birds at that time were referred to as 'she,' male and female. Maybe a vestigial memory of grammatical gender."

"Or an early example of gender confusion. But I wasn't thinking of Philip Sparrow, and this Philip is a parrot."

"Phillip Pirrip in *Great Expectations?* 'And then, Pip, what larks!'"

"No, it was Bear's idea. He named the birds after the British royal family."

"Then you'll need a Lady Di bird and a Charles. No need for the Queen, of course."

"No." Bunny smiles faintly. "Come say hello."

Philip perches on top of his cage and glares at me. He is a beautiful dove gray and quite large, about twelve inches long plus more for the tail feathers. He barks, sounding very much like a small, nervous dog. When I get too close, he lunges forward and growls.

"Be nice, Philip. This is a friend." Bunny speaks in a carefully modulated voice, as to a potentially violent psychopath.

"Hello, Philip," I say. He glares back. I point to a bagel chew-toy hanging in his cage. It is far gone.

"He ate the first one Bear bought him. He doesn't bite, though, not people." Philip's beak is sharp and curved, like a small scimitar or a large can opener.

I try a different tack and whistle. Philip cocks his head. I whistle again, higher, then lower, a variety of calls. Philip turns his head this way and that and shifts nervously on his perch.

"This is something new for him. Neither Bear nor I can whistle, so that mode of communication is out."

"Is it genetic, like tongue-rolling?"

"No, I just never learned. I didn't play with the right boys, I guess."

"I learned how to whistle from a little girl when I was four. Do you know that song about Grandma Grunt? We sang it in elementary school:

> Grandma Grunt said a curious thing—
> Boys can whistle but girls must sing.

It was a scandal, of course, because 'grunt' was our childhood word for 'shit.'"

"We didn't sing in school."

I try another whistle, starting on a low pitch and swooping up.

Philip answers immediately with a whistle that starts high and swoops down. We do this several times. It is a game.

"Maybe I should tape you so Philip will have someone to whistle with."

Thinking I have won his confidence, I take a step closer to the cage. Philip growls again.

Bunny busies himself around the cage, sweeping up cracked seed shells, and talking to Philip all the while like a conscientious nurse. Mostly, he repeats, "Hello, how are you?"

I look at books. I hear a flapping noise and turn around. Philip is gone from the top of his cage. A frantic scrabbling comes from behind the bench press.

"Oh, Philip, you'll hurt yourself." Bunny puts down the dustpan and goes to the corner. He bends down and offers his arm. Philip climbs on and rides back to his cage.

"I must have made a sudden move that frightened him. He doesn't know it, but he can't really fly. They clipped his wings at the bird store. One day I came home and found him on the floor, very unhappy. He must have taken a walk around the apartment because I found a trail of gray feathers."

I whistle some more but Philip does not respond. He puffs out his feathers and preens a little. He decides to eat a few sunflower seeds.

"Where is Bear, by the way?"

"Working. He's the assistant manager of a theater now. They have a new show going into previews, so he's been there late every night for a week. He's usually still in bed when I leave for work."

"You don't see much of each other, then."

"This is just until the show settles down. Time to go. Goodbye, Philip. Goodbye."

"Pleasure meeting you."

* * *

Bunny calls one Sunday morning to tell me he cannot make it to the ballet that night. His voice has dropped an octave: he has been home with the flu since Wednesday. He sounds miserable.

"Would you like a visit to cheer you up? I don't live that far away, you know. Is there anything I can bring?"

"No, no." Bunny sounds almost panicky. "I'm still contagious. There's no reason for you to get this." He coughs.

"Don't worry about that. I won't catch your flu. I know how boring it can be to be sick."

"I have the birds for company."

"Well, that's true. Can they catch anything from you?"

"No, there's only one disease in common, parrot fever, and that's passed the other way, to humans. It's fatal." In addition to being strangely low, Bunny's voice is hoarse and fails him from time to time.

"Philip must be falling behind on his lessons."

"He has a tape. Here." Bunny turns the phone away, and I hear his normal voice from a distance saying, "Hello, how are you?" Philip squawks a little and cracks seeds.

"Has he said anything yet?"

"Not yet. It takes several weeks."

"Let me know when he does, and get well soon."

"Okay, stay well."

I slip a new paperback in my sportcoat pocket and go to church. The book is a novel by Barbara Pym, so it should be acceptable, though no one will see it. The situation is one she would have enjoyed. The weather is fine, with bright sun and a promise of milder temperatures.

I have been to this church only once before, with a friend. It is a large, plain building in the collegiate Gothic style, with a small congregation. The rear pews are roped off so that we will be less scattered. Most of the others are badly dressed and older, especially older women. But I happen to sit in front of two teenage boys who whisper to each other all through the service. Their mother must have made them come.

The minister has a gray smudge on his upper lip, which I interpret as a trimmed moustache, and long sideburns, grizzled. He has an engaging manner. He does not preach from the pulpit but walks around the first few pews and talks in a natural way. He shuns intellectual tangents and sticks to simple metaphors, like Christ's parables, and real-life experiences that anyone can understand. He holds a book with a flexible black cover which he rolls like a newspaper, as if he were going to swat a dog and flourishes for emphasis. I did not expect to like him.

Silent prayer follows parish concerns. The minister repeats the names of members of the congregation who are sick or in the hospital and suggests that we include them in our prayers. I mentally add Bunny's, knowing he would think me foolish. I decide to visit him in his distress anyway, like a good Christian. It is a beautiful day for a walk.

Bunny comes to the door in a ratty bathrobe and dingy, frayed pajamas. He has not shaved for a few days and his hair is tousled. He steps back in alarm and covers his mouth with a sleeve. The apartment is dark and eerily still. The shades are half drawn. The birds are frisky, though. Andrew and Edward are playing leapfrog on the curtain rod over Bunny's head.

"Can I come in?"

He lets me enter but stays several feet back.

"I won't stay long. I brought you something inspirational to read." I take the book out of my pocket.

"Oh, thank you." Bunny is surprised. "I haven't done much reading lately. I haven't done much of anything, except video." Unaware of what he is doing, he presses the book to his heart and folds his hands over it, as if it were a prayer book.

"Where is Bear?" I have only seen Bear once or twice. He is eight years older than Bunny and bears a striking physical resemblance: he is simply a larger and grayer version. If he is Bunny's future, Bunny is equally his past, permanently young. In the dim light, Bunny still looks like a college student. We sit on opposite sides of the room.

"He went to brunch with some friends." Bunny coughs into the lapel of his bathrobe.

"Theater people?"

"Some." He gasps this word and coughs some more.

"Have you been eating?"

"I didn't have much appetite until today. Bear is never home for dinner, and it seems like too much bother to cook. Luckily, we have the microwave, but I get tired of frozen food. There's always Entenmann's."

"You can't live on cake alone, though I know you would if you could." Bunny can recite the list of Entenmann's bakery products like a poem by Walt Whitman. The names alone sound fattening. "How are you doing otherwise?" He enjoys talking about his symptoms.

"Still some fever but the ache has gone. For a while I felt like I had been run over by a truck. I wasn't even sure what time of day it was. It was all I could do to turn on the video. But I'm better today, almost human." He has another coughing fit, into his robe.

"Well, take care. It's getting warm outside. You might try to get some sun." I rise to go.

"Maybe. Come say hello to Philip."

I follow him, not to Bear's room but to the "video room," where Philip glares from atop his cage, next to a futuristic array of electronic equipment.

"Bear got tired of stepping on seed shells all the time," Bunny explains. "They crunch underfoot."

"Hello, Philip," I say. I whistle several times, with no response.

Philip deftly cracks sunflower seeds in his formidable beak.

"I guess he forgot. Come on, Philip, whistle for your uncle." Bunny blows through his lips.

I find the right pitch and Philip answers: swoop up, swoop down. I smile triumphantly at Bunny, who nods.

"I really should tape you." He is still clutching Barbara Pym to his breast. I point to the book.

"She's good, you'll like her. She writes about widows and the elderly, the poor in health and spirit, people who go to church. No birds that I remember, except a few stuffed ones."

Bunny shudders.

"Bye Philip." I reflect that birds evolved from reptiles. So far as personality is concerned, they did not evolve very far.

Bunny sees me to the door, keeping always at a distance, and watches me walk to the street. He waves weakly.

* * *

The ballet season is over, so I do not see Bunny for several weeks. I forget about his flu, then realize he must be well by now. One night, he telephones, very excited.

"Philip said his first word!"

"How thrilling. Put him on."

Silence.

"Say hello, Philip."

Silence.

"He's sulking. I'll have to tape him for you."

"His first word was 'hello,' I take it."

"Of course. That's what I've been training him to say. Actually, he says the how-are-you part, too, but too fast, so it comes out 'howerra.'"

"Well, that is good news."

"The first word is the hardest. After that, they can learn to say lots of things. I haven't decided what comes next. I should draw up a training program."

"There are so many possibilities: dialect, military commands, poetry . . . I saw a play recently in which a parakeet recites Gray's

Elegy. I think it must have been a tape. Everything is amplified in the theater these days."

"Probably. Parakeets can talk, but not that much. Maybe Philip could try out for the part. It would be more authentic."

"More visible, too. A parakeet is hard to see on stage. And you could be a pushy stage mother." Pause. "You sound all right now."

"Oh, yes."

I feel I should continue the conversation, that it is too soon to hang up.

"How is Bear?"

"He's fine. His show opened last week. It got good reviews. He asked me to the cast party but I didn't go."

"Why not?"

"I'm no good at parties. I don't know what to say, and it's uncomfortable with a lot of strange people around. I'm better off at home with the birds."

In spite of the fact that I ask all the questions, I sense that Bunny is drawing me into something. He drops bread crumbs in my path and before I know it I am headed in his direction. In the end I will be balked and just as hungry as before, and he will have demonstrated something as neat as a theorem, although neither of us could say what it is. Still, I nibble on.

"Is Bear home more often, now that the show is launched?"

"Not really. He tends to socialize and he has a lot of friends. He's quite sociable, not like me."

"What on earth keeps you two together?"

"Mainly the apartment. You know how hard it is to find a decent apartment in New York. But we have no problems."

"None at all?" I am playing my part.

"Well . . . Bear says I don't talk to him enough."

"How can you when he's never there?"

"That's not it. He's here sometimes. But he misinterprets. I don't talk to anybody that much."

"You're talking to me."

"I've known you a long time, longer than anyone in New York."

"That counts for something, I guess. But I can see what he

means. You don't make it easy. If I bring up something you don't want to talk about, you turn deaf. So I stick to what I have learned over the years is safe."

"What should I talk about?" He is peevish.

"Your job . . ."

"It's a boring civil service job. I work in the basement of an anonymous gray building with a lot of boring people. I conduct interviews and shuffle papers. There's nothing to tell."

"That's how you see it. What about reading?"

"I don't read much now. It's mostly video."

"I even *gave* you a book. Coals to Newcastle."

"I know."

"Well, what *about* video?"

"It's entertainment. It has no intellectual content."

"Then why watch it?"

"I like to be entertained."

"Fine . . . Then what about the theater — Bear's work?"

"That's his thing. I can't get involved with all those people. *Theater* people."

"It sounds to me as if you've dug yourself into a pit."

"We have the birds." He says this in a hopeful sort of way.

Brought up short, I begin to wonder if I've just been had. Is Bunny making fun of me, now that he has made me feel sorry for him? Or is he making fun of himself? Adept at irony, we are unable to deal with pity.

"Squawk. Hello, how are you?"

Ah, I think, Philip has at last decided to talk on the telephone. Then I realize that Bunny was imitating his parrot. "Was that him?" I ask, knowing better.

"No, that was me."

"Oh."

"He got distracted by something on TV."

This is all the explanation I am going to get; and, in a way, I understand. As much as I ever do with Bunny. "Well, thanks for the news, and good luck with your training program."

"See you at the next ballet, in October. I'll mail you the tickets."

"And I'll mail you a check for my half. Say hello to all the birds for me."

"Squawk. Hello, how are you?"

Peter McGehee

Survival

You wake to the sound of tennis balls. A window's open. It's warm. You roll over. You're alone. You wonder where that man is, the movie actor who has you here most Tuesdays. A white sheet trails from the bed. You hear the shower. You see the time. Your money's on the table. You get it and you go.

You drive across the city sipping coffee from a styrofoam cup. A little "v" is carved in the plastic top. The trip takes forever. In the hum and screech of the freeway you still hear the tennis balls.

You drive up a hill to this month's home, the pool house behind Barbara and Bill's. You figure you'd better try and sleep but you can't so you go out to the pool. Part of your job is to keep it clean. You've grown negligent.

You masturbate in the sun and wish it were midnight. You feel the smoothness of your chest and your scrotum tightens. Your feet point as the feeling gets better, a flexing habit left over from when you danced. You wish something were up your ass. You can almost feel it there. You pinch your left nipple, tickle it.

Someone is watching you. After you come, Barbara appears with a couple of drinks, Bloody Marys for the morning. She says, "Nice, Bruce, nice." You're not a dog, you want to tell her, but you dive into the pool instead. The gleam, the quick chill, and the glide back you up. Surfacing, you reach for your drink and smile.

She's naked except for toenail polish and pool shoes. She slips them off and tests the water with a toe. Inside, her lap dog is throwing himself against the glass doors, barking.

"Helmut, hush," she says, splashing water on her thighs.

You set the drink aside and go back under. You open your eyes. Her legs distort in the ripples like Olive Oyl with elephantiasis.

You float on your back thinking you're thinking of nothing but you're thinking of a painter you know who's gradually becoming famous. He no longer gives you pictures for free. You like art. You'd like to live in a house full of it, like Barbara and Bill. And you do, kind of.

"What are you thinking?" She aims at you with some of her water.

Slicking back your hair you say, "Nothing."

"Where were you last night?"

"Work."

She smiles. She thinks how precocious you are, how appealing and tantalizing your existence. She'd like to capture you and she's tempted but then the fun would be gone. She's fifty. She knows how to avoid self-destructive behavior.

You get out, dry off, and walk to a corner of the patio where you can almost see the Hollywood sign. If you could lean an inch or so further you could see it for sure. As a child you wanted to be a movie star. You remember that wish, you and a billion others. And you could have done it, but no longer cared. You get by; you live. You're a long way from Amarillo. That makes you smile. So what if you're lazy? Maybe you'll go to New York for the weekend, Fire Island, or even Rome. You need a break, and hell, you can afford it.

Barbara thinks how pretty your bottom is, so white compared to your tan. She watches your weight shift, the muscles along your spine. She considers your legs — lovely, the space between them as you stand there, your soft, succulent masculinity. "You ought to put on your swimsuit, Bruce. It'd be a shame to mess with that line."

You turn toward her, wrapping a towel around your middle. "Ready for your torture?"

"Soon as I finish my drink." The glass rests against her lower lip. She drains it, leaving lipstick on the rim. "Just give me a minute to get on my outfit."

"You're gonna do twice as many sit-ups today."

"Bullshit." She slides open the door. The lap dog runs out in a gust of air conditioning. You throw him into the pool.

"Really, Bruce. That isn't very nice."

* * *

Barbara has on a Jane Fonda outfit and several bracelets. She lies on the thick carpet of her dressing room. You sit with your legs in second position, leaning forward on your elbows.

"I hate having to exercise," she tells you.

"The sooner you start, the sooner we finish."

She stretches. She's feeling very matter-of-fact. "Do you love my husband?"

"No."

"Neither do I. I used to, but it didn't last. Not that it's supposed to."

"Lunge left eight times, be sure the knee goes over the foot."

She does so. "I don't know how you sit like that. It'd kill me."

"Flat back, now plié."

"This sudden fascination Bill has developed for young men is quite a mystery to me."

"Stomach in, arms out, shoulders down, and circle."

"He's never showed signs of homosexuality in the past, and he is over sixty."

You correct her posture.

"God this hurts."

"Then don't do it. It's for you, not me."

"I hate that attitude from a teacher."

"Eight more." You count them out loud to make her feel better.

"Actually, just between you and me, I've never found Bill a very sexual person. Works too hard. Not that there hasn't been the odd time, even the odd affair on both our parts—"

"Keep your hips straight. Face front."

She looks at you from the awkward position of a side stretch thinking she deserves more of a response than that. You agree. "I don't think he's very sexual either," you say.

She stand upright. "What do you do, the two of you?"

"He likes to watch me masturbate."

She's won. "So do I."

A plane flies too low, making outrageous noise, shaking the house. "That's not supposed to happen in this neighborhood," she informs you.

"Sixty-four sit-ups and we're done."

You feel paralyzed. You feel like everything you're half good at has been done a thousand times. You scold yourself for your lack of imagination and discipline. You resent belonging to a crowded generation. You resent the competition. You look at a crowd of people and see a billion single cells, each self-encased and self-sufficient. You're immobilized. Lucky you were born beautiful. Lucky to carry it off. That's the one thing you do well. Though it's work, it's an effortless kind of work. A talent, you decide.

* * *

"Rosita will fix you lunch when you're ready, Bruce. A nice salad? I've got my card game." She looks at you funny. "Are you on drugs?" She throws her car keys in the air and catches them on the jingle. This is her cheerio gesture.

You go back to the pool. When Rosita brings your lunch tray you say, "Gracias."

She tells you, "Speak English to me, please."

* * *

You've got on your swimsuit. You put the air mattress in the pool and slide on top of it. You think about taking a nap in the sun. You smoke a joint. You think how peaceful this part of the afternoon can be, so quiet, everyone gone.

You're stoned and daydream Sidney Ng, the day you met at the beach. There he was, a Vietnamese midget strolling the boardwalk in a top hat, tails, and carrying a cane. You thought you were hallucinating. He said "hello" with an effort against an accent. He told you he was in business, the funeral business, and you laughed.

"But I have great admiration for the American style with death," he assured you.

"Is that why you're in that get-up?"

"Please, what is wrong with my costume?"

You need to pee. No one's looking. You think about peeing in the pool. You've always done that and the act itself is like a safe memory. You wonder if anyone else pees in this pool, Barbara or Bill. The thought that they might disgusts you.

Your cock burns as the urine passes. Shit. You try to forget about it but can't. Your doctor's trained you well. You get out of the pool and pick up the pool phone. Rosita's talking to someone in a speedy Spanish. You hang up. A few minutes later she's off. You call directory assistance and ask for the number. You dial. Your doctor is expensive but you get an appointment for that afternoon. You bathe, masturbate, then dress.

* * *

The doctor's office is empty except for a homely male receptionist and one other patient. You check in. Your chart's already pulled.

The other patient looks at you cruisy. You like it until you think he's looked a little too long, too hungry you decide, and pick up a magazine — *The Advocate.* The headline has to do with AIDS. You put it back down. You pick up the newspaper. Reagan is visiting a Nazi cemetery, wants more money for the "contras" in Nicaragua, and is finally negotiating a date to negotiate with the Russians. You turn the page. "26,000 Blacks at South African Funeral — Does America Have a Stake in Apartheid?" You put that down too. You pick it back up to see what section the movies are in. The section you're looking for isn't there. You pick up a *McCall's* with two articles that interest you, one on Karen Ann Quinlan and one on Mary Tyler Moore. The other patient smirks at your choice and when he realizes you've seen him do it, genuinely smiles. You genuinely smile back. The receptionist calls you in.

As your doctor examines you, he tells you about someone he

knows who's casting a TV movie. He tells you this every time you see him. "And it just so happens they need a tall, dark, handsome sort of guy with icy blue eyes and excellent tan. Interested?"

"Sure, Doc."

"You really ought to be in show biz, kid."

You both laugh. He pats you on the ass like a father and tells you to do up your pants.

He looks at a slide under a microscope. "Nongonococcal," he announces and hands you medication from a metal drawer. "Stay out of the sun and no drinking."

* * *

You drive mindlessly through Santa Monica. You see a travel agency and park. You tell the woman in there you'd like to go someplace, someplace not too sunny, someplace in the rainy season. She suggests the Brazilian rain forest but you've already been there.

"Well, that's about the only place I can guarantee rain." She offers you a Marlboro. You take it. You only smoke when you're about to spend a lot of money, which excites you, and the cigarette calms you down. She flicks her lighter controlling the flame flirtatiously.

"I'd like to go someplace with a primitive culture," you say out of the blue.

She suggests a tour of Indonesia. "And they always have some rain," she adds.

"Not a tour. Just one place."

She shows you a pamphlet. You look at the map part, then the hotels, then the pictures. You pick the place with the least information, New Guinea.

She's taken aback. "I haven't any references in New Guinea."

"Just the ticket, that's all I want."

She seems put out, then remembers her commission. "First Class or Coach?"

"First."

"When would you like to leave?"

"Today."

She looks something up. "How long do you plan to stay?"

"I don't know."

"You can get a visa on arrival if it's less than thirty days."

"Twenty-nine then —"

"You'll need malaria pills. Oops, today's flight left at two."

"Then book it for tomorrow."

She fiddles with the ticket computer. "Quantas via Sydney. You can have a stopover if you like, it's included in the price."

"No thanks."

"Cash or charge?"

"Charge." You hand her Bill's card.

You go back to your doctor's. The homely receptionist says, "Forget something?"

"Malaria pills. I'm going to New Guinea."

* * *

That evening after cocktails, Bill visits you in the pool house. He stands with his lips an inch away from yours. His mouth is open and you are asked to simply stand there and breathe. He's Dr. Frankenstein. This ritual will eventually transfer him into your body and you into his.

He undresses you like a fragile doll. Your skin is so silky it frightens him. He tries not to touch it. You sprawl on the bed, touch yourself, and begin. There's no feeling. He asks, "What's the matter?"

You tell him you don't know but you have an infection.

"Good God," he says. He takes his drink and leaves.

The antibiotics have made you nauseous. You take a nap.

You wake in time to have supper with Barbara by the pool. Bill is elsewhere. The silver makes an eerie sound, hitting the plate, cutting the food. The ice in the Scotch glass cracks. The sky is orange and heavy with smog. Barbara turns on the pool lights, remote control.

"Bill tells me you have an infection."

"It's nothing really."

Dinner finishes. You ask for a joint. She gives you one of her best. You smoke. The silence is accompanied by nothing unusual, just a regular night. You sit still, stoned. You decide you like Barbara and smile. She smiles too. Your smiles are the smiles of children and the moment is sweet. You try to hold it, but the shuffling of dishes makes it die.

You rise, take off your pants for the pool, and walk to the lighted edge. You stand there, the night air around you, lost in thoughts unknown. You grip the concrete subconsciously with your feet, then pierce the water, splashless.

William John Mann

Cords of Love

He has the phone cradled between his chin and shoulder.
      Ringing...

He's wearing only a black leather motorcycle jacket.
Ringing...

His cock is lubricated and in his fist, and he's watching himself in a mirror.

"Hello?"

"I want to fuck you."

"What?"

"I want to fuck you."

Pause.

"Who is this?"

"Or you can fuck me..."

Dial tone.

Fuck them when they won't talk. Why don't they swear at me? Why don't they tell me to go fuck myself? I want to hear these straight boys say fuck.

"He's flipping through the phone book. His oily fingers are staining the pages. Who's the sexy guy with the Corvette? He runs his finger down the page until he finds the number. His cock is still fucking his fist, trembling to come off.

The tones made by the push buttons on the phone have come to excite him. So do the rings before anyone answers.

But no one answers. His cock can't take any more. He shoots anticlimactic cum on the mirror. He lies back exhausted.

Better luck next time.

His cum has started running down the glass. White water separates from the thicker blobs which dot the mirror. He wipes it off with Kleenex. He hangs up his jacket and gets dressed.

Outside his grandfather is mowing the small strip of grass in front of their building. Some black kids are playing stickball in the street. It is Sunday.

He sits beside the garbage cans and watches the yellow sweat roll off his grandfather's back.

"Why are you inside on such a nice day?" his grandfather asks.

"I'm outside now."

"You should cut this grass. I am old."

"I am young."

His grandfather wipes sweat from his forehead and puts his fingers to his mouth, tasting his sweat. "Too much salt," he says. "We eat too much salt."

"I hate the city," he tells his grandfather.

"So move away. Get a job and move away."

"Maybe I will."

The lawnmower has choked on grass. It sputters and dies. The grandfather turns it over and pulls out clumps of grass in his hands. He starts to sneeze.

"I'm allergic to grass," he says. "You should do this."

"You're not allergic to grass. You lie."

"I do not lie," says the red grandfather. "You lie. You lied about your mother. You made up a dirty stinking lie."

He gets up and walks away. He walks right through the stickball game in the street. His grandfather is yelling after him to come back and get the lawnmower started.

He stops outside the church. The young priest is saying goodbye to very small Italian ladies in black dresses coming out of Mass. He watches the priest make the sign of the cross over one of the ladies' rosary beads. They are made of blue glass. The priest looks up and sees him.

"How is your grandfather?" the priest asks.

"He's fine."

"Tell him we miss him at Mass."

"I will."

"And how are you?"

"I am fine."

"Will you graduate this year?"

"I think."

"That's good." The priest has come over to him. He smiles at him. His eyes are very deeply set into his face. "You know," he says, "anytime you wish to talk to me, about *anything,* you're welcome to do so."

"Why should I need to talk?"

"I said, if you wish to."

He doesn't answer. The priest puts his hands on his shoulders. "You mustn't punish yourself."

He likes the priest's hands on his shoulders. He wishes the grip would tighten. He wishes he could fall to his knees and bury his face in the somber black cloth of the priest's crotch. He wishes the priest would bear down and crush his collarbone.

"You did not cause your mother's death."

He looks up, quickly, at the priest's eyes, but he can't find them. His mother is in the way, hanging from the cellar rafter by her large wooden rosary beads.

He walks away, through the dawdling flock of Italian ladies.

"Please call me," the priest says after him. "Please call me if you need me."

He stops at the school and watches some boys playing basketball. He likes the way their legs move and the way their shorts inch up their asses when they shoot. He lets his hand fall to his groin and he rubs his cock through his jeans.

The boys stop playing and turn, pointing at him. They run over to the chain link fence that stands between them.

"Hey queerhead!" they taunt.

"Faggot, want to suck my cock?" One boy pulls down his shorts and sticks his cock through the fence at him. It is very small. It hangs through the fence like the trunk of a tiny sick elephant at the zoo. It disgusts him.

He moves away. The boys are calling after him. He runs through the traffic and heads home on the other side of the street.

He remembers once calling one of those boys on the phone. He remembers telling him he wanted to fuck his asshole because he was an asshole. He climaxed when he realized this straight boy was hearing *fuck* in front of his mother.

He remembers his own mother, who once slapped him when he said *fuck*. They were out at Christmas time, last Christmas, and they were pushing through the crowded sidewalks, fighting the mass of moving winter coats. It was cold and people were rude. He said, "Fuck."

She stopped, causing people to bump into her, and turned, her black eyes blazing. She slapped him, right there on the street, and her leather glove only slightly softened the sting.

He returns home.

In his living room his grandfather is asleep on the couch. His shirt is off. He smells of grass and sweat. He has a sunken chest covered with white fuzz. His chest rattles as he sleeps.

He moves quietly past his grandfather and lies down on his mother's bed. He can smell her, a smell of talcum powder. He remembers her on this bed, smelling like talcum powder and praying with her large wooden rosary beads, the ones she'd bought for him but kept for herself. She bought them from an Indian craftswoman, who didn't believe in the Christian god.

She never said anything about slapping him. But she bought him the rosary beads that day, about an hour later. She stopped when she saw the Indian, a street vendor with a small table and rugs spread out on the sidewalk. She picked up the three-foot rosary beads and held them in front of her. He was very cold standing there, waiting for his mother. His cheeks were red and hard. He kept his eyes on the old wrinkled Indian woman, wrapped in her colorful blanket, sitting there unsmiling, unbelieving in the Christian god.

His mother looked at the rosary beads for a long time, examining their big carved wooden beads and the leather crucifix. And then she smiled, her black eyes lighting. She handed the Indian two five dollar bills.

"Merry Christmas," she said to him, and gave him the beads.

Somewhere in the sidewalk crowd behind them someone cursed the fucking cold.

He remembers her praying with those rosary beads on this bed. He remembers her stroking each bead lovingly, and kissing the crucifix before putting it on each breast as she made the sign of the cross. He remembers watching her turn off her light and hang the beads from the bedpost beside her head.

He gets up and goes into the bathroom. He watches his pee swirl in the water of the toilet. He pulls on his cock. It gets hard but he can't come.

He stands in the hallway caressing his cock. He remembers sneaking out here many nights, the hallway striped by moonlight. He remembers watching his mother with men. Black men and white men and old men and young men. He remembers watching them *fuck* on her bed, wooden beads bumping against the bedpost. He remembers taking out his cock and whacking off, watching the muscular back of his mother's lover heave up and down. He remembers his mother's moans. And he remembers seeing her eyes that one time, appearing suddenly over the heaving back, her blazing black eyes shining in the moonlight, appearing just in time to see his cock explode in a thousand violent spurts.

He thinks of the phone and starts to breathe in quick little gasps.

He carries the phone into his room, locking the door behind him. He unbuttons his jeans and lets them fall to the floor, kicking them off from around his ankles. He lies down on his bed, rubbing his cock through his white Jockey underwear. He reaches under his bed and feels for his jar of Vaseline. It's almost empty, with lots of finger valleys and pubic hairs. He pulls off his underwear and slips one greasy finger up his asshole. He fucks himself a little and then pulls his finger out and smells it.

Maybe the Corvette guy is home.

The push button tones make his cock jump in his hand.

Ringing. . .

His eyes stare straight in the mirror.

Ringing. . .

"Hello?"

"I want—"

"What are you doing in there?" It is his grandfather, calling through the door.

"Hello?"

He whispers. "I want to suck your cock."

"Speak up. I can't hear you."

"What are you doing in there with the phone?"

"I want to suck your cock!"

"Who are you talking to?"

"Who is speaking?"

"Answer me! Who is on the phone?"

"Who is this????"

He throws the phone down. Damn them both! Damn them both to hell! "Let me alone!" he screams. "Don't I have any god-damn privacy?"

The grandfather mumbles as he moves away outside the door. "How he can swear at an old man who's just trying to be interested in his life I don't know."

He calls again.

"Hello?" There is irritation in the voice.

"I want to suck your cock."

"You want to do what?"

"I WANT TO SUCK YOUR COCK!"

Pause. *"Who is this?"*

"Would you like that?" His voice is breathy, and he's pumping his fist harder.

"No." Dial tone.

He slams the receiver. Damn him!! Why didn't he just say *fuck?*

He hesitates. He needs to climax.

He pulls out the soiled phone book and finds the number.

Push tones. Oh, God...

Ringing...

He pumps his cock, watching his erection.

Ringing...

Answer the phone.

Ringing...

Oh for God's sake, hurry up and answer the fucking phone!

"Hello?"

His throat is tight.

"Hello?"

"I want to fuck you."

"Excuse me?"

"I . . . I want you to fuck me."

"Oh." There is a long pause.

"Would you like that?" he asks.

"Would you?"

Oh, shit, he's talking. He can feel his cock getting ready.

"Do you have the right number?" the voice asks him.

"Yeah."

"Do you realize you're talking to Father Carson?"

"Yeah." He imagines those deep eyes and those black pants. He imagines the priest's hands bearing down on his shoulders, snapping his bones, tearing his cartilage.

"I see."

He needs to climax. He wants to hang up now.

"Why don't you tell me who this is?"

Shit, why can't I come? I want to shoot so I can fucking hang up.

"Why don't you tell me why you want me to fuck you?"

Jesus fuck he said it he said fuck and I'm coming I'm fucking coming! *Fucking* priest, he said *fuck!*

The cum shoots hard out of his cock and splatters against the mirror. He falls back onto the bed and groans into the phone. The cord is stretched taut across his chest.

He hears the priest say, *"I told you that you were welcome to call me if you needed me. What —"*

He jumps up and crashes down the receiver.

It is very quiet in his room. Silent except for the yelps of the boys playing stickball in the street.

Holy fuck. He knew it was me.

"Are you finished with that damn phone?" comes the voice of his grandfather through the door. "I need to call the radio station. I know the answer to this hour's prize question."

He just lies there. His cock curls up like a raw shrimp nesting ir his wet kinky pubic hair.

"It was Eleanor Powell! She was the wife in *The Thin Man.*

Bring me that phone! Did you hear me? Did you hear me?"

He waits for the phone to ring.

"Oh, forget it now. Somebody just called in with the answer. Forget it now. I was wrong. Just forget it now."

He cleans his mess off the mirror with Kleenex. He gets dressed and takes the phone to his grandfather.

"It was Myrna Loy," he tells the old man.

"Don't you think I know that? They just said it. Get outside and finish mowing the grass. Don't you think I know it was Myrna Loy?"

He doesn't go outside. He sits and waits for the phone to ring all day but it never does.

Contributors' Biographies

Robert Boucheron is a practicing architect in Charlottesville, Virginia. His stories and reviews have appeared in a variety of publications, and he is also the author of a book of poems, *Epitaphs for the Plague Dead* (Inland Book Co.).

Guy-Mark Foster III is a native of West Virginia who now lives in New York. He is a member of the black writers' workshop, Other Countries.

Patrick Franklin is a music critic and classical music broadcaster in Monterey, California. His work has appeared in dozens of magazines and newspapers and a collection of his short stories, *The Uncertainty of Strangers,* was published by Grey Fox Press.

Richard Hall has worked in publishing, advertising and filmmaking, and also as a teacher and music critic. His books include *The Butterscotch Prince, Couplings, Three Plays for a Gay Theater* and *Letter from a Great-Uncle.* Mr. Hall was book editor of *The Advocate* from 1976 to 1982.

Scott Humphries emigrated from the farmlands of Indiana to San Francisco, where he went to work in the computer industry. Although he is a published poet, "Tinky" is his first short story. Mr. Humphries was diagnosed with AIDS in 1986.

Lee Rosario Kincaid is a freelance writer who lives in the Boston area. "Coloring Inside the Lines" is his first published story.

Stan Leventhal has worked as music editor of the New York *Native* and currently edits *Torso* magazine. He has published a number of stories and he is the author of a novel, *Mountain Climbing in Sheridan Square* (Banned Books).

William John Mann has worked as a journalist in Washington, D.C. and Connecticut, where he now writes a film column for *Metroline*, the Hartford gay weekly. He teaches writing and film at the University of Connecticut. "Cords of Love" is Mr. Mann's first published story.

Peter McGehee is a native of Arkansas who now lives in Toronto. His stories have appeared in a variety of publications, including *NeWest Review, The James White Review* and the Toronto *Star.* He is also the author of *Beyond Happiness* (Stubblejumper Press) and two musical revues.

Alan Neff is movie editor of the *Seattle Gay News.* "American Dreams" is his first published story.

Scott W. Peterson lives in the Pacific Northwest. In addition to writing, his main interests are photography and history. He is working on a novel set in seventeenth-century France.

William A. Reyes is a Chilean-born writer who is currently a graduate theater student at the University of Southern California in San Diego. His stories have appeared in literary journals such as *Puerto del Sol* and the *New Mexico Humanities Review.* Mr. Reyes is also a playwright.

Robert Trent is a graduate of Williams College, which provides the setting for his story, "First Blood." A latecomer to writing, he has published a short story and an essay in recent issues of *Christopher Street.*

Tomás Vallejos, a native of Colorado, is a professor of English in Houston. In addition to articles and reviews in the area of Chicano literature, he is the author of a number of poems, stories and plays.

Bart Washington has published stories in *Mandate, Honcho* and similar magazines. From the closet, he has long published fiction under another name, for which he has been awarded two Pushcart Prizes. He teaches in the deep South, and engages in this polite deception in order to remain employed.

T.R. Witomski has written copiously for the usual magazines that are bought only for their photographs. He has also contributed to the books *Hot Living* and *Gay Life,* and the Boyd McDonald anthologies. Currently, to the delight of his creditors, he produces sleazy videos.

Other books of interest from
ALYSON PUBLICATIONS

Don't miss our FREE BOOK offer at the end of this section.

☐ **SOCRATES, PLATO AND GUYS LIKE ME: Confessions of a gay schoolteacher,** by Eric Rofes, $7.00. When Eric Rofes began teaching sixth grade at a conservative private school, he soon felt the strain of a split identity. Here he describes his two years of teaching from within the closet, and his difficult decision to finally come out.

☐ **ONE TEENAGER IN TEN: Writings by gay and lesbian youth,** edited by Ann Heron, $4.00. One teenager in ten is gay; here, twenty-six young people tell their stories: of coming to terms with being different, of the decision how — and whether — to tell friends and parents, and what the consequences were.

☐ **DEAR SAMMY: Letters from Gertrude Stein and Alice B. Toklas,** by Samuel M. Steward, $8.00. As a young man, Samuel M. Steward journeyed to France to meet the two women he so admired. It was the beginning of a long friendship. Here he combines his fascinating memoirs of Toklas and Stein with photos and more than a hundred of their letters.

☐ **THE MEN WITH THE PINK TRIANGLE,** by Heinz Heger, $6.00. In a chapter of gay history that is only recently coming to light, thousands of homosexuals were thrown into the Nazi concentration camps along with Jews and others who failed to fit the Aryan ideal. There they were forced to wear a pink triangle so that they could be singled out for special abuse. Most perished. Heger is the only one ever to have told his full story.

☐ **IN THE LIFE: A Black Gay Anthology,** edited by Joseph Beam, $8.00. When Joseph Beam became frustrated that so little gay male literature spoke to him as a black man, he decided to do something about it. The result is this anthology, in which 29 contributors, through stories, essays, verse and artwork, have made heard the voice of a too-often silent minority.

☐ **BOYS' TOWN,** by Art Bosch, $8.00. Scout DeYoung's four basic food groups are frozen, bottled, canned, and boxed — but this warm-hearted story of two roommates who build an extended gay family is a gourmet's delight.

☐ **AS WE ARE,** by Don Clark, Ph.D., 8.00. This book, from the author of *Loving Someone Gay*, examines gay identity in the AIDS era. Clark creates a clear and inspiring picture of where we have been, where we are going, and emphasizes the vital importance of being *As We Are*.

☐ **$TUD,** by Phil Andros; introduction by John Preston, $7.00. Phil Andros is a hot and horny hustler with a conscience, pursuing every form of sex — including affection — without apology, yet with a sense of humor and a golden rule philosophy. When Sam Steward wrote these stories back in the sixties, they elevated gay fiction to new heights; today they remain as erotic and delightful as ever.

☐ **QUATREFOIL,** by James Barr, introduction by Samuel M. Steward, $8.00. Originally published in 1950, this book marks a milestone in gay writing: it introduced two of the first non-stereotyped gay characters to appear in American fiction. For today's reader, it remains an engrossing love story, while giving a vivid picture of gay life a generation ago.

☐ **THE HUSTLER,** by John Henry Mackay; trans. by Hubert Kennedy, $8.00. Gunther is fifteen when he arrives alone in the Berlin of the 1920s. There he is soon spotted by Hermann Graff, a sensitive and naive young man who becomes hopelessly enamored with Gunther. But love does not fit neatly into Gunther's new life ... *The Hustler* was first published in 1926. For today's reader, it combines a poignant love story with a colorful portrayal of the gay subculture that thrived in Berlin a half-century ago.

☐ **WORLDS APART,** edited by Camilla Decarnin, Eric Garber and Lyn Paleo, $8.00. Today's generation of science fiction writers has created a wide array of futuristic gay characters. The s-f stories collected here present adventure, romance, and excitement; and maybe some genuine alternatives for our future.

☐ **BETTER ANGEL,** by Richard Meeker, $6.00. For readers fifty years ago, *Better Angel* was one of the few positive images available of gay life. Today, it remains a touching, well-written story of a young man's gay awakening in the years between the World Wars.

☐ **WE CAN ALWAYS CALL THEM BULGARIANS: The Emergence of Lesbians and Gay Men on the American Stage,** by Kaier Curtin, $10.00. Despite police raids and censorship laws, many plays with gay or lesbian roles met with success on Broadway during the first half of this century. Here, Kaier Curtin documents the reactions of theatergoers, critics, clergymen, politicians and law officers to the appearance of these characters. Illustrated with photos from actual performances.

☐ **THE LITTLE DEATH,** by Michael Nava, $7.00. As a public defender, Henry Rios finds himself losing the idealism he had as a young lawyer. Then a man he has befriended — and loved — dies under mysterious circumstances. As he investigates the murder, Rios finds that the solution is as subtle as the law itself can be.

☐ **GOLDENBOY,** by Michael Nava, $15.00 (cloth). Gay lawyer-sleuth Henry Rios returns, in this sequel to Nava's highly-praised *The Little Death.*
Did Jim Pears kill the co-worker who threatened to expose his homosexuality? The evidence says so, but too many people *want* Pears to be guilty. Distracted by grisly murders and the glitz of Hollywood, can Rios prove his client's innocence?

☐ **THE GAY BOOK OF LISTS,** by Leigh Rutledge, $7.00. Leigh Rutledge has compiled a fascinating, informative and highly entertaining collection of lists that range from the historical (6 gay or bisexual popes) to the political (17 outspoken anti-gay politicians) and the outrageous (16 famous men, all reputedly very well-hung).

☐ **OUT OF ALL TIME,** by Terry Boughner, $7.00. Terry Boughner scans the centuries from ancient Egypt to modern America to find scores of the past's most interesting gay and lesbian personalities. He brings you the part of history they left out in textbooks. Imaginatively illustrated by Washington *Blade* artist Michael Willhoite.

☐ **REFLECTIONS OF A ROCK LOBSTER: A story about growing up gay,** by Aaron Fricke, $6.00. When Aaron Fricke took a male date to the senior prom, no one was surprised: he'd gone to court to be able to do so, and the case had made national news. Here Aaron tells his story, and shows what gay pride can mean in a small New England town.

☐ **TO ALL THE GIRLS I'VE LOVED BEFORE, An AIDS Diary,** by J.W. Money, $7.00. What thoughts run through a person's mind when he is brought face to face with his own mortality? J.W. Money, a person with AIDS, gives us that view of living with this warm, often humorous, collection of essays.

☐ **GAY AND GRAY,** by Raymond M. Berger, $8.00. Working from questionnaires and case histories, Berger has provided the closest look ever at what it is like to be an older gay man. For some, he finds, age has brought burdens; for others, it has brought increased freedom and happiness.

☐ **LONG TIME PASSING: Lives of Older Lesbians,** edited by Marcy Adelman, $8.00. Here, in their own words, women talk about age-related concerns: the fear of losing a lover; the experiences of being a lesbian in the 1940s and 1950s; and issues of loneliness and community.

☐ **EIGHT DAYS A WEEK,** by Larry Duplechan, $7.00. Can Johnnie Ray Rousseau, a 22-year-old black singer, find happiness with Keith Keller, a six-foot-two blond bisexual jock who works in a bank? Will Johnnie Ray's manager ever get him on the Merv Griffin show? Who was the lead singer of the Shangri-las? And what about Snookie? Somewhere among the answers to these and other silly questions is a love story as funny, and sexy, and memorable, as any you'll ever read.

☐ **A MISTRESS MODERATELY FAIR,** by Katherine Sturtevant. $9.00. Seventeenth-century London is not accustomed to women such as Margaret Featherstone. A widowed playwright, she manages her own affairs, and competes with some of the most talented men in the realm. But she hides a secret, a secret that actress Amy Dudley shares, and that threatens to deliver them both to the gallows.

A Gertrude Stein-Alice B. Toklas Mystery

MURDER IS MURDER IS MURDER

by **Samuel M. Steward**
author of the Phil Andros stories

Get this book free!

Gertrude Stein and Alice B. Toklas, one of our community's most famous couples, go sleuthing to solve the mysterious disappearance of the father of their handsome deaf-mute gardener. Samuel Steward, who revolutionized gay fiction under the penname Phil Andros, has put together this unusual and well-written mystery, and given it large doses of realism based on his real-life friendship with Stein and Toklas.

If you order at least three other books from us, you may request a FREE copy of *Murder is Murder is Murder*. (See order form on next page.)

☐ **A HISTORY OF SHADOWS,** by Robert C. Reinhart, $7.00. A fascinating look at gay life during the Depression, the war years, the McCarthy witchhunts, and the sixties — through the eyes of four men who were friends during those forty years.

☐ **CHOICES,** by Nancy Toder, $8.00. This popular novel about lesbian love depicts the joy, passion, conflicts and intensity of love between women as Nancy Toder conveys the fear and confusion of a woman coming to terms with her sexual and emotional attraction to other women.

☐ **IN THE TENT,** by David Rees, $7.00. Seventeen-year-old Tim realizes that he is attracted to his classmate Aaron, but, still caught up in the guilt of a Catholic upbringing, he has no idea what to do about it until a camping trip results in unexpected closeness.

☐ **TALK BACK! A gay person's guide to media action,** $4.00. When were you last outraged by prejudiced media coverage of gay people? Chances are it hasn't been long. This short, highly readable book tells how you, in surprisingly little time, can do something about it.

To get these books:

Ask at your favorite bookstore for the books listed here. You may also order by mail. Just fill out the coupon below, or use your own paper if you prefer not to cut up this book.

GET A FREE BOOK! When you order any three books listed here at the regular price, you may request a *free* copy of *Murder is Murder is Murder*.

– – – – – – – – – – – – – – – – –

Enclosed is $_____ for the following books. (Add $1.00 postage when ordering just one book; if you order two or more, we'll pay the postage.)

1. _____
2. _____
3. _____
4. _____
5. _____

☐ Send a free copy of *Murder is Murder is Murder* as offered above. I have ordered at least three other books.

name: _____

address: _____

city: _____ state: _____ zip: _____

ALYSON PUBLICATIONS
Dept. H-36, 40 Plympton St., Boston, Mass. 02118

This offer expires Dec. 31, 1990. After that date, please write for current catalog.